KU-299-308

SAND BLIND

Recent Titles by Julian Rathbone

LYING IN STATE
THE PANDORA OPTION
WATCHING THE DETECTIVES

SAND BLIND

Julian Rathbone

This first hardcover edition published in Great Britain 2000 by
SEVERN HOUSE PUBLISHERS LTD of
9–15 High Street, Sutton, Surrey SM1 1DF.
First published in paperback 1993 by Serpent's Tail, London.
This first hardcover edition published in the U.S.A. 2000 by
SEVERN HOUSE PUBLISHERS INC of
595 Madison Avenue, New York, N.Y. 10022.

British Library Cataloguing in Publication Data

Rathbone, Julian, 1935-
Sand blind
1. Arms transfers - Fiction
2. Suspense fiction
I. Title
823.9'14 [F]

ISBN 0-7278-5565-4

All situations in this publication are fictitious and
any resemblance to living persons is purely coincidental.

Printed and bound in Great Britain by
MPG Books Ltd, Bodmin, Cornwall.

'Is this son-of-a-bitch really dumb enough to fight us?'

General Carl Vuono, Chief of Staff, US Army, 1 December 1989

(Quoted in The Commanders *by Bob Woodward, Simon and Schuster, 1991)*

Sand Blind is a fantasy inspired by history.

Only a couple of characters in this book relate in any way to any real person, living or dead, and even they are seen through the eyes of entirely fictional characters. *Sand Blind* is a work of fiction and should be read as such.

The historical inspiration was drawn from the following books and articles and from my recollection of TV news items: *Dangerous Liaison (The inside story of the US-Israeli covert relationship . . .)*, Andrew and Leslie Cockburn, Bodley Head, 1992; *Despatches from the Gulf War*, Ed. Brian MacArthur, Bloomsbury, 1991; *Saddam Hussein (A political biography)*, Efraim Karsh and Inari Rautsi, Futura, 1991; *The (1st) Gulf War*, John Bulloch and Harvey Morris, Methuen, 1989; *Trading in Death*, James Adams, Hutchinson, 1988; *Stealth Bomber*, Bill Sweetman, Airlife, 1989; *Secret Dossier*, Pierre Salinger with Eric Laurent, Penguin Books, 1991; *Unholy Babylon*, Adel Darwish and Gregory Alexander, Victor Gollancz, 1991; *The Commanders*, Bob Woodward, Simon and Schuster, 1991; *Desert Storm*, The Editors of Military History Magazine, Empire Press, 1991; *Why Bush Went to War*, Robert Brenner, New Left Review 185, 1991; *Realpolitik in the Gulf*, Christopher Hitchens, New Left Review 186, 1991.

Apart from history, Allan Isaacs attempted to get me to understand how advanced radar systems work. Probably he failed. Nevertheless I owe him a very big thank you.

JR

PART ONE

CHAPTER 1

My name is Salih K— and this is my Secret Diary, recorded on my personal PC in the small hours of the morning. The document will be hidden and only someone knowing the entry code 'Beast 666' will be able to access it. As a further precaution I am writing in English.

I have worked for most of my life as an archaeologist and archivist in the Assyrian Department of Baghdad University where it has been my privilege to unearth (sometimes literally) evidence of the heroic past of the Iraqi people. I learned the trade forty years ago at Cambridge University, England.

Unfortunately not only am I an assistant professor of archaeology, it is also my fate to be an Official Recorder of the Acts and Sayings of the Arab Redeemer.

There are three of us and we each work four hour shifts, four on, eight off, day and night, round the clock. It's an arduous business since most of the time off has to be spent writing up one's notes and presenting them to the Director of the Leader Archive who, of course, checks them for ideological impurities before filing them. An ideological impurity was the cause of my predecessor's decease.

Of course even a man gifted with the energy to maintain the tireless pursuit of his people's welfare and happiness that so gloriously characterises the Father-Leader must occasionally sleep, or indulge in practices which even he does not wish to share with an Official Recorder, and so it does happen that every now and then one can come off a four hour shift with nothing, or very little, to record. It is on these occasions that I shall find time to maintain my Secret Diary.

I entered on my new duties at half past nine for ten, yesterday morning, 20 March, 1990. Half past nine for ten? It takes that long to get from the outside world to the Presence. The process is brisk and efficient and involves a very thorough, humiliating, and even painful body search which includes an optical fibre probe down one's gullet and into one's stomach and another up one's back passage, an X-ray scan, a voice-print test, fingerprint check and so on. All this was done by white-coated technicians, some female, in an ambience of clinical austerity, in the outer of the six walls that surround the inner kernel of the Supreme Headquarters of the Revolution.

This, it turns out, is an inconvient forty-minute drive from the suburb of Amiriya, where I live with my wife and daughter, and is where Our Leader spends most of his time, using, or apparently using (see below) the more accessible Presidential Palace only when meeting visiting Heads of State.

Once they were sure that I was I and that I was only I and not also an envelope for bomb, weapon, poison or whatever, I was conducted through the outer shell, a six-sided edifice holding the bodyguard, logistical back-up, services and so on, along corridors and up and down staircases through what is clearly a labyrinth as complicated as that which housed the Cretan Minotaur. I suspect now, having been in and out of it twice, that I am taken on a different route each time, but it is difficult to be sure: the floors are uniformly marble, the walls ditto, the closed doors cedar of Lebanon with bronze fittings and the portraits, photographs and statues of Guess-Who monotonously repetitive.

At last we, my armed and khaki-ed escorts and I, came out into open air again, beneath the hot blue sky, and onto a wide alley twenty metres wide that separates the outer shell from the kernel or inner palace. This is a rectangular building, eighty metres by fifty, with no windows facing outwards below ten metres from the ground. And the few there are are small and barred. The space between kernel and shell, a dry moat really, is surveyed by CCTV, infrared scans and can be filled, my escorts told me, in less than ten seconds with a heavier than air nerve gas that kills unpleasantly but almost instantly.

A walk along one and a half sides, during which we were no doubt re-inspected for a last time, brought us to a large double door made of bronze and depicting in shallow bas-relief incidents from our Father-Leader's life. The door was opened according to some signal from inside or out — there was nothing on it as obvious as a conventional lock or handle — and I was passed from one escort detail to another and from one world to a very different one.

Everything was now light and airy. The long, high, ground floor halls are in effect glazed-in colonnades opening on to a large inner courtyard. Here a fountain plays, spilling bright sunlit water into four long rectangular pools that flow back to the centre of each of the four colonnades. Myrtles, ornamental citrus trees and slender cypresses fill the spaces between and white doves flutter amongst them, symbols of the peace the Redeemer so longs to bring to the Arab nation. Inside the decoration is minimal but reflected water and shifting light make up for the plainness. We passed from one hall into another, and as we did I heard voices, quiet but firm, and saw at the far end a crescent of three large sofas set round a low marble table. On the sofas sat five men, all in simple military uniform, and one of whom, the one in the middle, was, well, was Him.

It was, when all is said and done, an awe-inspiring moment, not least because I seriously believe that this was my first glimpse of Him ever. Incidentally, if these memoirs of mine ever come to light and are checked against media reports of the Leader's movements and are found to contradict them, no-one should feel surprised.

Our Father has two look-alikes always on the go at once who look after his public appearances for him. One, an actor, does the Haroun al-Rashid bit, the occasions when our Father, like the legendary Caliph, descends upon humble homes for a fireside chat with his people; the other is usually an ex-soldier who does the visits to the front-line, eats his warriors' simple food and shares their privations in the trenches. I say 'usually' because it is not always easy to find a look-alike with the right background and the turnover is fairly brisk — on average two are assassinated in every three years.

The hall had a sort of inner cloister along what would be the outside wall of the palace and we approached the Presence along it. About half way down there was a wide alcove enclosing another small fountain — a large basin scarcely raised above floor level beneath a high dome pierced with windows; a delicate tracery of stucco work, and stalactitic niches filled the spaces between. It was instantly familiar, but it was only during the course of the morning that I recalled why: it is a copy of the Fountain of the Abencerrages in the Alhambra, Granada, Spain. This is where Abu'l Hassan murdered sixteen princes of the Abencerrage family whose chief had fallen in love with the Sultan's favourite — Zoraya: a story to which the distancing effect of time has added a romantic tinge but whose ultimate horror is still recalled when one considers the russet iron stains in the fountain which are said by some to be the ineradicable blood stains of the murdered men.

The copy, which I had time to study since we halted by it for a moment or two while my colleague and his escort prepared to leave, seemed exact even to this last detail, though the stains here seemed stronger than I remembered those of the original to be — but, I reminded myself, it is now thirty-eight years since I made my one pilgrimage to Granada and the Alhambra.

Presently my colleague, a chap I know quite well by sight since he is a member of the History Faculty, was led down the cloister and past us — we smiled shyly at each other — and then I was taken on to the place he had vacated. This was a small desk at the top end of the hall, still in the cloister and so set apart from the magic semi-circle of divans. I could now see that the low marble table was mounted on ormolu claw legs and supported a model of a mosque, done in solid gold. My escort told me, in a whisper, that it was presented to Our Leader by Emir Jaber al-Ahmed al-Sabah of Kuwait on the occasion of Our Leader's victorious re-conquest of the Fao peninsula just two years ago.

Our Leader himself was reclining gracefully, according to my report, in the centre of the semi-circle. The word that sprang to mind at the time was 'slouched'. He was fatter than I had expected: a very pronounced spare tyre flopped over the webbing of his military belt and his khaki-coloured but silk shirt clung to the decidedly epicene roundness of his breasts. His face was darker than that of the two look-alikes I had seen on their ceremonial visits to the University, of which, needless to say, he is Supreme Chancellor, and had a sort of orangey glow that looked downright unhealthy, especially on cheeks so swollen with fat or blood-pressure that they threatened to give an almost oriental cast to his eyes. These, however, were remarkable.

They were dark, alert, alternately narrowed and widened in response to what was said, alternately questioning and demanding, defensive and threatening, true windows of a soul tormented by fear and rage. Although his mouth, beneath the almost Stalin-esque moustache, and with its petulantly spoiled lower lip, frequently smiled — either with a sort of shy charm, or accompanied by a bullish laugh with boys-together locker room brutality — those eyes never lost that look of beleaguered wariness.

For the rest it was his hands that drew my attention — large and strong, for most of the time they lay relaxed on his knee or the arm of the settee, though they occasionally reached forward to pat the shoulder or thigh of whomever he was talking to, and once playfully but painfully pulled a general's ear. They are, of course, the model for the new gateway to Baghdad: two fists holding crossed sabres commemorating our victory over the Parsee fanatics. It seemed to me these hands remained first and foremost weapons or perhaps wild and savage beasts, dominated by the will alone of an owner who might unleash them at any moment.

He carried a heavy automatic pistol, holstered and slung low against his right thigh.

Three generals, all wearing plain, unadorned fatigues, remained with him throughout my four-hour shift, other functionaries were summoned and dismissed, came and went. All entered as I had done, along the cloister. When they left they bowed deeply to the Leader and moved sideways, in a crab-like shuffle, repeating the bow, until they had passed through the arch in front of my table. Then only were they permitted to walk the long way back, past the Abencerrage fountain, to the door at the end of the hall.

There was another door up at the end where the Divan was being held, and occasionally a manservant would enter with coffee and sweetmeats. He always drank some of the coffee before serving it, and ate whatever sweetmeat the Father chose for him from the many on the chased silver tray. And at about half past one he brought in a bottle of Johnnie Walker Black Label — this he did not have to taste since it was a full bottle with the seals unbroken. More of that later.

CHAPTER 2

When I arrived Brigadier-General Hassan Kamal al-Majed, the Minister of Industry, was completing a report on what he described as a Super Gun.

'Both Forgemaster Engineering and Walter Somers of England have begun deliveries of the tubes we asked for. The last batch is due to leave England on 11 April. We have checked . . .'

'There was then no trouble with the British Government?'

The general laughed. 'Not at all.'

'Why not?'

'Why should there have been? The tubes are for a new petro-chemical plant we are building.'

'They *believed* that?'

'Of course not.'

Our Leader offered the sly, shy version of his smile and rubbed thumb and finger together in the traditional gesture. '*Baksheesh*? How much did it cost us?'

'No need even for *baksheesh*, at least not from us. The crumbling and effete British economy is such that they are begging for orders from anyone anywhere. I suppose it might have been necessary for employees of the companies involved to corrupt government officials, but if they did they did so at their own expense not ours.'

'And the propellant?'

'Your Excellency will remember that that is being provided by PRB, a British owned firm in Belgium.' A second general provided this information. 'Officially they are delivering to Jordan, Jordan will pass it straight through to us.'

'So. When can we expect the first test firing?'

'Dr Bull plans to be here on 10 April to supervise a scaled-down trial . . .'

'Ah yes. The excellent Dr Bull. I well remember his tremendous enthusiasm for my project — and his readiness to drink my whisky.'

'He has, Excellency, continued to oversee the whole project. For the trial he proposes to use only a twenty-metre barrel, so we have code-named the test-firing "Baby Babylon" but from it he will be able to extrapolate the data he needs for . . .'

And so it went on for an hour or so, technical stuff I would not pretend to understand, and I resorted to studying Our Leader, with the aim of making an objective assessment of his actual abilities. At first sight these seemed impressive enough. He appeared to have a fair grasp of the technicalities and recall of earlier stages in 'Project Babylon'. However, I soon spotted his characteristic ploy for presenting such an impression, indeed it is demonstrated in the exchanges above. Whenever his memory was nudged by a chance word and an opportunity for an informed intervention could be taken, he took it: witness, above, his reference to 'baksheesh' and the corruptibility of British officials, and Dr Bull's liking for whisky. Neither adds anything at all to the progress of the meeting, both are designed to impress his interlocutors with his grasp of what was going on.

After I had made this assessment I am afraid I grew even more bored and my mind wandered, as indeed I am afraid it does with increasing frequency these days, to the past, and particularly to my time at Cambridge University, England. It was the reference to the corruptibility of the English ruling class that prompted it. In many ways it was a pleasant time, but I suffered too, a great deal, from English snobbery and racism. The snobbery took several forms. I was enrolled at Fitzwilliam, not then a full college but a hall of residence. This was itself an object of quite unjustified scorn from almost everyone I was acquainted with. And then archaeology and anthropology were looked down on as not serious intellectual pursuits or even ones a 'gentleman' would involve himself with. Finally, the fact that I was Arab and Iraqi frequently brought suffering due to the deep-rooted racism of my fellow undergraduates. (Never, incidentally, were we 'students'. Students went to polytechnical colleges, undergraduates went to universities.) They firmly believed Arabs habitually bribe and cheat. We do. The racism lies in the fact that they believed that they did not. Yet during my three years there I heard many times how 'gentlemen' had bribed the police to drop prosecutions for speeding or drunk driving, how college servants were paid not to reveal the presence of women at night in men's rooms, of cheating in examinations, and even of large sums paid to examiners. And these were matters they boasted about!

Suddenly my reverie was shattered. The Father of the Arab nation was in a tizzy, a temper, up and striding round those huge sofas like a black panther, smacking his pistol holster and spitting with a rage that was all the more awesome because it was to a large extent contained. I make no doubt he would have been blazing away at us all if it had not been.

'Is he here? Has this traitor to the revolution, this Zionist parasite dared to show his face here in my Supreme Headquarters of the Revolution? Have him brought here immediately. I want him here now.'

A very frightened general scuttled sideways and backwards out of the circle and into the cloister, and I watched his khaki backside twinkling away through the barred shadows to the door at the far end before turning my attention back to the Leader and his ashen-faced minions. Our Father presently regained some composure and returned to his former place but now sat on the edge of the sofa with those large hands swaying and swinging between his knees while his flushed face swung like a tank turret from one to another of those who remained.

'So. What sort of system do we need to cope with this threat?'

'A Westinghouse Low Altitude Surveillance System might do. But as I understand it the best option is the Ferlinghetti AR 3D system, though even that would have to be modified, upgraded.'

'And who will sell us either of these systems?'

A cold silence spread over the whole group. Clearly the answer was — no-one.

'Jaber al-Sabah has three Ferlinghettis. But he won't sell. The Zionists won't let him.' This, eventually, from one general.

'They won't let anyone sell us an Air Defence System with that capability.' And this from another.

The Leader bit his thumb for a moment or two, then took another turn or two round the divans but this time deep in thought or calculation rather than anger. Finally he wheeled in behind the four men who had been sitting in front of him so they had to twist and crane their necks to see him.

'Use the phone, get on to your research department, find out what third world countries have the Ferlinghetti AR . . . whatever it was. Hassan, you have a team going to Santiago, yes?'

'Excellency, they leave in four days' time. They will complete the deal with Cardoen for Bell 206 helicopters equipped with missile guidance systems . . .'

'Then they must shop for one of these Ferlinghetti things too. Find out who has them and who might sell one to us.'

'But even if we find a grey-market seller, there are still bound to be endless problems . . .'

And so it went on: part technical, part on ways of circumventing the embargo on our nation which prevents us from buying anything that could be a threat to the Zionists. Presently the servant brought in two glasses (Waterford cut crystal, I think) and a sealed bottle of Johnnie Walker Black Label. At about this time a phone buzzed. One of the generals took the call and reported back that Ecuador have three Ferlinghetti ARSs and could surely be persuaded to part with one. And that Santiago was the place to make the deal. A man called Jabreel Mansur was mentioned as a likely broker.

A little after that the general who had been sent out was back, accompanied now by a small tubby man in civilian clothes — dark grey suit, white shirt, no tie, spectacles.

The Leader swung on him as he came through the arch in front of me.

'Dr Fuad al-Naqib?'

The poor man was speechless, rolling a big white handkerchief between podgy hands — all he could do was bob and mow, his face twisted in a grimace which expressed abject fear.

'Two years ago, doctor, I presented you with a concept that was universally received as a brilliant solution to problems we were having with the Persian air force. You know what I am talking about?' The Leader said all this in a friendly, quiet tone, not hectoring at all, but reasonable, sweet reason. There was no smile. Though his eyes were cool and calm, he seemed to be carrying some inner weight. We have a saying: a quiet man should not be made angry because he will be hard to handle.

'Your Excellency's extraordinary intellectual ability,' Fuad stuttered, overcame the stutter and stumbled on, 'produced the idea that a French Thompson CSF Tigre surveillance radar could be installed in one of our Soviet Il–76MD transports to provide not only an Airborne Early Warning system but also friendly fighter control. The brilliance of the conception was only surpassed by its actual performance in the final stages of the Persian war. It ranks by no means least as an example of the great gifts Your Excellency has put exclusively in the service of our . . .'

'I then asked you to prepare a report on the efficacy this system would have in giving us early warning of an Israeli strike, confident that it would provide us with the umbrella we require if we are to develop our nuclear ability and the means to deliver it.'

'Yes, Excellency.'

'And I never received that report.'

'No, Excellency.'

'Why not?' Still the gently enquiring tone.

'Excellency, there were three problems. In the first place it was almost impossible to keep the aircraft in the air round the clock and we could not spare a second Tigre surveillance system to make a back-up. Secondly, Excellency, the Zionists knew it was there and could shoot it down whenever they wanted to, and thirdly, Excellency, the Zionist fighter planes are now equipped with radar jamming equipment of a very high order, way beyond what the Tigre system can cope with . . .'

'I am waiting to know why the report was not delivered.' This said with an edge, and for some reason I could not restrain a shudder at the change of tone.

'Excellency, we decided it would be improper of us to submit a report which might be construed to belittle Your Excellency's profoundly correct achievement where the Persian air force was concerned. The fact is the Persian planes have no radar jamming facility of any importance at all . . .'

'Dr Fuad. Please come and sit here beside me.'

The little man did as he was told. As he did so Our Leader leant across the table, broke the seal on the whisky bottle, poured a substantial measure into both glasses and handed one to the scientist. All through this he continued to speak, but quietly again, the momentary asperity forgotten.

'Forgive me, Dr Fuad, but it seems to me that your judgement was clouded by what can only really be construed as cowardice. And as a result two projects, married together like an arrow to its bow, a sling-shot to its sling, namely a nuclear device and the ability to deliver it, both nearing completion, are as vulnerable to Zionist attack as Tammuz 17 was in 1981. And all the time I thought they were protected . . .' Here he leant back, and raised his glass before drinking — deeply, considering it was neat spirit. '. . . by a system that is worth no more than its value as scrap. Dr Fuad. You are not drinking.'

'Excellency, I do not . . . normally drink.'

'Please . . .?'

Not a word he uses often. Dr Fuad drank — a little, and coughed a lot. Our Father considerately patted him on the back until he had recovered.

'Now, you're getting used to it. A touch more? Yes? Think of it as medicine. Dr Fuad, was there, amongst your colleagues, anyone with the courage to suggest you were wrong not to make that report?'

'Yes, Excellency. Dr Nazir Fadel.'

'Then he shall have your job. Drink up, and let me see you on your way.'

At that point I think Dr Fuad believed he would survive with nothing worse than the sack, degradation, humiliation, poverty and a menial job as a hospital orderly as his punishment.

He stood up, unsteadily, the Protector of the Innocent supported him, and together they came through the arch in front of me and turned down the cloister. When they reached the replica of the Fountain of the Abencerrages, the All-Merciful Dispenser of Justice invited Dr Fuad to kneel over the low basin and drink some water. Dr Fuad did so and the Sword of Islam shot him in the side of his head so he fell forward into the basin.

I had no idea that a pistol shot in a large but enclosed area could be so loud. Nor had I realised that human blood released in volume, instantly, smells much like camel's blood when they cut the beasts' throats at the end of Ramadan, nor that a small cloud of gun smoke can hang in the air above a dead man for longer than it takes him to die.

The white doves outside clattered up into the air at the sound, wheeled above the fountain and the trees where the bright orange hung like a gold lamp in a green night, and then settled again as if nothing had happened.

CHAPTER 3

Three weeks have passed since I first opened 'Beast 666'. I have not told my wife and daughter about my new job — they still believe that I am going out to Babylon every day to supervise the reconstruction of the capital of the Mesopotamian Empire and sometimes, more often than was the case in the past, staying over night. I have also told them that a new military installation is to be built on a site of archaeological interest and that my department has been instructed to work overtime salvaging what we can of the past before the future moves in. Possibly my wife believes this is all cover for illicit amorous assignments, and it would be no bad thing if that were to be her interpretation of my absences. In the first place she can trot that out as an explanation if she is ever seriously questioned about my movements by the Mukhabarat, the Secret Police, and in the second place it might provoke jealousy which, in its turn, might provoke her to offer her favours more frequently than she does.

But this afternoon I am home again and alone since my wife and daughter are attending a meeting of the Amiriya section of the General Federation for Iraqi Women, where they are already discussing how to celebrate National Day in the most sycophantic way possible although it is still three months away.

I cannot say I am enjoying the work. Handsome and airy though the inner kernel of the Supreme Headquarters is, repeated shifts there observing an unrelenting flow of inner committee meetings, coupled with the hideous memory of that first day and the constant fear that a similar incident might happen at any time, have produced in me a deep antipathy to the place, an antipathy so intense that the palms of my hands and the soles of my feet come out in a psoriatic rash after I have been there for an hour.

No, there have been no more visits to the Fountain of the Abencerrages, though on at least two occasions it has been a close run thing. The Father of the Arab Nation is by no means the first ruler in Baghdad to have made a habit of cutting pieces off the bearers of bad tidings, and there have been several items of bad news in the last fortnight or so.

The first occurred three days after the events which I described when I opened this file. Apparently the Dr Gerald Bull who was to have been here a week later to supervise and evaluate the test firing of 'Baby Babylon' was gunned down in the entrance to his Brussels apartment. Clearly it was the work of a Mossad death squad, and when Our Defender heard of it I thought he was going to be taken away from us by reason of an apoplexy or stroke. The orangey hue of his face became purple then ashen then purple again, he picked up a silver tray of coffee-cups, pot and so on, hurled it against the wall, and finally stormed away into the private apartments. However, he was back within twenty minutes, much calmed and able to continue with the meeting, which was to do with the problem of gaining better access to the Shatt al Arab waterway. I suspect a fairly massive dose of beta blockers had been administered.

A similar outburst was provoked when news came in that British Customs at Heathrow had impounded krytron capacitors due for shipment to Baghdad. Now I have no idea what krytron capacitors are, but apparently they play a key role in the simplest sort of nuclear explosion. I, I must confess, felt some relief. I cannot believe our Nation's Father is any better equipped morally or intellectually to have control of such a thing as a nuclear bomb than was the late Harry Truman.

Finally, eight days ago and in spite of Dr Bull's absence, Baby Babylon, the scaled down prototype of the supergun that will put a satellite in space or a chemical shell on Tel Aviv, was test-fired . . . and the barrel split. A disaster compounded by the almost simultaneously presented intelligence that the remaining undelivered tubes from Sheffield Forgemaster, much bigger than the ones that split, had been impounded by British Customs, just when they were about to leave Teeside on a Bermuda-registered freighter.

The Lion of the Desert took this news quite well.

'Probably,' he said, 'they were also flawed. We should have gone to Mitsubishi.'

These last items were reported to him during a big meeting with all the heads of the ministries connected with the economy. The subject was nothing less than our ministers' failure to rebuild a country exhausted and impoverished after the titanic struggle against the fanatical Persians. It was a long and tedious meeting during which Our Ever Watchful Leader fell noisily asleep. The problem was that no-one was willing to tell the truth, or at least not outright, so each minister in turn made presentations of inordinate length and circumlocuity. It had already begun when I took over from my colleague and continued until three minutes before the end of my shift, when the Minister for Oil Exports cut through all the flannel with the simple statement that nothing could be done while the price of oil remained on the floor.

And why was it there? Because the Kuwaitis were overproducing and undercutting. Why did the sons of bitches do such a stupid thing? Surely they would get rich just as quickly if they sold dear and conserved their resources? No, Excellency. Kuwaiti wealth is no longer from their oil but from the petro-chemical industries they own abroad. These prosper on cheap oil.

Finally, to bring Beast 666 right up to date, yesterday there was a meeting of the military Chiefs of Staff from which I am glad to say, I was excluded. It ended half way through my shift, and, judging from the expressions of all concerned had gone badly.

As soon as the generals had gone a message was brought announcing that a certain Jabreel Mansur craved permission to present a report.

'Show the bastard in,' our Father bellowed, 'and let's have a bottle of Johnnie Walker and two glasses,' a request which brought the rash out on my neck as well as my hands.

However, I need not have worried. It was clear straight away that this Jabreel Mansur was an old crony and the whisky was out purely as a gesture of hospitality.

Mansur was about forty-five years old, and could have passed for a Mediterranean Arab though I understand he is a Yemeni by birth. He had coarse dark hair with a silvery patch above his right eye and on his forehead beneath it a small but deep scar. He had plump good looks only just beginning to deteriorate with dissipation, somewhat spoiled by a squashily semitic nose with a groove in the tip and the petulant cast of his angel lips. He wore a silky jacket with a tartan pattern, white shirt open to show the silvery black hairs on his chest, creased black trousers and Cordoban red loafers. In spite of the studied casualness of his appearance he had the oily shine that goes with good living and serious money.

The Leader rose to greet him, folded him in the warmest of embraces, and continued to pat his shoulders and arms as he made him sit with him on the central settee, a rare honour. He then cracked the seal on the whisky and poured a generous half tumbler for each of them.

'So, my friend, how is it going, what have you managed to get for me?'

'A Ferlinghetti AR 3D, only two years old. Sold new ex-factory to Ecuador in 1988. The Kuwaitis bought three of them at about the same time, so it's not rubbish.'

'And will it pick out the Zionist fighters for me?'

'Not without modification.'

'Explain.'

'Well, in the first instance the communications fit has to be replaced or rationalised with what already exists at your Air Defence Operations Centre, and with your interceptors and SAM sites. I can't get this work done until you release detailed specifications on all those areas . . .'

'Can't it be done here?'

'No. All along the line we shall have to buy in kit as and when our Project Manager needs it. At the moment the system, which fills eight containers, is in Malaga, Spain. The word is that Quito has leased it cheap to Mauretania. No-one can see why Mauretania should need it, except to keep up with the Joneses, but no-one much minds Mauretania having it and getting it upgraded. What's more they'll let us test it in the same patch of the Sahara where we tested your ICBMs. Just as important, no-one will stop our Project Manager from getting the kit he needs. If it was all here, in Iraq, you'd be struggling to buy the right size of spanner let alone anything else. So you have to give me those specifications.'

'You know,' here the Protector stood up and began to pace about pulling at his pendulous lower lip, 'I'm not sure we need this thing at all.'

Jabreel's face darkened, but he managed not to say anything.

'We needed it because we thought once we were close to a bomb and the means of delivering it the Zionists would send in their fighter-bombers again. But in the last three weeks they have set us back three years. They have murdered the man who would have built us the delivery system, they have persuaded the British authorities, whom we thought we had in our pockets, to impound essential *matériel* . . .'

'These are set-backs. And when you have overcome them, those F–15s with their new radar jamming equipment will be homing in again . . .'

'And this Ferlinghetti system can cope with them?'

'No. That's the second stage of the upgrading that will have to be done in Malaga . . .'

And so it went on, and I shall not pretend that I understood the half of it, but one thing surprised me — I have never seen our Protector so intimate and trusting as he was with this Jabreel Mansur. Clearly they had done a lot of business together in the past, presumably during our war with the Persians, and clearly it had all turned out well.

By their third glass of whisky they were concentrating on the security aspect of it all. Our Leader was still worried about letting Mansur and the Project Manager in Malaga have so much information about the defence systems already in place.

'Listen,' said the Yemeni, "You have French Thompson ADSs ten years old, SAM missiles, and MIG and Mirage interceptors. You don't have to be a spy working for the Pentagon to know what they can do and can't do. All you have to do is subscribe to Jane's Defence Weekly . . .'

He became aware that he had lost the attention of the Supreme Arab Intellect of All Time whose eyes had glazed, but who then suddenly stood up, paced about a bit, flicking his fingers as if checking off points in some interior argument. Finally he came to rest in front of the Arms Dealer, and wagged his strong phallic finger under his nose.

'Jabreel bey, listen carefully. To protect one installation in the desert from an Israeli strike one system is enough . . .'

'Yes. Sited as part of the installation it would provide a radar umbrella for four hundred kilometres in any direction.'

'And if I had three more, I could enclose just about everything in our country between the two rivers from Mosul to the Shatt al Arab waterway?'

'You know the geography of your country far better than I do, but I would guess so.'

'Can the Kuwaiti systems deal with the jamming devices the Israelis have?'

'No. No Arab country will be allowed to have them but...'

'Jabreel, could the work that is being done in Malaga, be applied to any Ferlinghettis anywhere?'

'I guess so. But I had enough trouble getting you this one...'

'And the Israeli radar jamming is the best, the best in the world?'

'Yes. It's called RASP, and was developed by... Oh dear me,' suddenly this Jabreel began to snigger, a most unpleasant sound that began life at the back of his unprepossessing nose, spread upwards through his sinuses and down into his mouth, finally exploding in a snot-laden giggle. 'Don't tell me. Let me guess. You're going to invade Kuwait, oh dear me, dear me...'

But my eyes were on those of the Sword of Islam. They shone with a satanic glitter, though he struggled to keep the line of his mouth firm and dignified, the way it should be when a World Figure in History arrives at a climactic decision. But then his laugh, a whoop of hyena-ish bravado, burst out and the two men embraced, rolling back onto the big settee, still howling with laughter until Jabreel knocked over the Johnnie Walker. The Butcher of Baghdad scooped it up before much of the foul stuff could escape, and slopped what was left into their glasses. He raised his.

'Let us drink. To the destruction of the Sabahs. Allah, how I hate them!'

PART TWO

CHAPTER 4

Philip Henley brought the Vauxhall Cavalier to a halt behind a big power boat on a trailer, and breathed a sigh of relief. For twenty-four hours he had been driving on the 'wrong' side of the road and he had not felt he had got the hang of it, especially on roundabouts: now, when he drove off the big car-ferry whose white hull and superstructure towered above the quay he would be back in a country that drove, sensibly, on the right. He sat for a moment, looked at his watch. Twenty minutes before embarkation began — time to stretch his legs and see if he could spot Cartwright. He pulled a comb from the top pocket of his dark linen jacket and pushed it through the still quite thick dark hair that circled the bald top of his head. Then, he opened the door, got out into the bright May sunlight and glanced up and down the long line of cars, campers and caravans.

Many drivers and their families were stretching their legs: he would not look conspicuous if he did likewise. He hitched his trousers, pants was the word he would have used, smoothed the sides of his jacket, patted the pockets checking for cigarette pack and Zippo. A casual stroll took him to the back of the line, still only three cars behind his. He turned, passed his own car and headed up towards the front. He was looking for a maroon Sierra, G registration, with male driver, no passenger. The man would be a young-looking forty, five years younger than Henley, at five feet seven below average height, fit, one hundred and forty-five pounds, dark-haired Caucasian, would wear glasses for reading.

No problem — there he was. Only seven vehicles in front, he must have arrived only minutes before. Henley strolled on past a small caravan towed by a Renault 5, then a big Mercedes camper, paused, lit a Chesterfield, smoked for a moment and let his gaze wander everywhere but back to the maroon Sierra. He took in the big silo at the end of the quay, the giant hoists mounted on rails and the big white ship he was about to drive on to, before allowing himself to turn and begin the casual stroll back. A small girl in a blue and white flowery dress almost stumbled against his knee, and her slightly bigger brother in blue t-shirt and gaudily striped shorts pulled her out of his way.

He stooped over them.

'Hi, there. You going on vacation?'

They looked bemused, uncomprehending — perhaps they weren't English at all, though the Renault had Brit number plates. Henley stooped, ruffled the little girl's hair and above her head took in, in a brief second or so, Cartwright's dark good looks, a face tired and a little anxious though his body was relaxed enough, shades pushed up on his forehead, elbow resting on the top of his open window.

Satisfied, Henley returned to his own car. Photographs and descriptions were never enough, but now he had seen his man it was all right. The image was a reality, he would never forget him, or mistake someone else for him.

Arnold Cartwright saw the brake lights flash on the back of the small caravan in front of him, realised the line was on the move, reached forward and restarted his motor. This was it then. Just about the most irrevocable of a series of irrevocable decisions, stretching back over the last four weeks to the morning when the Personnel Manager of Ferlinghetti Air Defence Systems (FADSI) UK had invited him to accept 'redundancy' rather than fight dismissal following the Ministry of Defence's new vetting procedures.

'Arnold, I really am sorry about this,' Bates had said, leaning back in his big chair and twiddling with a stainless steel executive toy, 'but behind it lies the Client, the US Pentagon. Whoever works on this next project is going to see specifications of the F117A, and someone, somewhere has decided you just don't match up for that privilege. Don't ask me who, or why, or what, because I don't know.'

Smarmy bastard.

Arnold engaged first gear, let out the clutch, and smiled grimly: no turning back now — one thing for sure was that once the men in orange overalls had slotted you into a niche on one of the car-decks, there was no way they were going to unslot you until the boat docked at Santander. He supposed they'd still let you jump ship, though even that might be difficult, and you'd lose the car, at least until the MS Brittany got back in a week's time. And Cartwright was not going to give up his car — apart from his brains, training and experience, and a couple of suitcases filled with clothes and a couple of cardboard boxes of reference books and hi-tech journals, all in the boot, it was his last remaining asset.

He could have fought Margaret for a half share in the matrimonial home, but what would have been the point?

The big mouth gaped Jaws-like, the ramps clanged and a man in a peaked cap murmured into an RT as Arnold slipped past him into the big well-lit maw. It always reminded him of the set of one of the earlier Bond films, with gantries men could run along and fall off, bang bang you're dead. One of the dockers in front, short ginger beard and oily hands, waved the caravan to the left, and when Cartwright tried to follow angrily waved him to the right.

I hate this, he thought. Already, after a separation only six weeks old, after six weeks of living entirely on his own for the first time in his life, his thought processes were more verbalised, had become a conversation with himself.

It's less than nine months since we were here before, on our way to spend a fortnight with Dad in Torrox, and no idea at all in my head she already had a bit of fancy on the side. No, it's not for the money, she'd said, when she took a part-time post at the Comprehensive, it's to give me a sense I'm still some use to the outside world. Use? To the outside world? It was the Head of Art who turned out to have a use for her.

Cartwright thumped the steering wheel with both fists and the docker who was waving him down the corridor of cars narrowed his eyes anxiously.

Cut. They always do that throat-cutting sign when they want you to stop. Stupid. No return to the car-deck once the boat has sailed so I must be sure to take up the right suitcase. Do I lock the doors or not? Do I leave the car in gear or not? Every time we made this trip, it would have been the fourth in three months' time, I asked her and she always knew and I'm blowed if I can remember now without her.

It's not the first thing there's been like that either, not by any means. She always kept the passport, the tickets, the cabin reservation, knew where they were and when and to whom they should be shown . . . Passport? I have to make do with a Euro travel document until I can get my own passport, and I always thought the one we all shared was, in the first place, mine.

What was it the Pentagon had taken against? Support for the local militant Member of Parliament the Kinnockites had wanted to deselect? But he only did it because it didn't seem fair. The Greenpeace decal on the back window of the car? The kids had put that there, not him, and it was Margaret who was the member. There was no rhyme or reason to it that he could see. Off-yellow suitcase with the straps, that's the one with toiletries and a change of clothes.

And he slammed the boot, locked it.

Smell of hot diesel, vibration beneath the feet, the tiny lift up to the Information Desk, it's all too familiar, I've done it too often before, and now . . . yes. I miss them. And it's going to be like that all the way there, and all the time I'm at Dad's. It seemed such a good idea, such a lucky coincidence that this job was going to be there, in Malaga, but I'm not so sure now, not so sure at all.

Cock-up over the cabin. Don't know the system, thought number three oh six was mine, that was the number on the reservation, tried to chuck out an elderly couple already installed, but three oh six turned out to be the number of the reservation not the number of the cabin. Margaret. She *always* knew about things like that. Case on one bunk and I sit here on the other, looking at it, wondering what the hell I'm doing here, how the hell I got to be here.

Telephone. Bates here. There's an ad in *The Guardian* appointments section might interest you . . . Project Manager, upgrading a Ferlinghetti AR 3D for commercial aircraft control, private firm based in Malaga, Spain. Canary Wharf office, one of the first to be let, slick post-modern glitz, views over the river. Gabriel Sur. Spic or Dago? No saying but his English was nearer Pak English than American. Of course I'll bloody take it: my marriage has bust up, I'm out of work. No, I don't want you to find me an apartment, I'll stay with my Dad and do my own house-hunting when I get there.

Boing boing. Mesdames et Messieurs . . . get off the boat now if you don't want to go to Santander, bon voyage, have a nice trip. They'll open the bar as soon as they cast off. Could do with a drink before lunch.

'Hi there, you on vacation?'

Cartwright lifted his head out of his half of Stella and looked round. Guy in a blue jacket over a blue sports shirt, dark-haired, going bald on top, a year or two older than him, looked okay. Deep Sean Connery lines from the sides of his nose past the corners of his mouth. Not a nutter or anything like that, just, like him, on his own. And perhaps American? That made him interesting.

'No, actually.' He regretted that. He wasn't the sort of person who said 'actually'. Bates, the Personnel Manager, had been to Oxford and said 'actually' all the time.

'Me neither. What's your line? Mine is security. Personalised security systems, especially premises surveilliance. I'm a salesman. It's what I sell. I'd give you my card but I left my business wallet in my business suit. Phil. Phil Henley.'

'Um . . . Arnold, Arnold Cartwright. Er . . . you sound American?'

'Canuck from Montreal.'

'I have cousins who live in British Columbia.'

'That's a helluva long way from Montreal.'

After self-service lunch, fish and chips (always had fish and chips, family joke: 'last decent fish and chips we'll get until we get to the chippy under Granpop's flat . . .'), Cartwright wandered from deck to deck trying and failing to blot out the memories. Nadine disbelieving that Drake had played bowls beneath that lighthouse. 'Only old men play bowls.' The place where Jimmy had dropped his choc-ice out of its wrapper and they had all walked away, as quickly as they could, smothering giggles, except for poor Jimmy who howled for a second. Then there was the map which lit up, bulb by bulb, marking their progress down the channel to that fist of Brittany that stuck up out of France into the Atlantic, and Nadine held his hand and asked him to explain it, tell her all about it.

The one place they never used was the cinema, video-lounge really, and as soon as it opened he went there. But it was showing *Indiana Jones and the Last Crusade* and was full of kids . . . just like his own.

'So, the Spaniards want customised premise surveillance?'

'Sure do. Well, not just the Spaniards, but all the firms, Euro and otherwise, who are moving in there right now.'

Their voices were raised against the rhythmic jabber of rap from the disco. It was a big room at the front of the ship, a sort of auditorium or arena funnelling down to the bow where a maniac DJ sheltered behind dusky glass in his tiny cubicle. Seating fanned back and up from him and the dance floor in front of him to the long curved bar at the top, the only bar on the ship. Early in May the boat was not full, and most of those on board were elderly — taking off-peak rates both on the boat and in the time-shared apartments they were heading for; but there was a sprinkling of younger couples and singles, enough to keep the DJ interested.

'You'd be surprised,' Phil Henley continued, 'there's a lot of very hi-tech development going on right now in Spain. Especially in the south which is attractive to high-fliers. Why just vacation there if you can work there too? It's Europe's answer to our Silicon Valley . . .'

But you said you were Canadian . . .

'And they need protection. From industrial espionage, for the most part . . .'

MC Hammer gave way to Liza Minnelli — Losing Her Mind.

'So. I have an apartment waiting for me in Torre del Mar, just down the road from Malaga, where the action seems to be, and I'll be operating out of there just as soon as I get my bags unpacked.'

'Well, I suppose that's some sort of a coincidence.'

'It is?'

'I'm heading for Laguna Playa in Torrox. It's the next town east of Torre del Mar. My father lives there now and I'm going to stay with him until I've fixed up a place of my own. And I suppose the outfit I'll be working for is much the sort of thing you're talking about.'

'Hi-tech, micro-electronics?'

'That sort of thing.'

And right now that's all he'll say about it, Henley thought. May be after a few more bevvies . . .?

'What's that you're drinking? Have another?'

'Euro-fizz. Stella.'

'Pint of Stella for my friend Arnold, and I'll have a

whisky sour. You get on all right with your Dad then?'

'Yes, very well.'

'Arnold, I envy you that. My Pop and I have been at loggerheads ever since I was eighteen. When he split from my Mom. Guess I've not seen him more than three times in ten years, weddings and funerals, you know the scene?'

Always make the Subject feel that it's me who is the talkative one, Henley thought to himself, me who's spilling the beans, me who's taken on board a bevvie too many.

When he was working one track of Henley's mind always stood apart, watched and commented, prepared a sort of first draft of the report he would write up later and file. Thus: I gave him an earful on what a bastard my old man is, all true, and soon he was coming back at me about what a whizz his father is. Toolmaker in the performance car trade, made redundant in the late seventies, borrowed money and know-how to set up on his own making computer hardware for a German performance car maker . . .

'That was one of the best times of my life — you see Dad called me in to write the programs, and so for a couple of years we worked together. Then he went public in eighty-six, ahead of the recession, took the money and ran. A cool half million. And last year the company went bust, right down the tube.'

'But he and your mom are safe and sound swanning about in the sun . . .'

'No mom . . . mother — died. Breast cancer ten years ago.'

'Shee-it. That must have been a bummer. I had an aunt who . . .' And I gave him an earful of equine faeces, right off the top of my head. I guess I have this creative streak I like to give an airing to every now and then. Then I twisted it back to where I wanted it to be.

'But this recession is something else again, is it not, Arnie? I mean like I was never a salesman before but a sales manager for a big refrigeration firm, that went bust too. A year ago. I guess it must have been something like that that set you on the road to the sunny south?'

'Not exactly.'

Henley waited.

'No. The firm I worked for will be in business for a bit longer yet . . .'

'But they passed you over.'

'Sort of. They said I had become some sort of security risk, but they had no reason to say that. So . . . I must have just rubbed someone up the wrong way.'

And he went into this Brit spiel about class distinctions, how he was self-trained, took correspondence courses to get the letters he now has after his name, and how the Ivy League guys from Oxford and Cambridge always keep the real plums for themselves. He got quite aerated on this subject, especially after I managed to get a double scotch into him.

'Never met a man yet from Oxbridge who wasn't a wanker. Certainly they've fucked up British industry over the last twenty years and not just on the managerial side either. Even when I was just a kid and still in a blue overall I was sorting out problems for the white-coats . . .'

He wasn't bragging, just bitter.

'I was section leader on a big project we'd just completed, a new contract was coming up in the same field and I reckoned I was on course to be Project Manager this time. There was no-one in the firm who could have handled it better than me. Indeed I reckon I was pretty well essential to it . . . they'll cock it up without me.'

And that was far as I could get. For all he was sick of them, for all they'd treated him like shit, and in spite of five or six drinks, and he was no hard drinker, I could see that, he wasn't going to tell me what line of business he was in, what the new project was, not even the name of the firm.

Half eleven and the teenies, nearly all girls, were going wild to 'Papa don't Preach'. A couple of them came running up the gangway from the floor, can't have been more than seventeen, flushed with the dancing, the holiday atmosphere, bare arms, beads of sweat on their breast-bones, runnelling down beneath the tops of their t-shirts, one in a mini, the other with an ass like a pear, snug in jeans. The smell off them was electric — deodorizers, duty-free scent, sweat and sex. They sang along with the record while the barman made up half-pints of lemonade shandy. Cartwright couldn't get enough of them. When they were gone he turned to me, his face pale now with tiredness and the booze, the lights from the show swirling over it.

'You know, Phil, maybe you won't believe this, but it must be about ten years since I had a really happy sexual experience.'

Well, when they reach that stage you know there's nothing useful to be got out of them before morning. I stood up.

'Can't stand Madonna, and I guess it's my bed-time. See you around, huh?'

Cartwright walked the length of the boat deck, down steps, and on to the sun-deck at the back of the boat. There was a moon, nearly full, Biscay was dead calm beneath it. Coming back last year we saw porpoises, can't have been far from where we are now. 'Porpoises?' a man nearby had said, without lifting his head, 'I've seen them on telly.'

Now a couple were heavy petting on the life-raft in the middle of the space, and the girl was beginning to ooh and aah. Whatever possessed me, Cartwright thought, to say that about sex to a stranger?

CHAPTER 5

Morning was sea mist, and an early breakfast. Cartwright again wandered the boat, trying out memories, see if they hurt. They did. Especially the ones that Nadine figured in. Presently the mist began to lift, creating for a short time a greyish sky, then, on the grey horizon a smudge, a dark line, Spain. The dark line spread. The mist or cloud lifted and suddenly it was a gorgeous sunny morning, sea ultramarine and bottle-green. Cartwright's mood lifted with it. Come on Arnie, this is an adventure, you know? Something good will come out of it. Not many men your age have adventures.

In the foreground a long promontory, green, partly wooded, with large houses, very grand. Islands to the left with strips of pale, bright sand, violet where a man or a parasol cast a shadow: already people were sunbathing and some even swimming, though the Atlantic in May is cold. Boats too, speed boats, dinghies, larger craft, and of course the gaily coloured sails of sailboards. To the right the promontory dropped into a basin filled with high rises and then the long jolly quay of Santander unrolled — palm trees, oleanders just coming into bloom, a wide boulevard, and the splendid late nineteenth-century commercial architecture one sees all over Europe, but not in England. What Jerry didn't bomb the developers pulled down.

The sky was now clear, perfectly, freshly blue. In the distance, behind the city, the mountains climbed into a purple haze.

'It's going to be hot,' he thought. Not hot like July, but better than the cold English spring he had left behind.

The map said: there's only one way to get from Santander to Malaga: Burgos, Madrid, Valdepeñas, Jaén, Granada. So I wasn't going to lose him and there wasn't a lot of point in hanging in behind him, except that I wanted to get to know him better, see what sort of things turned him on, get a bit deeper into his skull.

We were off the ferry just before one. I kept behind the maroon Sierra for just as long as I could, but it wasn't easy. Silly fruit lost his way coming through the industrial area, granted there were a lot of roadworks and new fly-overs under construction, all the same, the road to Madrid was well-signposted, and all the traffic off the boat was going the same way.

Even when we were clear of all that, progress remained slow. A long chain of villages, ribbon development, no by-passes, never more than just the one lane of black-top going our way, a long steady climb up into the mountains at the speed of the slowest and longest container that had come off the boat. At times the road hairpinned and I'd get a sight of him four or five vehicles ahead, for the rest it was a question of being patient. Pretty countryside though, very spring-green, lots of flowers in the steep hay meadows that looked like they could slip off the mountain-sides, streams lolloping through them down to the river below, good trout-fishing around here I guess, wasn't it round here Nick Whatsisname came trout-fishing in *The Sun Also Rises*?

Then, damn him, I passed him. Lay-by to the right, really steep drop to the left, and a small caravan slewed across the carriageway just above the lay-by with a little car in front of it, hood up, engine smoking. Some guy waving me on round the disaster zone, not much traffic coming down the hill fortunately, and the Ford Sierra in the lay-by. Why? What was he playing at?

'You look as if you could use some help.'

'Oh, God yes.'

'What happened?'

'Engine overheated, began to fail, I tried to reverse into the lay-by, caravan jack-knifed, tried to go forward again, could only get it to move by slipping the clutch . . .'

'And you burnt it out.'

'I suppose so. I'm really not very clever with cars.'

A little girl in a blue and white cotton dress stood under a small acacia tree and howled. The acacia was not quite in bloom, leguminous pendants of grey and white buds.

'Is she yours?'

'Yes. Poor thing, I told her to keep off the road while I tried to keep the traffic moving, and she's very upset. My wife, who speaks Spanish, is hitching back down for help. She's got our little boy with her.'

'Well. It's not a big van. We should be able to unhitch and let it slip back into the lay-by without too much trouble.'

'It's, er, quite heavily loaded. We've rented a house in Andalusia for a year, so it's got most of the stuff we'll need packed away . . .'

'All the more reason for getting it off the road. If we keep the brake on, just release it a little at a time, we should manage.'

'Do you really think so? You don't know what a relief it would be . . . My name's Chris. Chris Walker.'

'Cartwright. Arnold.'

It only took a minute or two, and then Walker got in the Renault 5, and let it slip back into the lay-by next to the van.

The little girl stopped howling, got into the caravan.

'Daddy, daddy, can I have a coke, let me have a coke.'

'A coke, *please*, darling. Would you like something, Arnold? I've got a beer . . .'

'No, I'd better get on. I hope things work out for you now. Have a good year in Andalusia. I'm on my way in that direction too, to a job in Malaga . . .'

'Oh really? Look, we won't be far away. In Capileira in the Alpujarra. This is the address and the phone number, if you're ever anywhere near us, then please drop in and have a meal.' He found a beer mat, scribbled: Chris Walker, Cortijo San Mateo, Capileira. 'You don't know how grateful I am, in your debt for ever, that sort of thing, so please drop by if you get the chance . . .'

Oxbridge accent, and an idiot with a car, but he seemed a nice enough bloke, so Cartwright thought he just might.

I pulled in at the top of the pass, Puerto Escudo, where there was a bar-café, and waited maybe twenty minutes in the parking lot before he came by. He didn't stop, and he didn't see me. I gave him three minutes to get clear and fell in behind. It was downhill now into the valley of the Ebro, much bleaker, few trees, lots of brown rocky hills and then prairie greening up with wheat. Then the long haul on past Burgos, across the Spanish *meseta*, good road, well engineered through the Guadarramas, *For Whom the Bell Tolls* country this I reckon, then the long straight road to Madrid — a towering rampart of apartment and office blocks beneath a pall of smog and an angry sunset. What's he going to do? Hole up for the night in a hotel or one of these road-side *hostals* we keep passing, or motor on for as long as he can?

The traffic thickened, the highway became a clearway, spaghetti junction after spaghetti junction, but the big boards clear in their directions: SUR, ANDALUCIA A4, even when I lost him I knew where he was headed, and I soon picked him out again. Then it happened.

He was about three ahead of me and in pole position at a set of lights. Three lanes and next to him a small white open-top driven by a guy who was lean and young, but had like silver hair. I guess something passed between them, a look, a challenge, because when the lights turned the open-top was away fast, and the young guy gave a sort of wave and Cartwright was off after him, ahead of the rest of the traffic, keeping on his tail. Then open-top's indicators blinked orange at almost the last moment and he swooped down a slipway, off the A4, and Cartwright followed . . .

Of course I was in the wrong lane. I guess it was silly, but I pulled across fast and I reckon I must have had a blind spot in the rear view mirror, since although we were now driving on the right, my car was still the Brit one I hired, and right-hand drive. Anyway a fucking great Volvo truck hauling thirty feet of container clipped my rear-end, turned me round, but, thank my guardian angel, not over, and into the crash barrier. Metal heavy on metal and loud.

A shunt is always a shock. Only one thing worse than a serious shunt, and that's a bullet wound. I know. I've had both.

CHAPTER 6

The early stages of the Madrileño rush-hour, on top of all the changes and shocks of the previous weeks, brought Cartwright to the edge of exhausted breakdown. The speed and noise of the traffic, the fumes and the garish colours of the bleeding sky reduced him to a soft and sentient blob, enclosed helplessly in a hurtling metal cage in a cataract of metal cages spinning along a mad roller-coaster of concrete and lights. Worst of all was a complete and uncharacteristic inability to make up his mind. Should he take his chance with a slipway signposted to places he had never heard of and look for a hotel, or stay with with the one illuminated word ANDALUCIA, white on blue, high up against the swirling blood of the skies?

But he had been brought up to believe men do not have nervous breakdowns, are not even indecisive in fast, heavy traffic. People of Cartwright's sort refuse even to rate exhaustion as much of an excuse for backing off. Whenever any of these things threaten they 'get a grip on themselves' which means that they look for a target to get angry with and then get angry, submerging the deeper horrors with one they can handle. And that was his first response the first time it happened.

He was braking for a red, when a small open car came up on his left shoulder, pushing relentlessly, almost touching, so he had either to slam on the brakes and let it in front or pull over to the right. The Cartwrights of this world, even the nicest of them, do not back off to small white cars. He pulled to the right too and kept level, causing the Volvo truck coming up on his inside with its thirty foot container in tow to brake with a great roar of its klaxon.

He turned with anger, ready to vent it, and found he was looking at a vision. The car was small and white, a VW Golf open-top. The driver had very short hair which shone metallically like silver beneath the harsh lights, looked young, no more than twenty, twenty-five at the most. For a moment Cartwright was sure she was a boy, but then took in the white, low-cut top, also shot with silver, and the bare honey-coloured brownness of neck and shoulders. No man Cartwright had ever known would wear such a garment. And she was almost smiling at him: a near smile that seemed to provoke and dare at the same time, offering a challenge and a promise.

The lights switched and the Golf immediately cut in in front of him, causing the anger to burn up again, like a sharp pain behind the breast-bone. He swerved back into the middle lane, without signalling, and the Volvo klaxon roared and the cataract of hot and shining metal thundered on under the sodium lights and the vermilion sky to the next junction, the next red.

Because the Sierra had a right-hand drive and the Golf a left, at the first junction they had been two car-widths apart. Now only a couple of feet separated them. This time her smile was more intimate, more sharing. Together they had had fun, but should it stop now? Shame if it did, if it did stop now, it seemed to say. As the lights changed she lifted her right hand and flicked it forward, just above the honey-brown shoulder. Light flashed from rings and bracelets. The meaning was clear: not ciao, adio, farewell, goodbye . . . but follow me.

He did, took the slipway and ignored the pandemonium of torn steel behind him as the Volvo truck clipped a Vauxhall Cavalier, span it round, sent it into the crash barrier.

His first emotion was gratitude — always a good basis for a new relationship, however transitory. He was grateful to be off the clearway, grateful to have had his mind made up for him. The white car swooped up a ramp onto a flyover, and suddenly the sunset blazed — the flags of an advancing army — straight into his eyes. Then the high rises closed in and narrowed his field of vision, as they dropped again to a new set of lights. There were trees in the avenue they were about to cross, startlingly viridian in the street lights, like plants on a distant planet, but friendlier than the aliens they had left behind. An illuminated sign pointed ahead. It read, simply, O'DONNELL.

It was a wide, long thoroughfare with handsome buildings as well as modern ones, slicing a grid of lesser streets. Always she hung back, made sure he was still there, refused to let other vehicles get between them: that way she made certain that he knew it was a genuine pick-up, not just his fantasy. Again there were occasional trees but less harshly lit, and bars, caves of light, one to every block it seemed, with people sitting outside on white plastic chairs, at white plastic tables. Then on the left, the far side of the street, there was a high wall and lots more trees beyond it, a big park perhaps.

The Golf's indicator flashed beneath a right pointing arrow and another sign: VELÁZQUEZ. He followed — into the grid, away from the park.

She must be, he decided, a prostitute. He had read, in girly magazines and tabloids, of how the Spanish capital is full of them — girls and boys selling themselves for the next sniff of angel-dust, the next whiff of crack. They haunted the asphalt jungle, so he had read, looking for joes who would take a stand-up in a service alley, a blow-job in the park. And no doubt the classier ones cruised the clearways looking for single men in the rush-hour.

She's pulling in. Not at the hotel but a block or two beyond. She has a slot, *en échelon,* beneath the plane trees, but do I? Yes. Six places on there is a gap. I have thirty thousand pesetas, roughly one hundred and fifty pounds in cash, less the cost of my lunch, and she can have all of it. If she wants more she'll have to take a Eurocheque or Visa. But I would like the deal to include somewhere decent to sleep with a proper breakfast.

Suppose, he went on to himself as he locked the door of his car, she wants five hundred quid: so what? I've just kissed goodbye to thousands. Five hundred would cover the music centre alone.

That's what he said to himself. But his real mind was churning with anxiety again and fear of the unknown. Almost his whole life had been spent rejecting the unknown, sheering away from it. But now? What had he to lose? Nothing. Some worthless money? Health??? I might have a condom somewhere, he said to himself, but if I do it's past its use-by date. Actually I don't care. But . . . the fears now dominant in his mind as he walked towards the doorway where he sensed she was waiting were threefold and nothing to do with the price she might ask, the diseases she might carry. Either he would not get it up or he would 'prem'. And the third was: what if s/he is a boy?

Joe E Brown, the last line of *Some Like It Hot*: 'We can't all be perfect.'

He remembered it and began to giggle, and when he saw her he began to laugh. She took one quick look at him, her face suddenly wary and calculating.

'Why are you laughing?'

'I thought,' he spluttered, 'I thought perhaps you might be a boy.'

'My name is Roma.' She pronounced it with a breathy, guttural, rolling sound on the R. 'It means "Exalted".'

'Arnold, Arnold Cartwright.'

She was standing, key in hand, on the stoop of what was clearly a luxury apartment block, with a retailer of oriental carpets on the ground floor. There was Arabic script as well as Spanish on the fliers above the window. And he could see at last what she was really like. Her appearance drained the laughter out of him, and the anxiety flooded back. She was too beautiful for him, too . . . classy.

Beneath the outlandish silver of her hair she had

almond shaped eyes, wide-spaced and very dark; her nose was narrow and straight above full lips painted a natural reddish brown. Her neck was long and shapely, her exposed shoulders thin and bird-like, marked with two small moles. Her torso was thin and small-breasted. She wore tight dark velvet leggings cropped short over shapely calves. Her tiny slippers were silver. She was not more than five feet tall.

In the lift she stood facing him, put her long-fingered be-ringed hands on his shoulders, and pulled them down across his chest to his waist. Her finger-nails matched her lips. Gold bracelets chimed like distant fairy bells. It was a firm caress, exploratory, finding out what sort of body he had, and he could not repress a shudder when it ended, with a squeeze, on his waist.

'There's no need to be frightened of me,' she murmured, then added: 'I would like it if the first thing you do, is to have a shower.'

Her English was slightly stilted and lightly accented. However, in the next twelve hours, she said very little.

CHAPTER 7

The next twelve hours surpassed every fantasy he had ever been capable of imagining, and as he took the long straight road across the Spanish *meseta* towards Valdepeñas late the following morning, he realised he did indeed feel exalted, deeply refreshed, more properly alive than he had ever been before. Everything seemed clearer, brighter, hard-edged, jewelled and enamelled. No doubt this was in part due to the fact that he had only ever travelled down this road at the end of July when all was brown and yellow, dried up, parched and hot, the wheat prairies covered with smouldering stubble.

But now the wheat was tall, and bluey-green, shadowed not by cloud but by the effect of breezy gusts. The roadside was filled with moon daisies, the hillsides with golden broom. Bee-eaters, red, green and yellow swooped in heraldic flight from the telephone wires, the poplars shimmered with fresh bright green leaf. He revelled in all of it but as a backdrop to the memory of all that had happened, for, by playing it over and over again in his mind, he was trying, as hard as he could to lock it there so every detail, every moment, would be part of him for ever, to be relived at will.

For a start, the shower. It was a large space, an alcove set without doors or curtains in one wall of the large, marble-faced bathroom, its floor a step below the rest.

Shy and anxious he kept his back to her, stepped down into the wide flat basin, and turned on the tap — there was only one. The first surprise was that the water hit him not only from above but from both sides as well. He found gel in a container, squeezed some out onto his right palm, and began tentatively to rub it into his left armpit.

Presently he looked over his shoulder. She was still at the far end of the room, leaning against the grey striated marble, still watching, assessing. He wondered what she was thinking, turned away and washed on.

She watched and thought. She had been told that he had been married for fifteen years and that the marriage had recently ended. He was clearly nervous, probably sexually inexperienced. Maybe he longed for a passive role in sex. Being passive did not mean that he would want to be humiliated, physically abused, dominated — just that the most sensual and exciting experience she could give him, the one that would create the bond she was there to forge, would be to allow him, for once, to be the one to whom it happened, rather than the one who made it happen. For the rest he had a strong back with a faded tan, no fat, a real waist, and pale white buttocks, small and tight, above strong legs with some dark hair, not much, good feet. She saw no reason why she should not enjoy what she was about to do.

He turned again and saw her straighten, put her arms above her head and pull off her top, give her silver head a shake. Her breasts were small and firm, the same shade of honey-brown as her shoulders, her nipples were large and dark. Then she stepped out of her slippers and, in one movement, peeled off the leggings and whatever she wore beneath them. She had a very faint bikini pallor over her buttocks; her pubic hair was rich dark brown, but with some red in it which echoed the coppery tones of her skin.

As she came towards him, he turned back, head swimming, heart pounding and he felt rather than saw her come in under the water with him.

She adjusted the flow, turned up the temperature a little, then squeezed a large dollop of emerald-coloured gel into her palm, and, still standing behind him, reached round and began to soap his stomach, his inner thighs and his genitals.

'Put your feet apart.'

He did, and his arms too, stretched out above his head so each palm pressed against the sides of the stall. Chin down, he watched her long brown fingers through the hot scented rain, saw how she was careful not to let her brick-coloured nails do more than tease the sensitive places. The hand in front closed round his prick and lubricated with gel and water began the primal movement along its length.

He knew he was going to come. He wanted to turn, but she resisted the movement.

'Let it happen.'

And he did.

She wrapped him in a thick white towelling robe, and slipped into one like it, then led him into a large warm room lit with candles and an oil lamp with a multi-coloured glass shade. The floor was again marble, but covered with rugs like the ones in the shop below, and many, many cushions. There were more rugs on the walls. There was a low circular marble table, rose-coloured, striated with quartz that glittered, and she asked him to sit on the cushions near it. Then she moved out of the room and left him alone. There was music, not loud, plucked strings and flutes, and subtle perfumes, some spicy, some with the sweetness of marijuana.

Cartwright felt sick with longing and shame that he had come so quickly, but physically he felt both relaxed and weak, a state he associated with childhood and recovery from flu, to being cosseted and looked after by his mother.

Roma came back with plates and dishes — a spicy pilaf with pine-kernels, raisins and shreds of garlicky lamb. There was no cutlery and she showed him how to scoop it up with his fingers and then dip them in a bowl filled with rosewater. Next she brought a tall glass filled with lemon sherbet and this time there was a spoon which she would not let him use, but fed it to him herself, coming close so he could smell her fragrances, and see the shadows between her breasts. They drank ice-cold sparkling white wine. Finally she brought out a plate of small dark cakes, oily and sweet, and with a flavour that echoed the marijuana in the air.

'What are these?'

'Kif.'

He did not know what 'kif' was, but suspected, rightly, that they contained hashish. He began to feel light-headed, little giggles floated up into his mouth like tiny birds trying to escape. And soon too he knew he would have no difficulty at all in achieving an erection as strong as the first.

She cleared the table, then knelt above him, shrugged off the bath-robe, and gently slipped his from his shoulders and arms, then she pushed him on to his back, knelt between his thighs and began to lick his chest and stomach, moving towards his penis. Then, just when he feared he might again come sooner than he wanted, she rose and lowered herself onto him. His head fell back and by turning his cheek he found he was in contact with a small area of cool marble; he pushed his hands through the cushions and found marble there too to cool his palms. The urgency and anxiety faded a little, and he felt strong and hard inside her.

Presently she lifted herself off him and turned right round so now she had her back to him and he was entering her from behind. She was more active now, rhythmically pushing herself up and down with steady acceleration, her head tossing, scattering shards of silver light. Her torso, rouged by the candles and lamp, began to glisten with sweat.

It was then he noticed the scars, a delicate tracery of thin white lines below her shoulder blades and above her buttocks and the sight of them overwhelmed him with tenderness.

'What's the matter, what happened?'

She had felt how his member had slackened.

'Your back, your poor back.'

'That was long ago, forget it, don't think about it.'

She straightened, her hands and arms came behind her and he fastened on to her wrists almost as if they were reins, but who was the horse and who the rider became totally blurred as each urged the other on. Never, when it happened, had he been so aware of a woman's orgasm, nor had he ever been so little aware of his own as something separate from it.

As he cruised into the low hills in front of Valdepeñas, geometrically patterned with hundreds of thousands of vines in emerald leaf, each with its clusters of pale green florets, or hard little buttons of embryonic grapes, the balance between euphoric triumph and anguished longing shifted irreversibly towards the latter. He recalled the pain of waking in the morning from the most perfect sleep he had had since childhood, a pain not assuaged when she took him to the shower again.

This time she faced him, stood close so her breasts touched his diaphragm, while below she again fondled his genitals with gel beneath the warm fine haze of water. Then, when his erection was strong, she looped her arms about his neck and with the suppleness of a gymnast, locked her knees about his waist, her ankles beneath his buttocks. After a moment of wriggling, he felt the warmth and silky wet softness sink over his phallus, closing and folding round it. He put his arms beneath her thighs, cradled her buttocks in his hands, let his fingers meet in the secret places between.

She was not heavy, not heavy at all, and the closeness of the embrace, the way she clung with her legs to him, filled him again with the rush of agonising tenderness he had felt when he saw the weals on her back . . .

The pain of parting had been compounded by his dreadful stupidity: he had put all his pesetas, nearly thirty thousand of them, under one of the cushions. Outside, when he put his hands in his pocket for his keys, he found she had put them all back. She knew he had found them and the smile she offered had forgiveness in it, but a hint of sadness too. When he was behind the wheel, with his window open she kissed her finger, reached through the car window, and planted the kiss on his cheek.

'Left when you get to O'Donnell,' she had said, and then she went — back through the stainless satin-finish steel which framed smoked glass between slabs of marble.

You live in a pad like that, you don't scrub around for a hundred and fifty quid.

Now, nearly three hours later, he topped a low hill and the town ringed with silver storage tanks waiting for the autumn's wine came into view.

'I'd do anything to be with her again,' he said, aloud. 'Kill, betray, anything.'

Her back and its scars, and that last embrace in the shower, which, he could not conceal from himself, recalled the way the eight-year-old daughter he had lost had sometimes clung to him, had sealed the bond, had made him Roma's whenever she should choose to have him.

CHAPTER 8

'You should have thought of me in all this. A little. I have some rights. Grandparents have rights you know. As well as responsibilities.'

This left Arnold confused, even distressed. He had arrived at his father's flat quite late the previous night, emotionally as well as physically drained, had eaten a sandwich, drunk a lot of Herbert's Soberano brandy and gone to bed. In a dark room whose window looked out on a similar window thirty feet away and down five floors to the *patio de luz* he had been left to sleep undisturbed for twelve hours.

Awake at last and in the kitchen to warm up coffee he had found his father already there, making *tortilla.* Spanish omelette, and clearly in a bad mood.

He watched the old man move with neat competence around the modern, immaculate kitchen, beating eggs, stirring the chopped onions and potato cubes which simmered gently in a robust olive oil.

'Where's the salt? Not where it should be.'

Arnold looked around, reached for the plastic tub and pushed it across the spotless work surface.

'Eggs, oil, salt: I thought you were meant to have high blood pressure.'

'Onions and garlic take care of the cholesterol, and I go easy with this.'

He took a big pinch from the palm of his hand, scattered it between finger and thumb into the orange mixture, then picked up a peppermill and ground that over it too, pocking it with black crumbs. His fingers were short and stubby with squared-off nails, his hands broad and on the upperside knobbled with the arthritis which had, initially, caused him to seek the sun. He wiped them down on his black and white striped apron and turned. A small compact man with close-cropped white hair.

'I were closer to a stroke than I ever have been from eating eggs, when I read your letter.' The accent flat, nasal, unemphatic, south Midlands, stronger than his son's. 'You should have given some thought to what it means to me.'

'Dad, you're talking as if this is my fault, something I've done.'

'That's just it. You've done nowt.' He turned back to his cooking.

'There was nothing I could do.'

'You let her have the children. My grandchildren.'

'Dad, I took advice. Proper legal advice . . .'

'Who from?'

'Frobisher. Tom Frobisher.'

'Arnie,' he turned away from the pan, waved that most essential implement in Spanish cuisine, an *espumadera*, a flat spoon or spatula, enamelled white, with holes in it, under his son's nose. 'Tim Frobisher is a wet fart.'

'Dad, Tim Frobisher retired a year after you came out here. Tom is his son, and he's very competent. And he simply laid on the line what I knew anyway. If the mother is not a heroin addict, a violent alcoholic, and has no record of violence to her children, is not certifiably mad and has the use of two of her four limbs, she gets custody. And that is that.'

'It don't seem fair.'

The old man, using the *espumadera*, spooned the onion and potato out onto a plate, poured excess oil into a mug, turned up the heat a little and poured the beaten egg into the pan.

'It's not fair,' Arnold agreed. 'But there's not a thing we can do about it.'

'I'll never see them again.'

'Yes, you will. Half of each school holiday. I'm entitled. Since you came out here, you only ever saw them for a fortnight in August anyway. Now you'll get three weeks. And, if I stay on here, more than once a year.'

Cartwright senior pushed the egg around for a moment or two, then let the soft onion and potato slip into the mixture. He spread them about in it, then left it all alone while a skin formed on the bottom.

'I still think you should have put up a fight. I tell you, if my mam had done that, my dad would have taken a pit prop and knocked the fancy man about with it and that would have been that.'

'And what would *you* have done?' Instantly Arnold regretted the question.

'Considering the sort of person your mother was, that's a bloody stupid thing to ask.' He paused, then realised an argument would help neither of them, returned to his cooking. 'This is the tricky bit.'

He slid the omelette carefully out of the pan and onto a plate, put another plate upside down above it, and turned them over. Then he slid the reversed omelette back into the pan so the uncooked side was now face down. It all now had the look of a perfectly round, well-formed eggy cake about an inch and a half thick.

'Cookery programme on Canal Sur taught me that. Turn the heat off now, there's enough in the pan to cook the rest, good thick tinned copper, leave it moist in the middle. And it should cool and settle before we eat it. Fetch a beer out of the fridge, our Arn, and we'll sit out for a bit.'

'Out' was on the one of the two large, south-facing balconies. The block was best Spanish modern, shiny small bricks, well-organised tiers of balconies, not a square but an ovoid tower. Inside the apartment there were two big living rooms, both with balconies: a dining room which the old man only used when his son's family came to stay; the other a big sitting room with comfortable sofas, low tables and a very large television with satellite dish so he could get all the English language programmes he wanted. That was not as important as it had been — in four years he had taught himself very reasonable Spanish, good enough to cope with Spanish TV.

There were framed photographs of his grandchildren in their school uniforms and a large oil, done from a photograph after her death, of Arnold's mother. Chrissie had been very pretty in an English rose sort of way and Herbert had worshipped her for her delicacy, her education and her forbearance. It was the tragedy of his life that she had not survived to enjoy the affluence of his later years: she had taught him to love beautiful things but by the time he might have shared them with her, she had gone.

The only other decorations were photographs and botanical paintings of orchids, Herbert's obsession. It had started as a hobby, initially inspired by the novels of Rex Stout. Rex Stout, Raymond Chandler and P G Wodehouse had been Chrissie's favourites, and were the only fiction writers he ever read. He had had the balcony beyond the dining room glassed in and that was where he grew his orchids. The obsessional element arose when he brought off his first true original hybrid and named it after his dead wife.

For the rest there were three large bedrooms, kitchen and bathroom, tessellated floors throughout which his cleaning lady ran a mop over twice a week, and solid dark Spanish furniture, which did not look dull or heavy since it all shone brightly, and the lighting, both natural and at night, was very bright.

Arnold carried two glasses of ice-cold San Miguel to where Herbert already sat in one of the two bucket-shaped white plastic chairs with a bowl of pistachios and another of plump green garlicky olives at his elbow. He bought the olives fresh in the little municipal market every November when they came into season, bled the bitterness out with brine and pickled them, enough for a year, some with garlic, some with rosemary he gathered from the road-sides in the hills behind Torrox.

It was all part of what Arnold jokingly called 'going native'. Herbert's riposte was to claim there was a lot more to Spain than sun and bullfights (though he loved both), and it was silly not to make the most of it. He hated the ex-pats who drank gin all day, gave themselves skin cancer in the sun, complained about the socialist government, and bought their olives in the same little jars they arrive in at Sainsbury's.

One o'clock and the sun was already warm, tempered by a slight breeze which blew off the emerald and sapphire sea and rattled the palm fronds below. There was a silvery jacaranda tree in full and gorgeous blossom, swags of lapis lazuli blue, which gave Herbert particular pleasure.

'It's certainly very handsome, but why are you so particularly crazy about it?'

Herbert chuckled, put down his beer, and came back with a very well-thumbed green and white Penguin, opened it at the first page.

'Second paragraph.'

Arnold looked at the cover first. *The Little Sister.* The last sentence of the second paragraph read: 'And in Beverley Hills the jacaranda trees are beginning to bloom.'

'I still don't get it.'

'Look, it says 'across the Hollywood hills you can see snow on the high mountains.' That's the Californian Sierra Nevada. And from here you can see snow on the Spanish Sierra Nevada, and a jacaranda in bloom.'

Arnold still couldn't see why this gave him such a kick, but he let it go, drank his beer. Perhaps it was because Herbert lived alone, perhaps it was the onset of senility, but at just seventy that shouldn't be a problem yet.

' "Daft git", that's what you're thinking. Never mind. Tell me about this job.'

When Arnold had finished the old man said nothing, got up, and came back with two more San Miguels with the tops off, waited till they had been poured, then . . .

'Arnie, it's got a whiff coming off it like rotten meat.'

'Why do you say that?'

'This isn't called the Costa del Crime for nothing.'

'What's criminal about upgrading a radar system?'

'It's a military system, isn't it?'

'Yes. But it can be used for peaceful purposes.'

'You told me a year ago how your rivals, Plessey, sold three military radar systems to South Africa and everyone including the MoD said they were for civil aircraft control. But when they got there they were deployed in Namibia on the Angolan border . . . on behalf of the South African backed rebels.'

'Well, we'll see. Anyway I've got to live, haven't I?'

'Ferlinghetti gave you a proper handshake, didn't they?'

'Of course.'

'You could have waited six months, a year.'

'Kicking my heels in digs, in Nottingham, with nothing to do? I'd have gone mad.'

'All the same. Bad enough you was working in defence. Never liked a son of mine in armaments. But at least it were legal.' The old man sighed, squeezed his aching knuckles. Again, one thing he didn't want, on Arnie's first day, was a row. 'Any road, not my business. I reckon we can eat that omelette now. Salad with it, all right?'

And he stomped off again, leaving Arnie feeling sour and empty. He shifted in his seat. Still a slight ache in his balls to remind him, but that would be gone by tomorrow, and then all that would be left would be the mental ache, the anguish.

'Roma,' he murmured to the breeze and the pendulous swags of blossom. 'Roma.' And he carefully rolled the 'r' with a breathy sigh behind it, the way she had.

Who would know in what language it was that those two syllables meant 'exalted'? Who could he ask, where could he find out?

CHAPTER 9

'Roma? Capital of Italy, that's all it means to me. I guess there may be one in Texas too. Why?'

'It's the name of a girl I met. The night after we landed.'

'Oh yeah? Where?'

'In Madrid.'

Well, I could have sworn it was a boy in the VW Golf, just before that mother of a Volvo nudged me off the clearway. (As usual Henley's mind ran a simultaneous scan on what was happening, fixing it for the detailed reports his employers required.)

'Tell me about it?'

'No, I don't think so.' Arnie cradled his nearly empty glass between his palms, his eyes solemn and far away.

'Okay! Here comes Pedro. Are you ready for another?'

'Why not.'

'Dos cervezas más.'

'I need a pee.'

'I won't run away.'

Café-bar Caracas, on the main drag through Torre del Mar. Four busy weeks later. Ten days in hospital, couple of crackedribs, broken collar-bone, facial bruising and shock. Then a car to be bought, new model Renault 19 this time, nice job — reasonable performance and there are about a million on the road in Spain, so not conspicuous. And the driving seat is in the right place. All in all it was nearly two weeks before I got down to Malaga and another three days before I located Cartwright's dad and Cartwright himself.

At that point I went to a local firm and hired a couple of gumshoes to take over. Two reasons: I didn't want Cartwright to spot me before I was ready or without my knowing he had; and if any other firm was on Cartwright's tail I didn't want them to know I was there too.

The gumshoes were okay, did a good job. Located where he worked, and nailed this bar as the one he always stops at on a Thursday night on his way home from work. Later he goes on to a Chinese restaurant round the corner. They even figured out why he does this on a Thursday. Thursdays Cartwright senior goes to a painting class. Flowers.

I moved out of the studio I'd taken and into an apartment a block away from the Caracas, so it looked as natural as anything in the world and not much of a coincidence at all when Cartwright came in and found me sitting in his favourite booth — the one furthest from the computer games and the TV. Which made it my favourite too.

And sure, he had been pleased to see me, happy to accept the coincidence. Apart from his dad and the guys at work, who, it seems, are an unattractive bunch, some without much English, he hadn't spoken to a soul since he left the boat. And Roma.

A one-night stand? A pick-up? The classier janes hunt the clearways for tricks during the rush-hour in all the best cities. But four weeks on and he was still thinking about her? Does that happen with a jane? Maybe, if the joe is an innocent sort of guy, and falls into it half by accident anyway. What did he say to me on the boat? Ten years since he had had decent sex? Something like that. Or was she something else again? He'll tell me. He brought the subject up so he wants to talk about it. Forget it, he said. But he won't. He won't talk about work, so what else can we chew the rag over? Here he is.

'Have you eaten?'

'Not yet.'

'There's a Chinese round the corner I go to. It's pretty awful but they will serve you before nine o'clock. I have to say I just can't get used to Spanish eating habits and I like my last meal of the day before ten o'clock.'

Pretty awful? It's dire. Well, when you know San Fran Chinatown, you get expectations about Chinese food. This place doesn't even have a dim sum trolley. The sweet is too sweet, the sour vinegary, the batter on the prawn balls soggy, and water chestnut in the stir-fry instead of on the side. All the clients are Brit and they seem happy so I suppose it's how they like their Chinese in Brit-Land. The liquor though was strong, good quality Chinese rice wine, and I managed to wean him off the Euro-fizz and get a half-litre of the stuff inside him.

'Brandy and coffee? My treat?' Back at the Caracas, quieter now, and we sit at the bar. Bar-buddies. Intimate, you know?

'I knew a girl called Roma once.' Making it up as I go along. 'In fifth grade. Big bosomy broad, let you have a look at them for a dime.'

'She wasn't like that. Not at all.' Dreamy look again, swinging the brandy round. I'd asked for a classy brand, Carlos V, so it came in proper snifters. 'The odd thing though is . . .' He looks up, a bit shy, a bit baffled. Is he going to go on or isn't he? Only thing you can do is wait, wait and hope. 'I think . . . I think I've seen her twice, here in Malaga.'

'Yes?' This is interesting, *very* interesting. But let him see that and he'll button up.

'You see, she has this extraordinary hair, like silver, I mean it really shines metallically. I saw it first driving home down the Paseo del Parque, through the trees, a gap in them. Just a glimpse.'

'But if the hair is that crazy, any time you see hair like it you're going to think it's her.'

'That's what I said to myself. But the next time was different. I like snorkelling. My father knows a place up the coast beyond Nerja where there are three or four unspoilt coves. It's where the road goes very close to the sea but high above it and the hillsides are very steep. Anyway it's great for snorkelling, because of the rocks, and the shingle bottom, the sand only begins beyond the headlands, so the bay itself is always clear. Do you go snorkelling at all? No? Well, on your own, it can be very, very restful. Just the fish and the sunlight and the water. It can be a bit scary too, if you're close to rock, in shadow, or if there's a lot of weed.'

I took a pull at my brandy and nodded. He went on.

'Well, most of the time you're looking straight down, because that way the snorkel stays at the right angle, and of course, if you get really caught up in it, you are totally unaware of what's happening on the surface, especially behind you. I was in about fifteen feet of water, with bright emerald weed below, and a shoal of bright fish silvering across it. Don't ask me their names, I don't bother with all that, I just like looking at them. Behind me and to my left I knew there were the rocks of the headland, climbing in untidy pinnacles to a hundred feet or so above the water, but with ledges and even small caves.

'I think I heard the splash, felt it even, the shock through the water, then there she was, gliding swiftly like a seal or a dolphin or something, beneath me, arms by her side, feet and legs flickering in a crawl movement, then arching up and away, long trail of silver bubbles. She was very close, not more than four feet below me, her body and legs striped like a tabby cat by the shadows the wavelets make. I couldn't see her face of course . . .'

'But the same hair.'

'Not only that. You see she had this . . . . like lattice work of very thin white scars on her back.'

'So what did you do?'

'I tried to get my head up, mask off, swallowed a ton of water. By the time I'd got my bearings and stopped spluttering, she was fifty yards away and swimming, well, like a dolphin. Far faster than I can, round the headland, into the next cove. By the time I got round the corner she'd gone. There was a small powerboat, glassed-in cockpit, couldn't see if it was just her in it, or if there was someone else. It didn't shoot off dramatically, it didn't have to. It just chugged out of the bay and was gone.'

He pushes down the end of the brandy, looks at his watch. Classy, old-fashioned Rolex Oyster, a twenty-first from his dad? It's his dad he's thinking of.

'Better get back now. Dad goes out Thursdays, but he'll be home by now, waiting up for me. Thanks for the drink. Next time, my shout, okay?'

After he's gone I lift a finger for the other half and while the barman pours, I say to myself, well, Phil, what do you make of that?

Entrapment it has to be. And it has to be connected with the work he's doing. Somebody wants to know: they could break in, stitch him up, harass him. What I know of Arnie makes me feel that won't work too well, unless they have a go at Dad. And you can't buy the Arnies of this world. But sexual enslavement, yes. Still young enough for it, coming out of a dull marriage, yep, that will do nicely, very nicely.

But who? Who wants to know all about it as much of even more than the firm I'm working for? Well, Phil, we'll just have to keep an eye on that angle too.

A week later and he's back at the Caracas, looking for me this time, waiting for me. I know a bit of what he has to say but of course I have to make sure he doesn't guess that. But I know why he now looks sort of gone over, paler than before, a touch dishevelled.

According to the bimbos I had working for me, Cartwright's apartment was broke into that very night before Arnie got back. No details, they didn't want to hang around with the Guardias all over the place. Bimbos? They work for me no more. Two nights ago I sent them over the wire into the compound where Arnie works. One got back out with a nasty flesh wound, but the dogs were just beginning to eat the other when the handler came out and called them off. I told them — dogs. They said — we know dogs. But they didn't, did they? So. Bimbos.

'Hi Phil,' he calls, making sure I'd seen him, he's that anxious to talk to me. He's drinking what looks like a large, long g and t. I take the banquette opposite and Pedro brings me my beer. After a coupla weeks he knows that's how I start — a small beer from the tap with a slice of the air-cured ham on a circle of plain bread.

'Phil, the last week has been terrible. I've had a really rough time.'

'And now you're going to get it off your chest.'

'First, last Thursday my Dad was burgled. Now these modern apartments here, the pricey ones anyway, are virtually burglar proof. So what the burglar did was wait until Dad came home, then came up behind him while he was tapping in the numbers on the electronic outer lock, gave him the time of day, so he thought he knew him, was a resident, and slipped in with him. In the lift he forced his keys off him, then bundled him into the flat, tied him up and gagged him. Seventy years old, and high blood pressure. They could have killed him.'

'What did this guy take?'

'Well that's it. Nothing. But he went through the place very quickly, searching everywhere, but most especially through all my stuff. And then he did the worst thing of all. Dad grows orchids, has about twenty, and he tipped out all the pots, looking for whatever it was they were looking for. It nearly broke Dad's heart. I got in not long after he gave up and left. He'd untied Dad, ungagged him, and he was on his knees in this conservatory place he's made out of one of his balconies, trying to clean up the mess, and crying. Yes, crying. He wouldn't go to bed until we'd got it to rights again.'

'Arnie, that's terrible, that's one of the most terrible things I ever heard. So what was it all about?'

'It has to be the job I'm doing here. He must have been trying to find some sort of clue, or work I'd brought home

. . . I don't know. But I am sure that there are people trying very hard to work out what it's all about . . .'

'What makes you say that, Arnie?' I ask, knowing too darned well what's coming next.

'A couple of nights ago, two men broke into the compound. Well, at night we have rottweilers patrolling the perimeter. These men had mace in aerosols, which I suppose normally might have worked, but our dogs have been well-trained to attack from all sides at once, and since there are six of them . . . Well. Sparing you the details, they actually killed one of the intruders, and began eating him before they were called off.'

'That must mean you've had the police in.'

'Yes.'

'Do they know who these guys were working for?'

'Apparently they were partners, small-time private detective agency.'

'But who employed them?'

'The survivor says they never knew. That they just got their instructions, their fee and that was it. The police have told us to put the dogs down and get more men in instead.'

Good news for yours truly. Arnie catches Pedro's passing eye and presently he's working his way through his second, if it was his second, large g and t.

'Thing is Phil, I can't risk a repeat of what happened to Dad. I've got to move. I've already found a flat, it's right here in Torre del Mar, but I need it to be secure. Now, on the boat, you said you were coming down here to sell security and surveillance systems . . .'

Life is not always a bowl of cherries, the plums don't always fall in your lap when you shake the tree, but just occasionally someone up there gets it right. In spades. I was so pleased I quite forgot to ask him if he'd seen the girl again.

CHAPTER 10

Corpus Cristi fell on Thursday, 15 June. A grateful management declared the week could end on Wednesday at seven p.m., resuming work the following Monday at ten.

Grateful? The first trial in the schedule had taken place at the end of the previous week, with the staff working round the clock for three days, running the new software through a test harness in the aeroplane hangar which was the biggest building on the site. Monday saw the start of a three day meeting during which the whole team of twenty managers, technicians and programmers, analysed the results of the trial. By Wednesday midday it was clear that Al Rashid, the new program and modified hardware, so far did for Haroun, which was what Gabriel Sur had decreed the Ferlinghetti AR 3D he had bought from Ecuador should be called, exactly what was wanted. In short the birth pangs of Haroun al-Rashid, an advanced radar system with three dimensional technology, capable of slotting into Iraq's air defence systems and of dealing with the latest in radar jamming, were well under way.

Not that anyone on the site knew that Iraq was involved: they had been told that the system was on lease from Ecuador to Mauretania, which was so unlikely no-one believed it. If they thought about it at all they thought of Iraq or Iran, but, though they were very definitely paid to think, thinking of that sort was not encouraged.

Cartwright declared a 'build', that is, he ordered the current status of the software to be frozen, and authorised the Quality Assurance Manager, a Korean woman of formidable mien and intellect called Tai-Won-Kun, to seal the software and prepare three copies of the source code and object code on RA72s: a working copy, a copy for quality assurance, and a back-up, known as the archive copy. At seven fifteen he locked up his office and drove the twenty miles back to Torre del Mar.

Routinely he opened his mailbox expecting no more than the usual handouts for dry-cleaners, a new hyper-market and fiesta discos at the local bars. But amongst it all he found a plain off-white envelope he might well have overlooked.

He opened it there and then, still standing in the street outside his block of apartments. There were three articles in it. The first was a simple, unadorned and unflattering photograph of Roma — taken in a photo-booth. It made her silver hair look tawdry and reduced the animation of her lovely eyes to a sullen stare, the glow of her skin to pasty sallowness. But it was she, not a shadow of doubt, the moles on her shoulders said so. The presence of it in the palm of his hand made his eyes smart, the back of his throat burn, while an intolerable knot of anxiety and longing formed behind his diaphragm.

The second article was a coloured piece of paper about two inches by four. Its thin outer border of purple framed a crude print of a watercolour depicting a *torero* in green and gold plunging his sword between the shoulder-blades of a big black bull. On yellow beside it, inscribed in brown and dark blue print he read: *Plaza de Toros GRANADA, 15 de Junio de 1990, 2600 ptas. SOL tendido 12. FILA 15 No. 13.*

The third article was a slip of lined paper torn from a tiny notebook. On it, in scrawled, untutored ball-point: 'Before you go to Granada please to leve Al Rashid Archive Copy on your kidjin table.'

Cartwright did not hesitate. Within moments he was speeding back down the motorway which carries through traffic in a loop through the hills before returning to the coast and the final stretch of dual carriageway, past the cement works and the brewery and so into Malaga. Ten minutes of frustratingly narrow roads still choked with rush hour traffic brought him into the wide one way avenue of the Paseo del Parque with its tall palms and glossy camellias, oleanders and evergreen magnolias, and so at last to the signs for Granada and Antequera which point north away from the centre and the quays. He made it back to the compound on the northern outskirts in twenty minutes. Twenty miles in twenty minutes — wicked, his son Jimmy would have said, even with the seven miles of motorway.

The site was part of a vast industrial estate lying between the main road and the railway, served by both, and on the north side occupying land that had once been part of a military airfield. Sur Industrias S.A. had come here not because it was part of Spain's silicon valley, but because the site, previously occupied by a now bankrupt manufacturer of small planes, had an aeroplane hangar in it.

SISA needed a hangar to house the eight containers and diesel generators that made up the Ferlinghetti AR 3D system and for closed circuit tests, like the one that had just been completed. That way they hid from the world, or at any rate that part of the world that has curiosity, small helicopters and aerial cameras, what they were up to.

The guard on the gate lifted the first barrier after the most cursory glance at his ID, the second opened the tubular steel gate mounted with razor wire as readily as if Cartwright had been Gabriel Sur himself. Why? At ten o'clock in the morning he and twenty others were expected. But at eight o'clock in the evening somebody should have been saying: why are you here?

He locked the car, trotted up a couple of concrete slab steps, unlocked his office door. He went straight to the Chubb safe, turned the dial in the reverse sequence of his birthday numbers and swung open the heavy door. The shelves were filled with folders and binders: the specifications of the Ferlinghetti AR 3D. On the top of one pile was a small leather-bound pocket diary. From 1 May to 30 October each day-slot carried, in neat fountain-pen, a six figure number, a different number for each day. The computerised electronic combination lock on the computer room door would respond to these open sesames only. Thus he alone on the site had the ability to open it each morning at ten o'clock when the day's work started. A similar diary was locked away in Gabriel's Sur's personal safe in his home near Marbella, kept in case Cartwright fell under a bus.

He relocked it all behind him. Out again in the warm evening air he thought: I'm bloody glad those dogs have gone.

He trotted up the computer room steps, four this time because the raised floor inside housed the cables that powered and linked the fourteen Digital computers and the pipes that carried the icy water from the plant above to heat exchangers sited at the base of each. In the gathering dusk, with mewing swifts scouring the luminous opaline sky above, Cartwright dabbed the numbers he had memorised from the diary on to the number pad by the door jamb. The door clicked and responded to pressure. The second door opened to a key on his key ring.

Computer rooms never sleep. The strip lighting, the air-conditioning and the fans that circulated the cool air had all been left on to maintain within narrow parameters the environment the computers liked best. They buzzed and clicked, and would continue to do so for nine more hours before they turned themselves off, converting the source code from the new software into machine code, producing the build from the programs that had been created during the previous six weeks.

Cartwright walked the length of the room to a rack of meccano-like shelving at the far end, past the VDTs with their keyboards in front of them on their metal tables, and the matching chairs. All were on castors for easy movement when access to the space below was needed, and one that had been left a little out of line with the rest swung and rolled a foot or so as he brushed it in passing.

The RA 72s were on the open shelving. They were identical apart from labelling: packs eight inches square three inches thick housing twenty five-and-a-quarter-inch floppies in impact-proof plastic casing. Each pack held one thousand megabytes of data. A novel of eighty thousand words requires half of one megabyte. Custom had not staled the sense of wonder Cartwright felt when he considered these capacities. He was old enough to remember the pre-micro technology when computers with this sort of capacity required, literally, acres of space. He opened his brief-case and into it slipped the one labelled *Al Rashid Build 1 (Archive).*

As he drove out of the gate, a stretched Merc 300 SE, silver with tinted windows, pulled in behind him. He was sure it had not been there when he arrived. But when he got back to the centre it took a right to the west, so he gave it no more thought.

As he drove back down the coast road, wondering if she really would turn up and sit beside him in the Granada bull-ring, he felt a niggling tremor of guilt. Not because he had betrayed his employer, but because he had promised to spend Corpus Cristi with Herbert. Every year for the last four years his father had gone to the Corpus Cristi bullfight in Granada. This year, partly as a result of the break-in, partly because of his blood pressure, he had decided to stay at home and watch it on Canal Sur. He had asked Arnie to spend the evening with him, share a six-pack like they used to on Cup Final day.

He'd have to cry off, and he doubted if Dad would take it well.

CHAPTER 11

'Dad? Arnie here. Look, the boss at work has given me a ticket for the bullfight, sort of bonus, with dinner and a hotel after . . .'

'Arnie, you must go. I'll miss you, but I'll keep an eye out for you on the telly. Come over and tell me all about it when you get back.'

'Of course I will. Thanks, Dad.'

That was all right. Then since they had kept up the Thursday routine, even though the original reason for it had disappeared when he moved out of his father's apartment, he rang Henley.

'Phil? Arnold Cartwright here. Look tomorrow's a holiday and I'm off to Granada for the fiesta so don't expect me round at the Caracas. Next Thursday? Okay.'

'Fine, Arnie. Don't forget to open Red Eye before you go.'

Red Eye was the name he had given to the security and surveillance system he had put in for Cartwright.

Cartwright was now too excited, overwrought and anxious to sleep, or at least not until he had fought his way through a third of a litre of Soberano. He spent a lot of time gazing at the photo, and then suddenly sickened of it. It did not do her justice. He put it, and the hand-written message, back in its envelope and left it on top of the cartridge on the kitchen table. 'Kidjin'? Kitchen, surely.

Then just as he was getting seriously drunk he scrawled a note of his own: 'Please make sure the RA 72 cartridge is here on Sunday: I must replace it before work on Monday. AC'

At last, staggering and bleary, and knowing he would sleep at last, he pulled off his clothes and rolled into his bed. Memory and fantasy merged into erotic dream. He woke briefly at first light with a hangover, thirst for water and a powerful erection. He drank half a litre of Lanjaron carbonated, masturbated furiously, then slept again, through to ten o'clock.

Spain takes Europe seriously, flies the blue flag with its circle of stars as proudly and as often as its own red and yellow flag. Less rationally it has adopted Euro-time even though it is on the western periphery of the community. This means that in summer real noon is about half-past two, the southern heat does not cease to build until five o'clock, nor get noticeably less harsh until two hours later. Five o'clock Franco-time, twenty-five years ago, is now seven o'clock Euro-summer time and the big bullfights begin at seven.

Nevertheless, Cartwright was on his way within an hour of waking for the second time, leaving Torre del Mar by the secondary mountain road that his map told him was the shortest route. It was a spectacular drive up mountain-sides covered in pink and white oleander and, higher up, golden broom. It was a glorious day, the air fresh and clean after the fumes and humidity of the coast.

At the highest point, on the border between the two provinces, he parked in shade beneath cork oaks, got out into the warm thyme and lavender scented air. Butterflies, long-tailed blues and saffron cleopatras, browsed the nectar from the flowers. He looked back the way he had come. Between and beyond the folds of the foothills he could see the sea still only twelve miles away as the crow flew but now four thousand feet below him so the very far distant horizon was higher in his field of vision than he had ever seen it other than from an aeroplane.

Rimmed in the foreground with bright bottle-green, the

more distant spaces, huge it seemed from up there, merged from deep ultramarine to deep violets, with small patches of dark purple where puffballs of cloud, actually floating below him, cast their shadows. And right in the very furthest distance a line of cumulus, at this distance a row of seed pearls, lay above a thin dark thread that seemed to mark precisely where sea and sky should merge. An optical illusion? He strained his eyes to make sense of it, even to be sure he wasn't imagining it, then: 'I'll be damned,' he said aloud. 'Africa!' He was looking at Africa! Deeply elated, he got back into the car and drove on.

He had been to Granada twice before, with his family, to see the Alhambra, the Cathedral and the mausoleum of the Catholic Monarchs, Isabel and Ferdinand, and a map of the city was among the things he had brought back out with him. He expected parking to be a problem, but arriving as he did at the beginning of siesta time, on the day of the city's biggest fiesta, it didn't take long to find a pay and display space on the small Plaza de Gracia.

He was hungry now, and with the car safely parked for several hours at least, ready for a beer or two. More of a problem than parking was finding a seat at one of the tables beneath the acacias, whose white flowers, heavily scented with a jasmine-like fragrance, were already crumbling apart to release drifting fluff. Just as he was about to give up and move on somewhere else, a family, English perhaps since the children were blond and the adults fair, scraped back their white chairs, showed sure signs of being about to leave. He moved in, hovering, with a half-smile on his face, not wishing to appear to hurry them.

'I say, don't I know you? Yes, I do! Darling, this is the wonderful man, the Good Samaritan who helped me get the caravan off the road. Arnold. Arnold Cartwright. Arnold, meet the wife: Jenny, Arnold.'

'And you're, let me see if I can remember, Walker, Chris. Chris and Jenny. You survived the ordeal then?'

Jenny was small, plumpish, with a nice open face and an easy laugh. She explained how she had successfully found a troll-like character with a workshop who made a good living off break-downs on the mountain. A few minutes of slightly awkward chat followed. How are you settling in? Are you here for the fiesta? And from the little boy: 'Are you going to the bullfight? We are.'

Which surprised Cartwright: Margaret had absolutely refused to go to bullfights, wouldn't let the children even watch them on Grandad's television.

Quite soon though, with typically British reluctance to develop a casual acquaintance, and very much to his relief, they moved off after repeating again the open house invitation if he was ever in their 'neck of the woods'.

After a plate of squid rings deep-fried in batter with a salad of tomato and olives and two beers he began to feel, for a short time at any rate, a little calmer, and conscious too that there were still four hours to kill. Attracted by the sound of Andalusian pop-flamenco he wandered up towards the cathedral and found all the little squares around it, and the larger Bib-Rambla too, filled with enclosures, *casetas*, each with a small area of tables and chairs in front of a stage and covered with white and red awnings. Thousands and thousands of large white and red paper pom-poms filled all the spaces between, strung from every small palm tree and lamp-post.

And the dresses! Margaret had vetoed a flamenco dress for Nadine on the grounds that only tourists bought them. He felt a sudden wave of anger at the thought of how wrong she had been in this as in so many other life-denying decisions. Nearly every Andalusian female he could see between the ages of three and thirty was decked out in the full rig: carnations and ribbons in the hair, lavish make-up, a wave burst of lace and flounces at each shoulder, low bodice, long tight waist, and then the layers and layers of swinging, swaying skirts, and the colours — raucous pinks, brilliant greens, turquoise and jade, orange, lemon and pulsating vermilion.

Best of all was the dancing. Sometimes to tapes, often to small live bands, girls, young and not so young, swayed and stamped and their long brown arms, wrists bent and fingers snapping or clicking castanets, made graceful windmills of delight.

It was too much, the *alegría*, the fine, high joy of it was too much, the anticipation was too much. Shaking his head, tears starting in his eyes, he blundered away, down the dark narrow alleys, seeking some sort of respite from the fiesta's relentless assault on the senses.

At half past six, when he arrived at the Plaza de Toros, the great drum of an arena was already a quarter full with people pouring in at all the entrances, and it took him some time to work out just what his ticket meant, but he got there in the end.

Look around, breathe in the atmosphere, Herbert had said, that's where the magic lies, the magic you never feel on film or telly.

The men were all in shirt sleeves but immaculately clean and pressed, most of the women wore summer dresses and many were *en flamenco*, especially on the balconies above and close to the ring below, where they could drape their fine embroidered mantilla shawls over the parapets . . . Then, oh SHIT. The seat to his left was taken by a huge Mama in a chintz that would have looked fine on a sofa and with a wide-brimmed straw hat which she used as a fan, occasionally flicking his ear with it.

Meanwhile, four very large fat men, with huge sombreros, Zapata moustaches and fluorescent shirts, jade and shocking pink, took the bench in front. One had a huge green and white drum, which he began to beat in tango rhythm while the others filled in with ferocious handclapping. Vendors came by with beer and sandwiches, friends tossed leather wine bottles up and down the terraces and one hit him on the side of the head, and now . . . yes, a small boy, beside himself with anticipation and clinging to the arm of his beaming, proud mother, an

Andalusian of stereotyped beauty whose scent was bottled carnation which threatened to overcome the fumes of the cigars, took the place on his right.

He couldn't argue, the boy actually showed him his ticket. Fila 15, No. 14. So. Roma wasn't coming. She wouldn't be there. He had accepted that she was a bribe, to get the RA 72 with the new programs his team had created on it. It had not occurred to him that she might be a cheat too. He was totally desolated.

A cornet squealed high and silvery, on the far side of the arena, heralding the procession of glittering *toreros* with their *cuadrillas* of *peóns* and mounted *picadors*. After saluting the president of the *corrida*, they shook out cerise and cadmium capes, spread them in the air, testing the breeze or lack of it, and then the cornet again, as the black caped, black plumed *alguacil*, pirouetting on his splendid Andalusian pony went through the ritual of handing over the key to the bull-pens.

The first bull, big and black, huge shoulders already engorged with blood from the anger and irritation at the ribboned dart that had just arrived in his back, thundered into the ring, head up, caught a *peón*'s cape in his vision and went for it. The *peón* scuttled away, and Julio Robles, the last great *torero* of his generation, having checked the bull came true, came out to take him in a perfect swirling veronica. The cape held the bull as its head went down, the *torero* moulding the lure to the speed of the animal's charge, and all done with that studied perfection of line that comes from a training as unremitting as a ballet-dancer's.

'Olé,' the crowd breathed the word, a caress on the air, full of expectation for what was to come.

Cartwright hauled in a huge breath of anguish and pain. Almost aloud, he said: 'I might as well go.'

CHAPTER 12

I'm sitting in my apartment, watching fucking soccer type football, there's going to be a helluva lot of soccer in the next four weeks on TV no matter what system you're tuned to, and wondering if I've done the right thing in staying behind. Perhaps I should've followed him up to Granada, but I'm feeling pretty certain that any action there's going to be is going to happen right here. I followed him yesterday when he scooted back to SISA, I saw the silver Merc that checked him out, and the input I've had since, checking out the registration and so on, is that it belongs to Gabriel Sur aka Jabreel Mansur. So I guess the whole shenanigans is a ploy to get him out of the way while they lift from his apartment whatever it was he went back to SISA to get. Odd business though. Why didn't Sur just go in and get it for himself?

Still, by three o'clock in the afternoon with highlights from yesterday's game between a load of crazy niggers from some unheard of place in Africa trampling on the Romanians while we wait for the match between Austria and Czechosolovakia to get under way, I'm still worrying as to whether or not I have made the right call. Then, bingo, a bleep from his apartment.

Only five minutes walk away, but I'm not going to stand around on the sidewalk as obvious as a banana in a coal-hole, so I pile into the Renault 19, and find a slot where I have a nice view of the stoop from the other side of the road. Can even see the mailbox from which he took whatever it was sent him running like a jack rabbit back to

SISA as soon as he had seen it. Twenty minutes and even with the windows down I'm beginning to sweat. Forty minutes and I'm wondering if I won't just go up and see who's there and why, when a black Peugeot 305 pulls up, right there on the kerb by the entrance. Just the one man, big guy, six one, six two maybe, well-built, two hundred pounds, black hair, sallow skin, white shirt. Gets something from under the dash, and well there are some movements you've made so often yourself you know what he's doing, and I'm right too, for the bimbo gets out before putting on his jacket which is on the back seat, and I can see in his waist band the butt of what even at that distance I'm pretty sure is a Browning automatic.

Five minutes, it took him that long to get past the lock, then another bleep, he's in. And then the gunshot I realise I have been waiting for ever since he disappeared. Muffled, could be a car back-firing a hundred yards away, but I reckon not. I know the difference. But not the Browning, something smaller.

And presently, there she is. Not a shadow of doubt at all — Roma. She's wearing plain black framed shades, a dark blue cotton top, no frills, but you can see her nipples, and the shape of a cute pair of boobs, white pants, jean cut, with a black belt and soft leather bum-bag, but worn not over her butt which is as cute as her boobs, but over her right hip, five gets you only one it's not a powder compact and lipstick she carries in it. Black leather lace-up bootees, no heel, but fashionable, I guess. And the silver hair. Now that is so unnatural, it has to be a wig, but clearly a permanent feature mounted on tight latex worn over a shaven head. I wonder if Arnie realises that.

Certainly she is very, very easy to look at, and I don't take my eyes off that sassy neat ass till she gets to her car, yes, the white open-top VW Golf, a block away beneath a palm tree. She pulls out, and is away. Choice? Do I follow her, or find out what's been happening in Arnie's pad? I choose the latter. Whatever else, she's a tough cookie, a skilled operator, chances are she'll spot me and lose me. Or shoot me.

Naturally, since I organised his alarms and surveillance, it's no problem getting in, I know what the locks are. In fact, on my advice, we didn't go for complicated locks, they never stop anyone who's really keen, and are expensive to replace. Instead though there is a micro cordless video camera with a wide angle lens mounted in the air-conditioning unit in the living room, which you have to go through to get to the rest of the apartment. Once the system is turned on it activates only when someone comes into the room and switches off as soon as it's empty again. The other feature is the bleeper. It emits a radio signal with a range of twenty-five miles and lets Arnie know if he has an intruder problem. Let's me know too, which is why I am there.

The big guy is lying on the floor with a look of surprise in his dead eyes, and a small hole in his right temple, almost no blood so he went very quickly indeed. And that makes Roma a very neat shootist indeed. His own gun is still in his waistband.

First I check out the apartment. Next, I turn off Red Eye, disconnect the camera, take out the cassette and slot in a blank. After all, I already have a supporting role, and if it runs much longer I'll get second billing.

Next I give the big guy a solid going over and come to the conclusion that he's Mossad, Israeli secret service. Nothing actually says so, it wouldn't would it? No more than anything I carry says what I am. But there are signs, not the least being the small gold Star of David under his shirt.

And finally I go back to the kitchen to check out that what I thought was there on the table really was there. Well, I'm no computer expert, but I've seen RA 72s before. There's also a note telling him to leave it on the 'kidjin' table, and a note from him saying he wants it to be there when he comes back, so I sit down and have a long think about it all during which I get bothered by a large blue blow-fly, which I smack with a rolled-up soft porn mag he's left lying around, making more mess than she did with her shooter.

Lots of questions: like why didn't she take the RA 72 with her? Like did that mean she might be back? Like why hadn't I brought some artillery with me? Like, surely she would be back, with help, to shift big guy? Or is she going to leave him there for Arnie to find when he comes home? All stupid questions, because no way could I find answers to them. A good maxim for guys in my line of work is 'the only good question is a question with an answer' and the only one of those I could think of is: what do I do with the RA 72? And the answer to that is so obvious it's not worth asking. But how?

I got on the phone to Madrid, used some clout, and even though it was way past bank closing time, they reckoned they'd raise something, would I like to call back in an hour? Most of which I spent in my car not wishing to be found in Cartwright's apartment if Roma did send in a disposal squad.

Which she did. Half an hour and a stretched Renault 21 hatchback, white, rolled up and two men went in with a big black bag and a stretcher, both folded, and came out ten minutes later with neither of them folded. I took the number. Feeling a lot happier now, I went back in, and eventually got the message back that the Malaga branch of the Banco de Bilbao had a Digital Equipment Computer that could take the RA 72 and copy it, and there was an operator over there waiting to let me in, even though the bank was closed. That's what real clout can do. I took the RA 72 into Malaga, brought it back. Then I went home and played the video cassette.

It showed her come in, go to the kitchen, come out. Then she moved about the living room for a bit fiddling with what looked like fine transparent almost invisible nylon line. Finally she put a chair against the wall by the door to the vestibule, where it would be part hidden by the door when someone came in, and sat on it, holding one end of the line in her left hand and a small silver pistol in her right. And she stayed like that for half an hour which I fast-forwarded through. When big guy came in she yanked the line and something, a glass maybe, tumbled to the floor in the kitchen, so that was the direction big guy was looking when she shot him.

I don't shiver that easily, but I shivered.

Seven o'clock, the Granada *corrida* is starting, live on Canal Sur, they say it should be one of the best so far this season so I guess I'll stay in and watch.

CHAPTER 13

Sickened not only by despair but by the terrible mess the *picador* made of the first bull, and the awful suffering inflicted on his horse, Cartwright decided the time had come to go. He placed both palms on the concrete bench and began to push. As he did so he felt a gentle pressure on his shoulders. Glancing left and right, he saw the hands he had dreamed and fantasised about for a month and a half — their thin length, the reddish ochre with a hint of a freckle or two, the fingers that could be strong or gentle, the rings, the nails the colour of raw meat.

Heart pounding, without daring to look behind, he seized the right one, turned up the palm and kissed it and held it against his face. Then came the warmth and fragrance of her head as she leant across the small space that separated them and put her cheek against his.

'Don't go.'

In spite of the applause for a competently placed pair of *banderillas*, the words, so closely whispered in his ear, dropped like jewels in a silent well.

Her hand carried odours — of discreetly scented soap, and behind it a merest hit of refined machine oil and burnt cordite. He could place the first, but the second eluded him.

The space between the rows of concrete benches in a bull-ring is very small. By sitting forward, she could drape her arms over his shoulders, or under his arms and caress his chest; she could grip his torso between her knees. And so she did, while Robles, in dove grey and gold, put together three strings of good passes, and the swell of olés began to rise and fall again as the crowd willed themselves into the hyper-trance that can be induced by a great *faena*.

On the second attempt at a kill the bull received the sword to the hilt as if it were a blessing or a release, but still refused to fall. The *peóns* dragged their capes in the bloody sand in front of it making the heavy head sway back and forth until at last the knees failed, and like a building dynamited and filmed in slow motion, he was toppled from within.

During the interval that followed the third bull, while the sand was re-raked and the drinks and sandwich vendors made their rounds, Cartwright turned at last, dared at last to look at his Eurydice. From above and behind, her full dark lips came down onto his, and cradling his left cheek in her right palm she gave him her first proper kiss. He felt her tongue tease his lips, and then she pulled back, and pushed him gently away.

'I'm hungry,' she said. 'And thirsty too. Beer, and something with meat in it. Not pig.'

Meat not pig proved a bother: he had to go inside the hollow wall of the drum, and search the grey, bleakly lit galleries before he found a stall selling beefburgers.

He was back only just in time to see Robles out again for his second bull, the fourth of the *corrida*, tempting it with veronicas, three, four o-o-o-o-lé, before spinning the cape round in the graceful swirl that leaves it held on his left hip and draped around his feet. He turned his back on the bull with his right hand flung in the air saluting the cheers of the crowd, slung the folded cape over his arm and sauntered, somewhat mincingly, but with style, back to the *barrera*. Behind him the panting bull pummelled the sand with his hoof, wondered where the elusive enemy had gone.

Cartwright turned, his mouth full of powdery white bread and real ground beef.

'Good?' he mouthed, and she smiled down at him,

delicately shifting a blob of chilli ketchup from the corner of her darker angel mouth. Then her eyes went back to the uncertain choreography of the ring.

This time Robles and the bull achieved the rare harmony that raises the cruel paganism of the bullfight to the level of the highest art. Taking the *muleta* he put together string after string of varied passes that mesmerised the crowd as well as the bull, and killed with a single sword thrust that felled him as if he had been struck by lightning. The crowd erupted, and Cartwright woke with tears streaming and mingling with Roma's, for her chin was on his shoulder, from a dream of perfection.

'Nothing,' she said, 'that is going to happen here tonight will surpass that. Let's go.'

For an hour or so they drifted among the *casetas* and watched the wild swirling dancing which yet was formal, not improvised like flamenco, so a dozen couples would turn at the same time, their skirts lifted to make breakers of white foam above strutting feet and calves, their arms windmilling together, and they stamped their feet as one. The colours of the dresses were even more vibrant now beneath the thousands of lanterns and the crowds watching them were dense. Vendors sold snacks of spicy kebabed pork from stalls, the smoke from their charcoal drifting in blueish clouds beneath the lights; others sold half chickens on paper plates, beer and cheap red wine. The noise was physical, palpable and beneath it thunder prowled. Sheet lighting lit the clouds above from beneath.

They pushed their way into a bar where Roma caught the immediate and wondering attention of bar-tenders who were ready to drop whomever they were already serving to do her bidding. She ordered, in very respectable Castilian, a half bottle of manzanilla, a very dry and very light sherry with a hint of the sea in it, and soft shelled Dublin Bay-type prawns, very garlicky, large enough for the claws to be worth cracking, and the shell soft enough for teeth to do the job. They came with a small basket of chopped bread, hard-crusted and floury.

They spoke little: 'All right? Of course. You have the last one. No, you.' But smiled a lot, sometimes shyly, sometimes knowingly, and once when she caught him looking at her with what could only be described as greed, but greed elevated to passion, her giggle swelled and exploded into a laugh, so she had to reach for the chrome serviette dispenser.

'Do you have your car here?'

'Yes,' he laughed too, 'In the Plaza de Gracia, and I have no idea how to get there from here.'

'We'll get a taxi.'

Again, out on the Gran Vía, her silver hair and her marvellous behind caused a cabbie to accelerate away from an elderly couple he had slowed for.

'*El parador.*'

'*¿En la Alhambra*?'

'Sí-í.'

The last drawn into two syllables the way Spaniards do to make a simple 'yes' into 'of course — what else?' Cartwright began to wonder: was she Spanish after all, perhaps with Moorish blood in her — hence, the Arabian ambience of the Madrid apartment?

The taxi swung into Reyes Catolicos, strung with lights representing the jewelled pyx that holds the Host of Corpus Cristi, and still with drifts of rose petals from the processions that had passed earlier. They took a right at the top of the street, climbed a narrow dark alley, passed through a big stone gate and into the dark steep woods that lie below the Moorish citadel and palace. The walls also contain the Parador San Francisco, a monastery converted into a luxury hotel.

Leaning back in the soft leather of a ten-year-old Merc, holding her hand on her knee, he murmured, not without anticipation: 'Do you have a room there, booked?'

'No.'

'It'll be full.'

'So?'

Puzzled and a touch anxious, he waited.

A second big gate, grey stone, floodlit, set between high walls made from big blocks of reddish brick, and a guard. But the taxi-driver leant through the window, nodded towards the couple behind him, and said simply. 'Al Parador,' and they were waved in. Cartwright had a brief sense of a steep twisting climb between walls and buildings. Cypresses and cedars closed and then opened out again for the hotel. The taxi dropped them in front of the lit bevelled glass and shiny brass of a revolving door but as he paid off the taxi (Roma seemed to have no money and indeed nowhere to keep any), she whispered: 'Follow me.'

She circled the building, found a service area at the back with big heavy-duty plastic bins. She took his hand, her palm was dry and cool, and led him along the bottom of a wall that dripped with ferns and ivy-leafed toadflax to the foot of a very steep grassy bank.

'Up,' she said. They had to scramble with their toes and at one point she began to slip and he got his palms beneath her rump and gave her a bunk up. Then he had to grab handfuls of dryish grasses and hope they would hold. She glided along the top for a moment, almost he lost her apart from the gleam of her hair beneath the spreading boughs of a huge cedar, then she caught his hand, pointed down. They were on top of a second wall, a seven foot drop to a narrow gravel path.

'You first.'

Reminding himself to land on the balls of his feet and bend his knees, he jumped. He flexed too much and caught his chin on his right knee, hurting both.

'Come on!'

He overrode the pain, stood and spread his arms above his head, just in time to catch her and swing her to the ground. He stood, holding her for a minute or two until the pounding in his ears faded and his breath was back to normal.

'Where are we?'

'In the Alhambra, of course. Listen.'

Water, trickling, chattering, splashing lightly. Crickets. And then, picking up from where their arrival had interrupted his flow, a nightingale: Lu-lu-lu-lee-leee.

'Smell.'

He breathed in. Jasmine and roses.

'Come on.'

There was a three-quarter moon, high and rosy in the hazy sky, and from outside and below the buildings were floodlit, casting cut-outs of bright light through tracery casements and across the battlements. Holding his hand she led him on past a wide rectangular pool whose water was ebony black yet carried the reflection of the perfect pavilion beyond it: a wide central arch between two smaller ones on each side was supported on slender marble columns, the spaces between filled with a patterned tracery.

'We are in the harem,' she whispered, 'Queens and princesses only. You had better hurry before the ghost of a eunuch catches you.'

But there was no hurry: they strolled from moonlight into purple shadow, down an alley of low box into a small patio. They climbed wooden stairs, passed through three empty rooms, one with a fireplace.

'This is where the American writer wrote his silly stories.'

They came to a square room, set in one of the towers, so three sides faced outwards, pierced with windows, again with the marvellous tracery, and filled with light from the floodlighting which was full on it. She kept him in the shadow, but made him look up at a small dome whose stucco had been carved into five thousand empty honeycomb cells, climbing to the apex.

'The Queen's Room.'

Beyond it, the Patio de Leones whose huge alabaster bowl supported on the backs of ten small lions he recognised. Twice he and Margaret, with the children, had been here in August, and always, against the best advice, in the morning. 'In the afternoon, it will be far too hot for the children.' But the palace had been built for heat, and all the coach parties, dozens of them, a chain of them trundling up the hill outside, came in the mornings. Twice he had been in this wide perfect courtyard, but always with hundreds of other people, and moved on by attendants fearful that the Germans and the Japanese, queuing in their thousands, might take the place apart with their bare hands out of intolerable, overheated frustration. Yet he had sensed a private, quiet magic, patiently waiting for the many legged monster to wind its way out again before re-asserting itself. And he, as part of that monster, had never felt it, only sensed it was there. But now . . .

As they walked down one side of the cloister he marvelled at the domestic scale of the place: the complex, intricately carved capitols of the columns began no higher than the top of his head, and yet he felt moved by a wonder greater than he had experienced in, say Salisbury Cathedral or Ely. The blueish marble of the floor was dappled with tiny overlapping ovoids of light cast through the tracery that separated the arches. It was like walking on, no, floating inches above, the bottom of a sun-filled sea and he was put in mind of her most previous, fleeting epiphany. He said nothing but squeezed her hand.

Presently they turned the corner, and came upon two small thrones, Cordoban leather slung between hoops of black wood. They sat there for a moment, and reaching across the space between linked fingers.

'Jimmy, I'm sure those are ornamental and not for use. Get off.'

With the memory of that other voice in his ear, he looked down a narrow channel of black water that occasionally glittered with gold, to the central fountain. The channel ended in front of them in a small round ebony pool set in the marble. It ran through a desert of gravel.

'You look sad. Why?'

For Nadine. And Jimmy. And for beauty.

Roma went on: 'These silly Spaniards. This should be a garden. All gardens remember Paradise and so they have four rivers. This is one of them. There should be orange trees in fruit and bloom. Aromatic herbs, lilies and roses. That is how it used to be.'

But then where would be no room for the Beast with Ten Thousand Legs that comes here every morning.

She gestured across the spaces in front of them. 'We did okay, yes?'

'Yes.' So she is Moorish. But he checked: 'We?'

'The Arab Nation.'

He thought for a moment, sought for something that would please her.

'It's better than the Parthenon.'

'Oh yes!' Her laugh was tumbling water. 'Much better. Come on.'

She stood, turned, traced six inches of calligraphy in the carved stucco behind her. '*Wa-la ghaliba illa-Llah.* There is no Conqueror but God.'

There was one grey moment. Passing down the next side of the Patio de Leones, they came to the Fountain of the Abencerrages, with its iron stain in the basin.

'I do not like this place.'

'Because of the slaughter here?' It was the sort of thing that stuck in your mind when you were part of a Beast with Ten Thousand Legs.

'There was no slaughter. That's all just Christian propaganda. That's what I do not like. The Christians come here and marvel. But the silly legend leaves them the chance to continue to feel superior.'

The manzanilla, exhaustion and excitement, prompted a sequence of imaged thoughts that lacked logic and which he kept to himself as they wandered on, past walls covered with white roses, back to the pavilion and pool they had first encountered. Sure it was a lie that Jews had ever ritually crucified Christian children, that the Germans in 1914 threw Belgian babies in the air to catch them on bayonets. But in that case then perhaps the Indonesians have not committed genocide in East Timor, perhaps the Killing Fields in Cambodia are grossly exaggerated and the Americans hardly ever napalmed young girls. And in the middle of it all he remembered the scars on her back. And in front of the tower that is haunted by the ghost of the Princess who loved her Father too much to elope with her Christian lover, he turned her towards him in the moonlight and asked for a kiss she was unwilling to share.

Indeed she broke away from him and taking him by surprise bounded lightly up the path that follows the curve of the battlements, disappeared through a big stone arch. He pounded after her, but stumbled on steps, nearly fell, saw her silvery hair gliding swiftly across a short stone bridge. More careful now he followed, found himself at a junction of black-top paths. He remembered the earlier visits. Left up the hill to the Generalife gardens and summer pavilions, right down the hill to the big carpark and entrance. He chose left.

Presently he found himself on a long parterre filled with small gardens, each like a separate room walled with clipped cypress, but linked by a stone channel of slowly moving water. On one side a purple forest climbed to a star-strewn sky, on the other the floodlit palace and fortress they had just left floated magically on a bed of darkness. All around the sound of water, and more distant now, the nightingale sang on. He turned, looked for her, and caught his breath at the sight of distant snow, new fallen in the thunder that he had heard earlier, clinging to the northern slopes of the highest peaks of the Sierra Nevada, a ghostly presence beneath the setting moon.

Gravel skittered lightly, he spun towards the sound and saw her, her hair and the whiteness of her jeans, flitting away from him, up into the woods. He followed, and she made sure he would, until they were clear of the formal gardens, and beneath tall lean elms and beeches on a steep incline covered with dry moss, beechmast and leaf litter.

Twenty yards above him she stopped, turned, spread her arms.

'Arnold,' she said, using his name for the first time. Then her silvery laugh exploded again as if she found the name unbearably funny.

She ran at him, full-tilt into him, almost knocking him backwards, and as his arms closed round her she seized his face in her hands, pulled it down to hers, and stormed it with kisses, hard, quick, passionate, her tongue flickering in his mouth. His hands slipped down her thin, fragile back, his fingers seeking to get under the waistband of her jeans. She pulled back but no more than an inch or so this time and only for as long as it took for her to release her belt and then his. His hands slid down beneath silk and onto her cool buttocks; still kissing him, her fingers found a way through zip and cloth to his prick and he began to ease her loosened jeans down her thighs.

Firmly she shifted his right hand to her front, where his middle finger threaded the curls beneath her small neat stomach to find her warm, wet sex; the kisses became slower and longer. Eventually she made him lie on the sun-warm ground. Then she stepped out of her lower garments, eased his down a little, and then mounted him. Beyond her head he could see stars and galaxies sown across a gap in the thick canopy of leaves, and still the water and the nightingale sang on. Never, ever, had he been so happy.

PART THREE

CHAPTER 14

'Okay. I guess all the input on that one is seamless, box it, and stick the right label on it. What's next? Mark?'

The ex-Colonel of Marines, a stocky man, neat in a pale double-breasted suit, tilted back his swivel chair, cloth upholstery because he was only an ex-Colonel, made a prayer of his hands and beamed round.

The three younger persons in front of him sighed, whispered, delved into brief-cases on the floor beside the high-backed chairs they sat in, pulled out files and slipped them onto the polished veneer of the oval table. Four hours the meeting had lasted and they had all hoped the Colonel would pass the last three items up, let them go home. But he was looking over his shoulder and down two floors into the five-sided space of paths and lawns below, and saying to himself: if we clear the backlog this session, I'll get an extra day on the farm, whup some sense into that colt who thinks he's god, not me.

Mark, a ginger-haired young man, fair eyelashes, not to be trusted the ex-Colonel's mother was wont to say, flattened the sheaf of papers he had hauled up with a sweaty hand, cleared his throat and longed to clear his sinuses which were playing up no end. He found a handkerchief and rolled it between his palms. It was always the same, the centralised, computerised air-conditioning system could not cope with an unexpected rocketing of temperatures at the end of June, had had a brainstorm. They sweated, somewhere else no doubt guys froze.

'F three three stroke A stroke six E, C, D one oh three

nine two eight. We now have a breakdown of the copied RA 72 from Malaga, Spain.'

'Sorry, guys, I'm behind the curve on this one. Fill me in.'

Mark looked across the table, raised a pale eyebrow. Louella, in beige tailored suit, sweatmarks in the armpits, scrabbled in her hair. Her two colleagues both men, the bastards, had taken off their jackets, an option not open to her as all she had underneath was a nylon slip, see-through on the lacy bits. She picked up the file and bounced the papers level on the shiny surface.

'This was started in Santiago, Chile, in March, this year. Lot goin' on there then . . .'

'Helluvalot,' the ex-Colonel agreed.

'Well, in amongst all the rest of the shee-it,' she drawled, 'we tagged the fact that someone was using Jabreel Mansur to get theirselves an advanced radar system with three-dimensional orientation.'

'Someone?'

'The guys down there fumbled about a bit, and came up with Iraq.'

'Go on.'

'Mansur bought a Ferlinghetti advanced radar three-dimensional system for Ecuador, no problem. But next thing was Langley, who monitored the deal in Quito, got wind it was to be shipped not to Aqaba, Jordan, for onward transit to Baghdad, but to Malaga, Spain, and the cover was that Ecuador had leased the system to Mauretania. Moreover, using his SISA cover and his Gabriel Sur identity, Mansur was buying a lease on workshops north of Malaga, including an air hangar facility . . .'

'An upgrade?'

'That's right. Now to do an upgrade on that system you need an expert, someone who knows his way round it, one of the originators for preference. A project manager who came to it cold, however smart, would put months on it, by when you'd be past the sell-by-date. So Langley went to FADSI (UK), who created the system back in eighty-eight to see who they'd lost recently, and bingo, one of their top men, a guy called Arnold Cartwright, had just jacked in his job and packed his bags for Malaga. They put an asset on his tail, a freelance who calls himself Philip Henley, with the brief to find out all he could about Cartwright and what he was up to. He did very well. Do you want all the details?'

'No, I guess I have the main frame on line.'

'Okay. The cherry on top is that Cartwright took an RA 72, the archive back-up of the new programs his team had created, home to his apartment and Henley got it copied without him knowing. And it's the analysis of that back-up that is the subject of the report. Back to you, Mark.'

'Thank you, Louella.' Pale eyelashes fluttered across the table. 'Okay. It seems Cartwright's team are doing two things. One, they're compatting the system to the comms and shooters, interceptors and surface to air missiles, Iraq already has. Which is what you'd expect. But it's work that could be done in Iraq, makes little sense to do it in Spain. That's not all though. A very smart anti-radar jamming program seems to be under way as well, specific to RASP 3. RASP 3 is the latest in radar-jamming and only one force outside NATO has it.'

'Israeli F-15s.'

'Precisely. They used RASP 1, 7 June 81, when they took out Tammuz 17, Saddam's nuke facility. They've had the upgrades from us ever since as they came on line.'

'Thank you Mark. Especially for keeping it short.'

Pencilling a note on the paper in front of him, the ex-Colonel carefully avoided looking at the third person at the table, a tall saturnine character, not long out of Harvard Business School, younger than the others, ambitious. Two factors here: he'd want to cock his leg, squeeze out his drop of piss, make sure that if their report was going to the top someone up there knew he'd contributed. Second factor: he was part-Jewish, liaised unofficially with Mossad, a two-way deal, and since a threat to Israel's ability to drop bombs at will was in the air he would probably over-react and keep them all at the table an hour longer than was necessary.

'Bob, Your turn. Political assessment.'

But Bob had got the message.

'Not in our part of the park. Mossad has its eye on it and I guess they're not too worried. Two things Israel might want to zap in Iraq. The nuclear plant again, and the supergun. Saddam thought both projects were doing well, so he decided to give his radar a pre-emptive update. But Mossad got a spin-doctor on it. They tipped off British Customs and deprived him of the krytron capacitors he needed for his bomb, and then the tubing for the gun too. And they wasted the guy who was running the supergun project. Neither is a threat now, nor will be for years.'

'So why is Saddam carrying on with this radar upgrade exercise?'

Bob shrugged.

'Who knows? Maybe he just forgot about it. Maybe, no, for sure, he wants to keep Mansur sweet, and definitely Mansur would not like it if he cancelled when it was this far down the line. Anyway, Saddam likes having fancy toys: he definitely suffers from a "my pecker is bigger than your pecker" complex.'

'Right. A one page digest, marked "no action required", to the Vice-Chairman, Joint Chiefs of Staff office, just so we're on record. Next?'

Ginger shuffled up the next file.

'The Langley guy in Baghdad, the one who thinks he's got a deep-throat right out of Saddam's Supreme Headquarters. There's an archivist works there who has a PC modem linked to the archaeology department of the University, where he used to work. He made contact through the Dutch Embassy, saying he was no friend of the regime, gave his modem number and the password to the file where he keeps a secret journal of what happens at the Headquarters. Our asset in the Dutch embassy regularly accesses it and has come up with this: he reckons Saddam is getting together a plan to annexe Kuwait . . .'

'That,' said the ex-Colonel, very firmly, 'that has to be loony tunes. Not even Madman Saddam would do that. How does Langley rate this source?'

'Low-grade and unreliable. The journal itself is intermittent, quirky, even jokey. The guy has a flawless record as a Saddamite Ba'athist, he wouldn't be where he is if he didn't. It's either deliberate disinformation, intended to distract us from some sort of move he's planning against Israel, or a joke.'

'Like I said — loony toons. Okay, pencil it message received, but pass it up as a no-no. Next?'

'Sir?'

'Louella?'

'I guess it doesn't have to be loony tunes? Last month, the Arab Summit in Baghdad?'

'Yes?'

'Referring to the low oil prices and Kuwait's refusal to keep within quotas, Saddam said, and I quote,' she made rabbit ears on either side of her head, '"War is also done by economic means, this is in fact a kind of war against Iraq." Unquote.'

'Louella, none of that adds up to a can of beans. He knows we won't let him snatch Kuwait. That man's just full of shit, and sometimes it shows . . . Next.'

And you're not? Louella said to herself. And don't you mean *row* of beans? And can't you see there may be a connection between having an Advanced Radar Defense System and a plan to invade Kuwait?

But the three men continued to ignore the anger and frustration of a person they all thought of as two tokens in one, a female black, and the Sub-Committee Mid-East 3, Defense Intelligence Agency, moved on to other business. Outside the shadows lengthened across the pentangular paths that criss-cross in the centre of the Pentagon;

suddenly the room felt chill and the men put their jackets back on.

Next Monday, one floor higher and one wall further round so it got less sun, in a room where the air-conditioning worked, Vice-Chairman (Joint Chiefs of Staff)'s Sub-Committee, Middle-East Intelligence, met. All men here (apart from a captain of marines who was really a stenographer): five military with stars on their shoulder flashes, two army, one air force, one marines, one navy, and a civilian political adviser from State. The room was smoke-filled (much to the disgust of the State Department official, who liked to be as politically correct as his position allowed) and two of them had had lunches liquid enough to leave the smell of stale alcohol on the air. In the absence of the Vice-Chairman the senior general present was in the chair.

'Right. Next,' he growled, pushing on one side the Afghanistan file they had been discussing. 'Conflicting reports passed up from DIS regarding Mad Saddam. Seems he's switching targets from Israel for the time being, and maybe planning something naughty against Kuwait. He has several grudges against Kuwait which are not our business. Question is, if he does go in, what sort of response is the National Security Council going to ask and should this committee alert the Chairman JCS.'

'Sir, with respect, what you are suggesting is way beyond the brief of this sub-committee.' The civilian from State spoke wearily. Again and again he had to remind these desk-bound warriors that their role was purely advisory and to the NSC alone. 'What we have to do is evaluate militarily the intelligence we have in front of us. But even here, I think the macro-situation has something to say to us about how we look at this very particular and possibly not very reliable intelligence.'

One of the army generals, a Texan who prided himself on speaking straight, cleared bourbon-flavoured phlegm. 'Is there a way of saying that in plain American?'

'I think,' Navy intervened here, suavely and without patronising, he knew better, 'what State is saying is that the National Security Council already has an overview of the situation and they don't require as of now anything that is going to have them think again.'

'It would help us formulate an interpretation if State would fill us in as to the nature of this overview.' Air force's contribution was punctuated, made almost incomprehensible, by heavy puffing as he got his pipe going again.

State batted the foul stuff away from his face, shuffled papers, coughed.

'Saddam badly needs a hike in the price of oil, currently held low by Kuwaiti and United Arab Emirate overproduction. OPEC meets third week of this month, in Geneva, to review price and quotas. Prior to that meeting we expect Saddam to bring whatever pressure he can on Kuwait to drop production and raise the price. He has territorial claims too, and wants Kuwait to cancel his debts. So, along with a lot of diplomatic and commercial activity, quite naturally he's making belligerent noises too.'

Suddenly he wished he had not given up smoking. He went on.

'NSC reactions are several. One. Whatever else we think of Saddam, the President sees him as a stabilising force in the area. He keeps the lid on Shi-ite fundamentals. And while he's around there is no chance the Kurds will remove from US influence the oil-fields round Mosul and Kirkuk. Two. We can trade grain, electronics, defence *matériel*, all sorts for Iraqi oil. Almost everywhere else it's petro-dollars, which in effect means yen and marks we can ill afford. Three. A reasonable hike in the price of oil, as of now, wouldn't hurt, and in fact would be a bonus in Texas and south of the border.'

'You mean like win votes?'

'And campaign funds from the Tex-Mex oil barons.'

Silence, then Chair sighed, lurched forward on the

tiltable chair (leather for generals), elbows on the table, palms flat between them.

'I think we all are on the curve. What it is required of us to say is the signals we are getting that Saddam is positivising a military threat to Kuwait are not seriously intentioned. They should be noted and in the situation as it spins as of now, should be given low-grade consideration. Right?'

'Right!' They all agreed. They all knew that the National Security Council, of which the President, the Vice-President, the Secretary of State and the Secretary of Defense were the only executive members, was as prone to negative response to bearers of bad news as the ancient Caliphs of Baghdad had been. Confrontation with the man who bought grain from threatened farmers, defence *matériel* from a threatened defence industry, and paid with oil, was not something they felt they ought to recommend.

'Navy said: 'We have a carrier, I forget which, in the North Indian Ocean. We'll put that up the Gulf if he really looks like cutting up rough.'

'Fine,' said State. 'Why not?'

He fastened the clasps on his case, set the electronic locks.

'Er . . . just one thing.' Air force had found a sheet in his portfolio which he was reading for the first time. 'It says here he may be clandestinely working on an upgrade of his air defences.'

They all rummaged back, looking for their own copies.

'Yeah. Ant-i a possible Israeli pre-emptive.'

'The Israelis have everything we've got air-assault protection-wise bar Stealth. If he's got or getting an Air Defence System that can cope with them, then we have to recognise that, and be prepared to deploy Stealth.'

'Look.' State rebuttoned his case. 'Nothing like that level of escalation is about to take place. This guy is making a legitimate play to hike oil prices, and maybe annexe a cuppla islands at the mouth of the Shit, I mean Shatt al

Arab waterway. It's not a worry. Let him get on with it. Okay?'

'Okay. But let's keep a check on that Advanced Radar System, look at it again if or when our boys have to fly.'

'Okay. Okay then.'

Air force looked at the Captain of Marines (black, female) stenographer.

'On the record?'

'On the record. Sir.'

CHAPTER 15

17 July, and I have an hour or so with The Beast 666, aka My Secret Diary. The Day of the Nation, the twenty-second anniversary of the Ba'ath Revolution, and my wife and daughter are at a mass-display of unison flag-waving and elementary gymnastics put on by female school children under the guidance of the General Federation for Iraqi Women. They won't let the poor girls go home until they have achieved a perfection equal to Red Square on May Day under Stalin or Tiananmen Square under Mao, a perfection that will not disgrace them when the display is shown on television. Last year the recording wasn't in the can, as they say, until two days later, and never got shown at all.

Today we had an outing from the Supreme Headquarters of the Revolution. Very soon after I arrived there, it was off in the helicopters to the heliport on the roof of the National Assembly, a building not much used normally, but bedecked for the occasion with flags and huge portraits of Guess Who and ringed with tanks. You can always tell when the real Father of Our Nation is in town. Huge areas are cleared of people, spot checks are carried out on the peripheries, both for weapons and documentation, and an inner circle of tanks, personnel carriers, and plain clothes members of the Mukhabarat with RTs is formed up round the building where the Presence is about to manifest itself. *Au contraire*, when an Actor is out and about, crowds of cheering flag-wavers, many of them children, throng the streets and the police and military presence is reduced to what is necessary to round up the assassins after the attempt has been made. Whether or not the attempt is successful is a matter of little importance to any one except the Actor — who is readily replaceable.

Just how easily replaceable became obvious after I had taken my place in the great hall, to the side of the rostra and podium but with a good view of the two hundred and fifty members. About fifty of these are women — doctors for the most part but with a sprinkling of lawyers and senior cadres from the General Federation. Of the remaining two hundred men all those dark-haired, of thickset build and reasonable height, bushy eyebrows and sallow complexions, between the ages of thirty-five and sixty-five, say some fifty in all of the total there, had grown Saddam moustaches and aped his general mien and physical habits, some almost to perfection, so I was given to wonder once or twice if Haroun al-Rashid Mark II had not slipped in anonymously to hear what they were really saying about him.

But then the hubbub died down as the thirty or so strong Revolutionary Command Council, all in best military uniform, came onto the rostra below the podium, and filed into their pew-like places. The hubbub rose again, more a sussuration this time, wind in the poplars on the banks of the Euphrates, as the members could not restrain themselves from speculating who's in, who's out, who had gone up a place or two, who down. These things are important — one's own position depends so much on the shifting hierarchy of potential patrons above one.

The RCC, the senior organ of the Ba'ath Party, was once only seven strong and a real power in the land. Indeed it was as a check on its power that . . . Well, this is all now irrelevant. Suffice it to say, that by altering its constitution, increasing its size, stacking it with stooges and murdering the recalcitrant, the All Merciful has converted it into the creature of his will — though many of his closest advisers are members, so it still does influence national events.

And how here at last he is. Trotting with practised ease up onto the podium, he raises his big hands in salute and gratitude for the overwhelming applause that breaks out, applause that has been well-rehearsed, actually by a senior member of the Royal Shakespeare Company, to be dignified and sincere. This is not some tinsel pop-star to be raved over, it says, nor are we such slaves to his will as to go mad: no, we are rational educated human beings, welcoming the architect of prosperity and enlightenment, and our plaudits will be solemn and weighty, though, of course, prolonged. The model is the sort of ovation a Party Leader gets at the annual British Conservative Party Conference, also, so I am told, ably orchestrated by professionals.

He is wearing khaki, but certainly not the coarse stuff his soldiers wear, with a Field Marshal's insignia on his shoulder straps, and of course, his black beret.

This, I have to say, is a mistake, since it never seems to sit quite as it should, but is always either too flat on top, or pulled like a sort of badly kneaded and burnt loaf to one side.

He drops his hands, the applause subsides, the television lighting comes on and we wait. He coughs, and a technician springs to his feet as if electrically galvanised, and wheels the hitherto unnoticed tele-prompts into place. I should not like to be in his shoes, indeed I were he I'd be rummaging in the medicine chest for the hemlock as soon as I got home and running a warm bath.

All now sit back for the traditional paeon of praise for the Arab Nation, the paternal wisdom of the RCC, the Voice of the People as here represented, the army, the forces of law and order and so on and so on, oh yes, and Allah too, but above all for Yours Truly, for bringing Iraq through another year of growth towards prosperity and freedom, in spite of the efforts of the US-Zionist conspiracy and the selfish greed of the oil monarchies. But in fact the celebratory mood which reached such exalted heights in 1988 when 17 July so coincidentally coincided with the triumphant end to the Persian War, was not sustained. Why not? Because, frankly there was very little to celebrate. Not that he actually said as much.

Why not? Well, Kuwait and the United Arab Emirates were to blame. They are trying, he said in the slow, rather measured, and one has to say basically rather boring, delivery he has, to undermine Iraq after its military triumph. Instead of rewarding Iraq, which sacrificed the blossoms of its youth in the war to protect their houses of wealth, they are severely harming it. By exceeding their oil quotas they had pushed the price of oil down to $14 a barrel. And so on.

After an hour or so of this he reached for his peroration: 'Raising our voices against the evil is not the final resort if the evil continues . . .' Nor did he raise his voice, rather it sank to a hoarse and menacing whisper, which, amplified, rattled round the hall like the tail of a rattlesnake . . . 'There should be some effective act to restore things to their correct position . . .' Now his voice did rise, he rose, and sliced the air beneath his neck with the flat of his heavy hand, and shouted: 'Cutting necks is better than cutting the means of living.'

Shattering applause broke out at this *bon mot* of peasant wisdom, referring I believe to the killing of laying hens in times of famine, and with it the Butcher of Baghdad (the epithet at this moment seemed more than usually apt) stormed away from the podium followed in a scurry of rubber-soled soft leather combat boots by his bodyguards and several members of the Revolutionary Command Council.

It was my cue too to be up and off, for my brief was to stick throughout my shift as close to the Almighty as possible unless told to do otherwise. But where was he going? He had left from the opposite side of the hall to the one I was on, and the exit was already blocked by the people who were trying to follow him so I took the way out by which I had come in and the lift to the roof. It was the right move, and I got there only just behind him, for he had taken the lift on the other side.

The upshot of all this was that I found myself bundled not into the draughty Chinook I had been brought in, but into the Presidential Chopper itself. Up, up and away into the limpid blue empyrean, the grid of downtown Baghdad diminishing and swinging like a censer beneath — an image I am quite pleased with since here and there and especially in the shanty towns on the fringes, columns of smoke rose from rubbish dumps, accidental fires and the homes of dissidents routinely torched by the Mukhabarat.

In spite of the sickening swings, which I feared would bring back the coffee and dates I had had for breakfast, this was indeed luxury after the Chinook. We were in, I gathered, a large Messerschmitt-Bolkow-Blohm, customised for presidential use with soft red leather banquettes and porthole windows set behind the crew's blister, enough to seat two advisers and four bodyguards two of whom had to share a banquette with me, crushing me up against the porthole. Clearly I was indeed *de trop* but nothing to be done about it now. Unless they chose to chuck me out — a thought which again brought back the taste of date-flavoured bile.

Presently the manic see-saw effect ceased as the Pilot of Our Nation relinquished the controls to someone better qualified and with a more humdrum attitude to the job. Instead he took a seat, more a throne really, still in the blister and raised to give him an all-round view. The adviser behind him passed him a large hip-flask, from which he took a prodigious swig, Johnnie Walker no doubt, and on we went. Palms, fields and orchards swiftly gave way to desert, and slowly the horizon in front filled with a cloud of dust and diesel fumes. We lost height and flew into it.

It was, I suppose, a stirring sight. Certainly the Warrior Leader thought so. His smile was grim and dignified, I could see it in the mirror placed above his head so he could keep an eye on those behind him, but when for a moment he half stood and half turned to keep a particularly pleasing item in sight, it was clear he was in a state of physical excitement usually associated with Venus rather than Mars.

We were flying at only a hundred feet or so above a long column of large squat tanks with round turrets like squashed buns and huge guns, whose dust and fumes, shot with the sun so the sand sparkled and glittered, swirled towards us, sucked up into our blades and shredded behind us. They flew scarlet flags from their radio antennae, and goggled soldiers, one to each, some in black berets, some in the red chequered headdress favoured by supporters of the PLO and the anti-Zionist cause stood in each turret, arms raised in salute as we passed above.

They were on the move, heading south-east, and in earnest. The signal that had activated them was our Chieftain's battle-cry heard not only across the land but in their earphones too: 'Cutting necks is better than cutting the means of living.'

We came to the end of the column at last, soared, banked, and headed straight into the setting sun, leaving my entrails a kilometre or so behind us. A supreme mental effort on my part pushed them back into place. It was now twelve hours since I had eaten and six beyond my normal four-hour shift in the Presence. Blinding sunlight, searingly vermilion when I shut my eyes against it, flooded the tube behind the blister which seemed to collect and focus it like a laser. The noise of the motors thundered in my ears, the thigh of the thug sitting next to me relentlessly pressed against mine and some part of his ordnance bruised the flesh between my pelvis and my floating rib. I longed to be anywhere other than where I was.

Twenty minutes of this had to be endured before we landed on the innermost roof of the Supreme Headquarters of the Revolution. I was last out of the MBB, indeed a heavily armed flunkie in combat gear almost shut me in for the night: he was hoisting up the drop-down hatch with its fold-up steps just as I was putting a tentative foot on the topmost rung.

Again I did not know what to do. Was I still 'on the job'? Would anyone notice or be bothered at this moment of national crisis if I tiptoed away from it all and went home? Fortunately, very fortunately, common sense came to my rescue. I was due back on duty anyway in something less than two hours. I took the lift back down to the ground floor and explained the situation to the senior security officer there, who for once turned out to have average ability in comprehension and an ability to make up his own mind under difficult circumstances. He found me a room to sit in, brought me some food and coffee and ushered me back into the presence when my time came round again. I even managed to doze off for twenty minutes or so . . .

CHAPTER 16

'Dad? What on earth is this?'

Cartwright held up a small yellow cardboard box. *Condimento para Pinchitos* it said, above a picture of a red-turbanned Moor breathing in the aromas from three skewers of meat cubes. Herbert had just shaken it over the two large pork chops he was about to barbecue, covering them with a liberal scattering of a coarse dull yellow powder.

'Just what it says it is, Arnie. A condiment.'

'What's it got in it?'

'All sorts. Oregano, cloves, tumeric, cumin, garlic, nutmeg. Made in Granada. Reckon with the Alhambra and irrigation systems it's one of the last remnants of Arab civilisation left in Europe. Does wonders for a pork chop, better than sage and onion, any road.'

'Presumably not what the Arabs used it for.'

'Why not?'

'Pig.'

'Oh aye.'

Not in the least put out the old man used his *espumadera* to plant the chops on the grill above a brazier filled with chunks of oak charcoal, already white except when the slight breeze made them glow red. The blue smoke that billowed round the balcony brought tears to Cartwright's eyes, and not just because it was smoke. The aroma was precisely the one which had filled the squares of Granada after the bullfight. Nearly three months gone and not a sign or a word.

He turned, beer glass cold in his hand, and looked down the wide patio that stretched to the sea. Yellow dates now in the palms, the jacaranda blossom replaced by unattractive bunches of black pods, and the last of the holiday-makers — all old, the children gone, including his own, back to school. They struggled up from the beach or down to it, in either case in costumes that seemed to get skimpier each year and laden with parasols, rattan mats and bags filled with sun-lotions, before and after, tar removers and pills against the gastro-enteritis that almost inevitably followed if you accidentally swallowed the seawater and was a certainty if you were tempted by the seafood.

'Not many left now.' There was satisfaction in his voice. This year he was going to be among the ones that stayed.

'Less each year.'

'Really? Why?'

'English recession, Spanish boom. Half the Brit-owned properties, and there are a lot of them, are up for sale. Pity your lot couldn't come now. It's nicer when it's not so crowded and August was, well, too hot. Especially this year.'

'Dad, I've said I'm sorry. What more can I say?'

It had been hell for all of them. SISA had suddenly demanded, back at the end of June, that they work flat out, thirty-six hours in every forty-eight. Cartwright had wanted to cancel but Grandad wouldn't hear of it, had sworn he would manage. But it had all gone badly wrong. Seeing their Dad only intermittently and for short spells the children quickly got out of hand and in very different ways. Nadine got in with a gang of nine- and ten-year-olds who bombed about the big patios and the promenade throwing cheap balloons filled with water at anyone who they reckoned couldn't run as fast as they could; Jimmy got badly parent-sick and took to phoning his mother at all times of the day and night. Grandad's blood pressure soared and in the end they aborted the holiday after only twelve days, paying an extra three hundred pounds to get them on a scheduled flight to Heathrow, foregoing their bucket shop returns to Luton.

'It's a bloody shame, it really is. A bogger.' He flicked the chops over, smoke and the smell again.

'I know what you mean, Dad.'

And he did too. If the children had been able to come out for the last three weeks of September instead of August they would all four have had a whale of time together, rebuilding the broken relationships, enjoying the cooler weather, exploring the mountains inland and using a beach you could move on without falling over near-naked broiled flesh.

'And you really will be free by the end of next week?'

'Should be if it works the way it should. Tomorrow the containers are shipped to Mauretania for testing. I follow by plane three days later. If all goes well then that's it.'

'And if it all works and you are through, what then?'

'Hang around for a bit. They've paid me enough. Living as I do at the moment I needn't work for a year. I'll hang around, see what turns up.' Roma? Oh God, I hope so. Without any really good reason he had got it into his head that she would be part of the bonus if the test went off properly.

The old man raised the level of the meat and squirted water on the coals, lowering the temperature.

'Let's see how those chips are doing.'

Cartwright followed him back through the airy sitting room and into the kitchen. Herbert lifted down the door of the eye-level oven. A good-sized double helping of chips sizzled gently on a tray, just beginning to take on colour.

'Best thing since sliced bread, these oven-bake chips. Have you learnt how to make a decent salad yet, our Arnie?'

'No.'

'But you haven't forgotten how to take the top off a San Miguel.'

'No again.'

'Help yourself then.'

'Are you having one this time?'

'No. Doc said two in the evening was enough. None at midday.'

'Blood pressure not dropping then?'

'Not enough. He wants me to go to Malaga hospital for echocardiography, see if I'm suffering from left ventricular hypertrophy, but I'll not bother.'

'D-a-ad . . .?'

'I'm not arguing, Arnie, so shut it. I'm not in a hurry to go, but I'm not that fussed about hanging on either.' He sliced cucumber with professional rapidity. 'But one thing I'm not going to put up with is slow deterior, deter . . . getting worse, surgery, losing it all bit by bit.'

Cartwright looked at him sharply. That failure to get his tongue round the word . . . had he already had a minor stroke and wasn't letting on? His own heart lurched.

'Dad, you take care. You've all I've got now.'

'Well, maybe you'll spend a bit of time with me, once this job's over. Be a good lad and check those chops for me, eh?'

They ate out on the balcony, with the green awning down to give them shade and the glass door open behind them to keep the air moving. The chops were brilliant, Cartwright said so.

'Aye. It's leaner here, pork is. They kill them younger. And you can't beat proper oak charcoal.'

'Nor the old *condimento.* Dad, what do you make of this Kuwait lark then?'

'Don't ask me, son. I'm no sort of expert.'

'But I am asking you. Who's right, who's wrong? You know I'm illiterate where politics are concerned.'

'This has nowt to do wi' politics. It's about greed, pure and simple, nothing else. Number one. The Kuwaitis are the greediest people in the world. Jack Arbuckle worked there for a bit, remember Jack? And Doris Stevens went there teaching kids, British kids in the special school they set up. It's a nasty place, ruled by nasty people. Both said so. Number two, the place should never have happened anyway. One thing Saddam has got right is that on any of the arguments put forward nowadays to justify where a line should be drawn between countries, Kuwait should have been in Iraq.'

'Why wasn't it then?'

'Oil. Give the cream of Iraq oil to a family of bedouins or whatever they are, we can keep control of it, was the way they saw it in 1960 or whenever it was they set the place up.'

'This Saddam is a murderous bastard.'

'Bush is a murderous bastard.'

'I don't recall ever reading that Bush goes about emptying pistols into the back of people's heads.'

'I don't recall ever reading Hitler did likewise either. And I don't recall Bush ever condemned the Contras in Nicaragua who did, nor the death squads in El Salvador.'

Cartwright eased the top off his third San Miguel, leant back and looked out at the palms, the dark sea, the geriatrics hobbling up from the beach.

'If,' he said, 'Bush had let Saddam get away with this, if Bush had kept out of this, what would have happened?'

'A meeting of Arab heads of state who would have urged Saddam to withdraw. And he would have done, taking some loot with him, and keeping the oilfield he says is his and those two islands in the waterway. Kisses, you know how they go on, between him and Sheikh Jaber. And a *duro* on a litre of petrol.'

'A what?'

'A *duro*. Five pesetas. Tuppence-ha'penny.'

Down below a pair of buttocks in day-glo pink retreated towards the sea and caught Cartwright's attention. The skin above and below was nicely tanned. He couldn't make out any sign of a bra strap or halter. One thing though. The hair was definitely not silver. Just white. Amazing how some of these old biddies kept their figures, at least until you got close enough to see the wrinkles.

'There's ice-cream in the freezer.'

'No thanks, Dad.'

'Your Nan always used to say a meal isn't a meal without a sweet.'

Cartwright laughed.

'So she did. And you're the only one of her brood who made it to seventy.'

'Brandy? I've got a good one. Domecq. Something they don't put about all that much. Won it off a Spanish mate of mine chucking arrows.'

'Later may be. You still play darts?'

'Only against the locals. Robbing the blind. I tell you though it's catching on here, darts is. All the best pubs have a dart-board.'

'Well, maybe I'll try it. The brandy I mean.'

'On the sideboard. Help yourself.'

Back on the balcony Cartwright sniffed and sipped.

'This is . . . smooth. You know, for a time I thought this thing I've been working on was for Iraq.'

'Crossed my mind.'

'But it can't be.'

'Why not?'

'This blockade they've put down. Closed up Aqaba. No way they're going to get eight containers into Iraq.'

'So where are they going, our Arnie?'

'Christ knows.'

'But you're going to Mauretania, Arnie, and even in early September the Mauretanian Sahara is going to be . . . hot. Take some sun-cream.'

CHAPTER 17

It was. Very hot. As soon as Cartwright saw the temperatures expected between ten in the morning and eight in the evening he ordered the containers to be painted with aluminium reflective paint, to be sealed at nine, with their cooling systems turned full on and constant monitoring of the temperatures inside. If these rose above 40° the programs would be wiped. All through the long hot hours the diesel generators rumbled almost noiselessly and the sun bounced off the reflective silvery surfaces. He and the crew of thirty, including drivers, cooks and bottle-washers, tried to find ways of making the time go by without going mad. The only ones who slept were the drivers, small dark men with lined faces and strong hands.

They had tents hired from nomads, portable air-conditioning, and a gallon of cold water per person per day, salt tablets and soft porn videos, but it was scarcely enough. The relief when eight o'clock came round and the purple shadows stretched across the sand, the taunting mirages faded and the ripple effects deepened almost to black, was enormous. As the first stars punched holes in the darkening fabric of the limpid sky all bustled briefly, packing tents, cooking equipment, water tanks back into the big Russian four by fours, the Volvo trucks were reharnessed to the containers and within an hour they were off, just as the sun dipped behind the distant dunes and the sky went black.

For three nights they roared steadily across the desert following the one unmetalled but ballasted track that headed north-east towards the Algerian border. The headlights of the lead vehicle swung across the desert landscape, but the rest were dipped because of the dust cloud they created; each driver locked his gaze on the red tail-lights of the vehicle in front. They maintained concentration by talking to each other constantly on short-wave radios, about everything and anything. Occasionally Cartwright's driver in the lead vehicle would burst out laughing, and then, since he had very reasonable English, he would repeat whatever it was one of the others in the procession behind had said. Usually the funny bits were elaborate obscenities describing what Saddam Hussein had done to the Sabah family and was about to do to Bush and the Jewish state: their unanimity on the subject was seamless.

Around three in the morning the pattern would shift, the airways being handed over for the hour before the very first light to just one driver who would relate a rambling tale of feuds and romance, ascribed to a great grandfather and offered with folkish embellishments.

It was a remarkable endorsement of modern technology, not the high-tech sort but the more down-to-earth production of cooling systems, tyres and diesel engines, that nothing broke down at all during the whole week.

On the fourth morning, at a little after three o'clock, the guide who shared the front bench of the lead vehicle with Cartwright and the driver suddenly pointed ahead, issued a staccato order which made the driver dip his lights and reached for the microphone that spoke to the whole convoy. There was a glow in the black night of the desert, four miles away.

When they came up with them they found three Mitsubishi jeeps and a couple of pitched tents lit by diesel-generated electricity. Beyond the light, other shapes, other vehicles. Figures spilled out: tall Algerians in djellabahs, soldiers in desert fatigues and three Europeans in shirts and shorts. One, lean, blond, fit, welcomed Cartwright as he stepped down into the cool night.

'Cartwright, Arnold? Stefan Wörtche. Whoops, mind how you go.'

Because his leg had gone to sleep, Cartwright had to turn the handshake into a support.

'Are you all right? Good god, man. The needles and pins? Ah yes . . . Now. You have just three hours to deploy your system. Is that enough time?'

'Yes, yes I think so.'

'We are giving you a 180° sector with a median eight degrees east of magnetic north.' The English was that of a well-educated German: almost flawless, with flat short vowels and self-conscious if slightly idiosyncratic deployment of upper-class idiom. Cartwright reacted badly to it. 'The target plane will penetrate your two hundred and fifty mile perimeter at exactly six o'clock, but you must of course be prepared for it to come from anywhere in the sector. No second chance.'

'No problem if it's using RASP 3.'

'Well, we have done our best. Of course we could not get authentic RASP 3, but we have fitted RASP 2 upgraded according to our best information about RASP 3. The plane incidentally is an Algerian F-15. We have been working on it for three months, and I suppose we have it about right.'

'Okay. Let's get on with it. Who are these?'

Three more men had appeared from one of the tents. All wore yellow combat fatigues, black berets, and two sported thick black moustaches. They were in their forties, wore a colonel's stars on their shoulder straps and two of them had air force wings above their left breast pockets.

'My dear chap, these are our masters. At any rate our paymasters. Best not to ask where from, I think, but those moustaches say it all.'

Cartwright felt a sudden chill, and it was not just the night air, now polluted with the diesel fumes that swirled around their knees. Whatever else, one thing was sure: in the four days and four nights he had spent in Mauretania he had seen no Mauretanian who resembled them in any way at all, apart from having black hair. But they didn't actually have to be from Baghdad, did they? And so long as no-one actually said so, then he supposed he could get on with the job in hand. He shook hands with them, muttered banalities which he was sure they could not understand.

Feeling slightly sick, and with a steady burn of anxiety building up inside, he set about deploying the containers in a circle, like the wagons in a western. He put the actual radar antenna on its eighteen-foot trailer, precisely in position on its four jacks at the top, pointing the designated eight degrees east of magnetic north and next to it the radar transmitter and receiver. It was not a round dish but a slice from a parabola made out of a highly polished brass-like alloy, mounted vertically, sixteen feet high. Then came the brains, a full thirty-footer stacked with computers, ageing PDP 11s, which processed the incoming squawks, and, once a target had been fixed, computed its distance, height and speed.

The next contained more computers, which converted the old direct blip on a cathode ray tube familiar from films into a processed image, and five display consoles to show it.

The fourth, at the far side of the circle, carried the main displays and was known as the 'Director's Chair'. Here the displays were enhanced and controlled by computers that activated alarm programs if, for some reason such as radar jamming from the in-coming aircraft, they lost the target. In that case the alarm programs continued to predict where the aircraft was until the proper signal was picked up again. This was where Cartwright would be, and, he supposed, the Clients. It was here that they would first pick up the intruder, identify it as hostile, lose it as it activated its radar-jamming devices, and recover it as they counteracted them.

The circle was completed by two more containers carrying the communications equipment which would, in a 'real' situation, feed the information back to a command centre, which in turn would be connected to airfields where interceptor aircraft would be on permanent standby or surface to air missile sites. The gaps were filled with diesel generators and power conditioners. The spaces above were laced with aerials and antennae. Cartwright had questioned the necessity of bringing the onward communications containers: since there were no interceptors to be scrambled or missiles to be aimed and fired, what was the point?

He had been overruled by a higher, but shadowy, authority.

As the minutes ticked by towards six o'clock he became more and more aware that Stefan was a pain, a pain in the arse. He not only clung to him all the time, occasionally he seemed deliberately to distract him from what he was doing.

'Frankly, old chap,' the German insisted, 'I have done a damned fine job and I have a wager with my friends the plane will get through. If so, our clients get a damn fine attack aircraft capable of penetrating most defences, even if they lose out on a decent defence system themselves.'

There is then, thought Cartwright, a touch of the old needle here. With renewed energy and purpose he set about checking out Haroun al-Rashid's systems. Presently he realised that Tai-Won-Kun was finding a lot to talk about in a language he could not understand with the other two Germans.

He had learnt to respect Tai-Won-Kun's intelligence, and even more her ability to work for thirty-six hours in forty-eight. Apart from that there was nothing likeable about her at all. He rationalised, or at any rate explained to himself, the revulsion he felt along predictable lines. She always wore the same clothes: a denim jacket above a denim skirt with chocolate-brown tights or possibly stockings and Reebok trainers with the tongues pulled up. She was not exactly fat, because she was also compact — like a T–62 tank. She had funny eyelids and the hazy beginnings of a moustache. She carried with her a sour odour — not sweaty, and certainly not the sickly sweet urinal smell one associates with twenty-four carat BO — just sour. Because she so grossly offended every conception he had about what a woman should or even could be, he had for a time told himself that the distaste he felt was inexcusable: the knee-jerk reaction of a racist MCP. Then one day he had the sense to ask himself: would I like her any more if she were a Caucasian male? Since the answer was an unambiguous no, he stopped feeling guilty about it.

But he did concede her intelligence, her capacity for work and her knowledge too. She knew it all. Indeed, he sometimes wondered why he was needed. She could have done his job as well as he. And now it was becoming apparent to him that that was precisely what she was doing — his job. When he came to check out areas in the whole complex link-up he found she had been there before him.

'Aw light, Meester Arn-old. Eees done awleddy.'

Benny Hill could not have done it bedder.

At five-thirty, with just the merest glimmer that the rich black of the Saharan night, scattered with a billion jewels, might not be permanent, he boosted the power from the generators. At five fifty-nine he turned the system on. It emitted a signal which hopped adroitly between 2,000 and 3,000 megs, peppering the hemisphere in front of it with oscillating squawks from horizontal or 0° to 60° with a range of two hundred and fifty miles. Almost immediately he got a bleep and a dot on the circular screen in front of him, coming in from the West. The computerised systems worked out distance and height algorithmically, working between each pulse. Relying on the Doppler effect, other systems calculated the speed of the incoming aircraft. Five hundred and seventy knots, one thousand feet, two hundred and thirty miles, closing.

Watching it all, in the command container filled with display consoles, Cartwright turned to Wörtche.

'We're getting no IFF signal.'

Identity, friend or foe. Every plane that flies faster than a hundred and fifty knots is meant to send out a signal from a transponder saying who and what it is.

Tai-Won-Kun pushed a lock of greasy black hair off her sallow moist forehead.

'A plane that fries without IFF is a rogue,' she murmured, 'deserves what it gets.'

Cartwright shrugged. Then suddenly the blip was gone, for about a second, then came back red.

'He's turned on RASP, the image we are now getting is the predicted one. Now here goes.'

He flipped a couple of switches. The blip returned to its original colour.

'Gotcher.' Satisfaction, successful culmination of sixteen weeks work. But what did she mean — 'deserves what it gets'?

'Well done, English.' Stefan on his other side, patted his shoulder. 'I lose my bet — only fifty marks, not a big deal. In a minute or so he'll be visual. I think I would like to have a look.'

Suddenly Cartwright was alone. They had both gone, clattering along the metal floor of the container, out into the pre-dawn gloaming. Then the noise came, dulled by the walls around him, but alive and frightening, a sudden swift monstrous whoosh of a noise and a moment later a second smaller blip appeared on his screen.

'Oh, shit, it can't be,' Cartwright cried. 'Abort it, they've got to abort it.'

But no. Twenty, fifteen, ten seconds, at a combined speed of something close to two thousand miles an hour they were heading for impact. He knew now precisely what was happening.

The missile was homing on the return radar signal it itself emitted. The F–15 was issuing a jamming signal to scramble the return signal the missile was getting. The missile then switched to another system to home in on the jamming signal. The pilot of the F-15 should then receive a signal which said that the missile's original radar had been switched off. He could then switch off his jamming signal and take evasive action. And judging from the way the blip was weaving that precisely was what was happening. Finally the pilot turned into the start of a hundred and eighty degree turn. But he was too late. The pulsing glow on the screen marked two arcs which swiftly grew to a meeting point, not unlike the arcs described by a bull and the running *banderillero* up to the moment when he plants the barbed and fluttering darts in the bull's back, but this time the blips simply met and went out. The reading said that impact had occurred twelve miles away.

Anxiety tightened its knot in his diaphragm. He wanted to cry out, to scream, to stop what had happened. But still part of his mind refused to believe it. He looked at his watch. The sweep second hand had just passed the ten. In sixty seconds, when it reached the ten again, there would be a bang. He hauled himself out of the swivel chair, slowly crossed the floor of the container and cranked the chrome handle that released the airtight seals. He pushed open the heavy door and sat down on the steps and watched the second hand.

Five, four, three, two, one, and crack! Out of the cloudless sky a distant thunder-clap. The time was 0621.

He felt sick, dizzy, his knees were cotton wool. He sat where he was, his face buried in his hands. He could not bring himself to get up, get out, face the others, all of whom were now utterly hateful to him. But presently he knew that someone had come back inside the container and he forced himself to look up.

Tai-Won-Kun was reaching for switches and controls, closing the system down.

'What was it?' he asked.

She looked at him. Her face was no longer inscrutable, indeed it expressed a muted inner radiance. She was high, high on it all.

'A HAWK. A Homing All the Way Killer. Latest version. It was a shame you missed it.' There was scorn now as well as the high. 'It was magnificent. They are velly pleased. Come.'

He hauled himself to his feet and followed her, stumbling, out into the open. The colonels in their black berets closed round him, shook his hand repeatedly, slapped his back, even tried to embrace him. They smelt of stale sweat, garlic, cheap tobacco. The technicians hung about in the background, but they all looked pleased, excited too. Stefan Wörtche took his arm, urged him through a gap in the corralled containers, out into the desert.

They were on a sort of gentle eminence, higher than most of the land around them. The wind-rippled dunes they were on rolled away from them into a distant pearly haze. Beyond the haze the ridge of a low brown plateau, fifteen miles away, already caught the golden sunlight across its eastern flank and along the serrated escarpment. From a patch of dark, plum-coloured shadow a fireball of orange pumped a plume of black smoke into a sky that deepened from opal to blue in the moment or two he stood there. Then the heat of the risen sun hit him, like a blow, and he turned back into the enclosure.

'I'd like tea,' he said, and he heard the faltering in his own voice, almost a whimper. 'A cup of proper English tea. With sugar.'

CHAPTER 18

'Dad, you never killed anyone, did you?'

They were up in the mountains, sitting in the Ford Sierra, looking at a grey blank wall of vapour. Cartwright had driven his dad up to the point where he reckoned he had seen Africa, back on 15 June, to prove to him it was possible and to give him an outing too. But this time at fifteen hundred metres they were in cloud. With damp mist falling from the trees and a weeping sky he had suddenly found himself telling the story of his trip to Mauretania.

His dad looked down at his arthritic knuckles, massaged them for a moment, shifted tired thin buttocks on the upholstery.

'You're asking me because you think you did. But you didn't. You unwittingly aided and abetted. Unwittingly.'

The old man pulled in a heavy, quavering breath, went on.

'Aye, our Arnie, I did. You know I were a squaddie, National Service, and '46 to '47 you know I were in Palestine. Bought the filigree necklace of silver and gold flowers there, in Jerusalem, and gave it to your Mam when I got back. She were only sixteen then and by god she were pleased. Well, yes. I killed a lad, same age as me I daresay. Terrorist. Jew-boy. Reckon he'd be in their Cabinet right now if I hadn't got to him first. Never told anyone, not even your Mam, though I often wish I had. Not much we didn't share, your Mam and me, and she could have carried it, help me carry it.'

Clearly he was disturbed.

'Dad, don't go on if you don't want to.' Cartwright's voice was as gentle as he could make it. Outside the cloud shifted and a scrap of cork oak forest on the other side of the valley briefly appeared: tall trees with dark foliage; the red wood exposed to halfway up their trunks where the cork bark had been stripped. With the mist swirling round them they looked like ghosts marching to perdition. Then they were gone.

'It's something I have to say. After all these years. I've not got much longer . . .'

'Da-a-d!'

'It's the truth son. I feel she's coming closer. And I dream a lot of your Mam at night, she's closer too. Any road I'll get it off me chest. Time I did. Haifa backstreet. Upstairs room, tiny, whitewashed walls, a little metal bed, don't remember anything else. He was on the bed when we got in, asleep. Young lieutenant we had in charge, he was National Service too, didn't know his arse from his elbow. Started rabbiting on about "Are you Jacob Ben this or that, and I must ask you to accompany me . . .", didn't even have his revolver out. All the time this Jacob whatever had his hand under his pillow, the way you do when you're asleep, and suddenly it wasn't there any more but coming out holding something black and sort of snake-like it's always seemed to me since. Reptilian anyway. So I blew his head off.'

Silence filled the car. Herbert sighed again.

'Thompson sub-machine gun. Tommy-gun. Made . . . made a mess. All he had was a tiny German pistol. Two-two. Pin-fire. Probably wouldn't have gone off even if he had pulled the trigger. Mind you though, four days earlier he lobbed a grenade into the market the Palestinians used, took out a couple of kiddies amongst all the rest, eight in all. So we'd been told. That's why we were there.'

'Dad. That doesn't seem to me to be something you should worry about, feel bad about.'

'Well. I don't know. I always have. Felt bad. I could have

just . . . hit him with the butt. Or something. They shouldn't have told me about the kiddies in the market.'

Nearby, on the bough of a pine tree, a small dark bird with a red breast and a pert upsticking tail began to sing its heart out.

Cartwright started the motor, shifted the gear.

'We're not going to see Africa today.'

He set the car in motion.

Presently they came out of the cloud and into the sunlight. Below them the road wound down to a copse of scarlet mountain ash and silver trunked poplars with leaves like gold coins. They were clustered round a bar-restaurant: whitewashed walls, red tiles, wrought iron gratings on the windows, patio with vines and a creeper with small delicate white flowers.

'Pull in, Arnie. I'll buy you lunch. We've picked a good day for it.'

'How do you know that, Dad?'

'See the missus over there, by the side of the house?'

A plump corseted woman in a black dress, white apron, hair in a bun, up to her elbows in a big zinc bowl, heaved and pushed and scrubbed what looked like a vacuum cleaner hose made out of white rubber.

'That's tripes she's washing. That means they've killed summat this morning, and that makes it worth stopping.'

Wiping red hands on a large cloth she waddled ahead of them through the dark dining room and out into the patio.

'Take away the electric light, the coffee machine, the ice-cream cabinet and it could be AD 90. Pity it in't.'

Herbert asked if they had *vino de la costa* and the owner brought out a terracotta jug covered with a small lacy mat. The wine was a sort of brownish rosé, tangy, slightly metallic, very strong, and Herbert insisted they should dilute it with Casera lemonade, the best, really just fizzy water with a hint of lemon and lime and only slightly sweetened.

'Spain's best kept secret, this wine is,' Herbert said. 'It come from up the coast, the mountains above Motril. It don't bottle well, won't travel. No additives, see? Nearly a year old now and a bit dry and tart, it's just about fermented right out. Best time to drink it is in the spring. Have a glass for me next April if I'm not around. And don't pull that long face, Arnie. Knowing she's getting closer puts an edge on things, makes things seem brighter, cleaner, better.'

'She? Who is this "she"? That's the second time you've talked about a "she" getting closer.'

'You know what a sarcophagus is?'

'Sort of marble coffin?'

'That's right. Romans used them. Carved usually. Common figure is a draped female form, cowled, hand holds the cowl over her face like a veil. That's who she is.'

Cartwright shivered, the old man covered his hand with his own, dry and hard, squeezed.

'Now let's enjoy this. It's going to be good.'

And so it was. They ate T-bone steaks from the young steer freshly killed that morning by the owner in contravention of who knew what EC regulations, charcoal grilled, very rare. The chips were cooked in fresh olive oil, everything in the salad apart from the olives had also been alive that morning.

They got back to Laguna Playa at about four o'clock. A stretched Mercedes, silver, was parked outside the front door of Herbert's block, and as they approached it the driver got out, leant against the limo, elbow on the roof, keys on a fancy ring dangling from his brown hand. Although he was not in uniform his pale blue shirt over slightly darker trousers, shiny black shoes, heavier than you would expect, said chauffeur, driver. Black corrugated hair, dark eyes that looked dead and a smile that hurt, said other things: minder, bodyguard, muscle... may be worse.

'Mr Cartwright? Gabriel Sur says the containers just got back from Africa, and there's more work to do on them. I'm to take you over to his place. He's got a new contract waiting for you. The terms are advantageous. Very advantageous. Okay?'

He opened the passenger door, so it blocked the sidewalk.

'You'd better go, son. Keep in touch. Let me know how it works out.'

Cartwright got in, felt the languid embrace of buttercup yellow soft hide closing on his back and buttocks. Herbert was still fumbling with his keys as the big car slipped away. The driver unholstered a radio-phone, thumbed a memory button.

'Abdul? Tell the boss he finally showed. I'm on my way with him now.'

CHAPTER 19

The luxury of the car did little to ameliorate the ride: Cartwright had no wish to be re-employed by people he knew to be murderers; although no force had been used or even threatened he felt he had been kidnapped; fifty of the sixty miles they travelled followed one of the most depressing roads in Europe. The sea on one side and the mountains on the other were like two beautiful women on the arms of a diseased lout: they clung to the hot ribbon of poisoned air that threaded urbanisations and *pueblos*, factories and wasteland, from Torrox to a motorway exit past Malaga, just short of Marbella.

As they got through all this, much in the way a miniaturised camel might be expected to pass through the magnified eye of a needle, the driver, 'Call me Josh — it's not my name but it's what people call me', indulged himself with a monologue in praise of his employer.

'Jabreel Mansur. Maybe now the richest man in the world. They used to say that about Adnan Khashoggi, but his Saudi brethren let Khashoggi down and he got in an expensive muddle with the FBI, US Customs. You speak English English, like they speak it in England? Yeah, so do I. Two years I did in Brixton. Crack rap.' He half-turned his head, grinned, exposed gold molars. 'Anyway, North was a wanker so Khashoggi got stuck with it. Jabreel too got into bad odour, how do you say, a stink? With almost everybody. Had a nice pad north of Marbella, but the one he's got now is even better. Lots of pressure on him, but he got out from under. Too many locals had too much to lose, and others in Washington. So they sent him away. To Damascus. To the Crimea, would you believe it? Cooling off period. But now he's Gabriel Sur. With some sort of ex-Spanish Sahara ID that makes him legal.'

Away from the motorway and the coast they climbed low foothills through abandoned olive groves where dried grass and scrub had invaded the fertile soil beneath. Each crag and steeper slope was dominated by its unfinished urbanisation, often just the cuboid frames of reinforced concrete, stacked pigeon-holes waiting for a flock of monstrous tin harpies with cries harsh like screaming metal to come and build nests out of the tin drums, twisted discarded girders, heavy-duty polythene and glass-fibre wool that littered the forecourts. Many of the hoardings bore the logo of Sur Industrias SA, SISA.

The road climbed a little higher, left what had once been honest farmland behind, threaded rocky outcrops covered with broom and cistus, all now dry and seemingly dead although in early summer they had covered the hillsides with silver and gold. There was some rosemary though, which the September storms had brought back into bloom, spikes of tiny pale blue stars, the colour of Nadine's eyes. Cartwright had wanted to call her Rosemary, but it was a name Margaret held to be common.

Presently the right hand side of the road was fenced — eight feet of chain-link topped by razor wire, then a gate appeared, or rather a gate-house: heavy sheet metal flanked by round concrete pill-boxes like hat-boxes with horizontal slit windows, manned by four guards in para-military uniform. They all carried Heckler and Koch MP 5s — cybernetic extensions to their right arms. While two of them covered the road in both directions to make sure the car was not a decoy distracting them from an assault that might be coming up behind, the third checked the car, under the hood, in the boot, underneath, and the fourth its occupants.

He was thorough, bantering with 'Josh' whom he clearly knew well, but taking no chances. He had them both out and frisked them, and finally checked back to the house that the car was expected. Then the gates were opened, silently, electronically.

The road, now no longer a potholed mixture of concrete and crumbling tarmac but black velvet, wound back and down into a high valley. The sea appeared again and the coast, from this height and distance a necklace with Marbella as the jewel in the middle. The plants were no longer agricultural or wilderness but exotic and planted for effect, many of them tropical — lush clumps of scarlet and yellow flowers in beds beneath palms. There was a grotto with a waterfall that fed a small lake set between landscaped lawns on whose emerald velour a world-class golfer would have been happy to putt, and, finally, set in a clasp of thin black cypress and spreading cedar, a villa. It was large, vaguely Roman in style with ochre stone walls and red-tiled roofs, two storeys, three blocks placed in a 'U' with a simple Doric colonnade enclosing a fountain: three nude Graces pouring water from urns. Their marble was too white, their buttocks too rounded and their breasts too pert to be anything other than Marbella kitsch.

'You were upset. About the plane you so skilfully destroyed. And of course the pilot. Actually he was an Israeli. Got caught in Kuwait sleeping off a hangover. Several Israeli pilots in Kuwait, said to be instructors but really they were the only ones there who could fly the planes at all . . . shall we say, aggressively? Most had the sense to get out during the build-up.' Jabreel Mansur, Gabriel Sur, reached for ice-cold buttermilk, pushed the silver forelock into place with his other hand and continued to wax expansive. 'Anyway, he was good. We told him what he was up against, he did his best. You did better. You should feel proud.'

The way Dad feels proud of shooting the head off an Israeli terrorist back in 1946?

'I felt . . . I still feel sick at the thought of it.'

Mansur's heavy arched eyebrows lifted in wonder or

disbelief. His fingers, podgy, the left pinky ringed with a diamond not as big as the Ritz but big, drummed for a moment on the carved arm of his chair. Like everything else in the big, wide, airy room it looked rare, old, expensive. Louis something or other, Cartwright supposed.

'You are not, I am sure, going to allow the distress you feel to interfere with any future you might have with SISA.'

Cartwright said nothing, remained standing, then made up his mind.

'I really don't want to have anything more to do with you or SISA. I would appreciate a lift back to the motorway. That's all I really want from you.'

The look in the Yemeni's dark eyes combined cold anger and hate in an evil mix that suddenly frightened him. Mansur reached for the small silver bell on the occasional table at his elbow, gave it the briefest of shakes. A door behind Cartwright opened, he felt a presence.

'Josh. Hurt Mr Cartwright. But not his head or his hands.'

The first blow, it could have been a kick from one of those heavy black shoes, was accurately placed on his left kidney. His back arched with the pain but worse was the sheer psychological shock that this was actually happening to him. The second kick caught him exactly on the pelvic bone half an inch above his anal sphincter and this time the pain overwhelmed everything else. He rolled to the floor, tried to make a foetal ball of himself and failed. The third kick found his scrotum, the fourth the pit of his stomach, the fifth his diaphragm, winding him, so on top of the agony he felt for a moment that he would black out for lack of air. Through the roar of the blood in his ears and the rush of air dragged into his aching lungs he heard Mansur's voice and the scorn in it which cut like a knife.

'He's dirtied himself. Get him out, quick. Before he spoils the carpet. Clean him up, tell Efraim to check him out.'

Hands like heavy duty vices bunched the collar and back of his woven cotton shirt, the other took a grip on his belt so his trousers tightened and he felt . . . yes, the bastard was right. As they reached the double door, the voice barked again.

'Stop.' Mansur came out of his chair, walked up to them, took Cartwright's chin in his hand. 'Look at me, Cartwright. And believe what I am going to say. If we are not in total accord with each other by this time tomorrow, then Josh will be on your father's doorstep Saturday morning when he goes to buy that English newspaper he has once a week. And he will do to him exactly what he has just done to you.'

Josh half dragged, half walked him out into a big circular marble hall lit from a glass dome above. Round the walls were niches with busts of classical figures — Roman Emperors? He just had time to see the squat denimed figured of Tai-Won-Kun turn from one of these as Josh got him through another door, down a corridor and into a small room with a shower-stall and toilet where he dropped him, let him fall to the floor and left him.

There were towels and soap. If there had been a razor he would have cut his wrists or his throat. He considered using his belt to hang himself from the shower fitting but in the end turned on the water, and slowly, painfully, dragged off his filthy clothes.

CHAPTER 20

There were carrots as well as sticks. Nevertheless, three days passed before Tai-Won-Kun felt able to tell Mansur that she was ready to believe Cartwright was working properly and would continue to do so.

The first twenty-four hours they were very careful with him. After he had cleaned himself up Josh showed him to a small but very comfortable bedroom where a doctor was already waiting for him. He was a small tubby man with spectacles who claimed, as he ran strong but sensitive fingers over Cartwright's body, to have spent two years at the Fenwick in Cambridge, studying what he called 'small battle lesions' — everything from the results of beatings through knife wounds to small arms bullet wounds and shrapnel. All this after qualifying in general medicine, *summa cum laude*, from Cairo University.

'The trauma, psychological as well as physical, will continue to affect you for months, perhaps years, after the bruising has quite disappeared. As to the actual lesions I am saying there is no cause for worry. Josh is very experienced in this sort of work. I would have preferred the blow to the kidney to have been just a little less percussive, but I detect no symptoms of rupture and the prognosis is good. I am sure it will recover almost as readily as the rest . . .'

The doctor left Cartwright, lying under a silk coverlet, dosed with painkillers and tranquillisers. He slept for nearly twenty hours.

At one o'clock the next afternoon they woke him with

coffee. Folded on a chair by the bed a Pierre Cardin short-sleeved shirt lay on top of a pair of lightweight trousers with a Savile Row label. They were only slightly too large for him. At two o'clock a Filipino girl less than five feet tall and dressed in a starched white overall took him downstairs, back to the big room where it had happened.

Mansur and Tai-Won-Kun looked up at him as he came in. They were sitting opposite each other on low settees, with a table between them laden with dishes filled with a wide variety of seafood and *picante* dips. There was also a silver bowl filled with ice, and Lanjarón mineral water.

'Is . . .', Cartwright dragged in breath heavy with apprehension. 'Is my father all right?'

Mansur smiled, the corners of his angel mouth lifted archaically.

'My dear fellow, of course! Give him a buzz, check him out.'

'No . . . no, I . . . Perhaps later. If you don't mind.'

A half glance flashed between Mansur and Tai-Won-Kun. It said — this man is already broken.

'Then come and sit with us. Enjoy the meal.'

Presently Mansur opened the discussion. The pretence that the Ferlinghetti was for Mauretania was no longer maintained.

'There is no longer a problem,' Mansur began, waving the leg of a small lobster, 'about shipping our Ferlinghetti to Iraq. Quite simply it can't be done. But the Kuwaitis had three Ferlinghettis *in situ*, identical to ours, that is ours before you made your excellent improvements. The problem is how to get these three unimproved Ferlinghettis up to the same standard as yours in a very short time.' He cracked the leg with gold-capped molars, dipped the ends in a coriander and chilli sauce, sucked out the flesh. 'Any ideas?'

Cartwright saw the obvious possibility straight away, but refrained from jumping in too quickly. He wasn't hungry, he still felt sick and was still in pain. He felt weak too. He toyed with an anchovy, fried, crisp but cold, put it down, waited.

Tai-Won-Kun cleared her throat.

'The telephone? Modems? Modulator-Demodulators?'

'Problems.'

They waited.

'Well. First of all the development systems will have to be re-configured to download our new builds. Then, you have to realise error-free reception over telephone lines and satellite is extremely critical. And one single error will render all the information useless.' He paused. 'I can envisage ways round these problems.'

Tai-Won-Kun sucked an unsuspecting oyster out of its shell.

'We can split it all up into small packets, add extra data to check for errors,' she said. 'We'll have to prepare data transmission programs to cope. And we'll need a copy of those at the other end.'

Cartwright turned to Mansur.

'What can be got into Iraq? People? A disk-pack?'

'If we move quickly, both. As long as Saddam has some of the Human Shield in place that's just the sort of thing he can trade off. Pop-star, Muslim boxer ex-world heavy-weight, ex-president, whatever, comes to plead for the hostages he's particularly interested in, he could have a disk-pack strapped to his body, better still . . .'

'Yes?'

'If he's got some sort of diplomatic immunity, if he's still part of the Arab world that still sides with Iraq, then maybe a diplomatic bag . . .'

Mansur beamed. And not just because he had answered Cartwright's question. He knew the man was hooked. Giving him a problem to solve in his particular field was a bait, a carrot. Give him a problem that was subversive, overrode the rules, and he was your man.

'We'll need more than that. More than just a disk-pack. Someone at the other end who knows the whole development system.' Cartwright looked at Tai-Won-Kun, expressionlessly, hiding the dislike he felt. Then back to Mansur. 'Can you get her in? She's the only person who knows it well enough.'

'Sure we'll get her in. Fix her up as a Red Cross nurse. Better still, the Japanese Prime Minister is on his way, she could go in as one of his aides.'

The Korean was angry.

'I am not,' she said, 'Japanese. And I do not look like a Japanese.'

Mansur beamed at her. 'Try the prawn balls. They're very good.'

The technical discussion went on for an hour before Mansur interrupted it again.

'Take a break, Arnold. And why not give your dad that buzz right now? Use the phone on the cabinet by the window.'

Cartwright tapped in the number. Herbert answered on the second beat, as if his hand had been hovering over the handset.

'Dad? It's Arnie. I... just wanted to check if you're okay?'

'Arnie? I'm all right. But are you? Listen, that man who drove you off yesterday, he's back here now. Parked opposite the outside door, just as he was yesterday. I thought he must have brought you back to your place. I rang there, but no answer. So why is he here? What's he up to?'

Sticks and carrots.

The following morning Josh was back to drive Tai-Won-Kun and Cartwright out to the SISA lot, north of Malaga, where they sorted out the procedures he would follow to create new subsidiary data transmission programs with built-in error checks, handshake signals and so on. But it became clear Cartwright was still virtually a prisoner, at least until they felt completely sure of him. Josh agreed to take him out to Torre del Mar to pick up a change of clothes from his apartment, but he was not allowed to go to Torrox for his car.

Back at the villa that evening the final carrots were on offer in Mansur's office, a functional room on the first floor. The Yemeni sat back in a huge black soft leather armchair which enclosed him like a fat padded glove, responding every time he moved. If he leant forward towards his desk it came with him; when he weighted his left elbow with his left forefinger against his cheek, it tilted too.

'Arnie, how do you feel today? Still a bit stiff? A word of advice? Look on the bright side of life and tell yourself it could have been worse. A lot worse. Now . . .' He put his finger ends together beneath his chin. 'Something new has cropped up which would work very much to your advantage. You are looking at half a million sterling. What do you say to that?'

'I don't need that sort of money.'

Mansur ingored what he clearly took to be childish petulance rather than a sincere statement of fact.

'You were sacked by FADSI (UK),' he went on, 'at a crucial moment in the history of the Ferlinghetti empire. They were, were they not, just about to embark on a major project.'

'Yes.'

'A project which you expected to manage?'

'There was no-one else in-house who could have done it.'

'Sit down and tell me about it.'

The only other chair, an upright with a stainless steel tubular frame, was in front of the big picture window, which, partly shaded by adjustable vertical panels, looked out onto the pool with its grotto and waterfall, lawns, flower-beds and the big black trees. Cartwright leant forward with his hands on his spread knees, then stretched up to ease the ache in the small of his back.

'I'm sure you must know about the Stealth program developed by the Pentagon.'

'Pretend I don't.'

'All right. There are two versions in production. The Lockhead fighter-bomber designated F–117A and the Northrop bomber, the B–2. Both use the same technologies to make them virtually undetectable by radar, even advanced systems like the Ferlinghetti. Now, it's conventional wisdom in the Pentagon that you don't invent a new weapon, particularly a new offensive weapon, without at the same time developing the technology to counter it. The reasoning is that if we can invent and produce this weapon, then so can someone else. Or even they might just steal it. The contract FADSI was about to sign when they sacked me for a ten million dollar R and D project for a radar system that could detect Stealth-protected aircraft.'

'Is it possible? Can it be done?'

'I think so, yes.'

'Could you do it? Given the sort of facilities you know SISA can put at your disposal.'

'I could have a damn good try. But I don't want to be responsible for the deaths of any more pilots.'

'But you like the challenge — to do here what you were not allowed to do legitimately.'

Cartwright felt a surge of excitement. It echoed something he had first felt when he was barely thirteen years old, and just beginning to realise that the physics and maths he was being taught came far more easily to him than they did to his fellow pupils. The actual lessons became a bore, and not just because he was usually ahead of them but because they were routine, programmed, followed a pattern set by others. Whereas free speculation and experiment away from school, even when it came to nothing, had thrilled and frightened him as much as the discovery of his emergent sexuality.

He straightened again, rubbed his back.

'Yes,' he said. 'I like the challenge.'

'And as for the pilots . . . Three things. One. This time they will be shot down not as part of an experiment but because they will be on their way to kill people, many of them perhaps civilians. Two. If the US knows Saddam has an air defence system capable of downing Stealth protected aircraft, then they won't be flown. Three. You forge the sword. But you don't wield it. No more than you did in Mauretania.'

Cartwright turned in his chair, elbow over the back, looked down and out over the lawns.

'If you hurt my father I'll find some way of making you pay for it. At the very least I can kill this project.'

A bank of flowers, very pale blue, almost white, something like gladioli but bigger than any he had ever seen before glowed luminously in the dusk beneath a huge spreading cedar. Beyond them the shadows were purple and deep, deep prussian blue, almost black, and through them she seemed to float, dressed in a simple sleeveless long white gown, her skin dark above it, beneath the glimmer of her silver hair. He rubbed his eyes, looked back at the spoilt, ageing, handsome face, the big dark eyes that glittered above the archaic smile.

'Am I hallucinating?'

'No.'

He turned back, but she was gone. Silence filled the room.

'I don't understand. Does she belong to you? Is she part of the package?'

Mansur laughed quietly, sardonically, almost wistfully.

'Roma is not for sale. Not to anyone, not even to me.' He shrugged. Amber worry beads strung on gold, the thirty-three names of Allah, trickled slowly between the podgy thumb and forefinger of his right hand. 'Almost from birth she gave herself, body and soul, to a memory.'

'Of what?'

'Of an olive grove beneath whose branches wild lavender, daisies and poppies bloomed among the grasses on which her grandfather grazed his sheep. There's a supermarket there now and a shoddy little town as ugly as anything I have built here on the Costa del Sol. And there, over there, believe it or not,' again the sad laugh, 'the people speak Russian. Tell me. How will you set about building a radar system that can detect Stealth?'

Cartwright took a deep breath, overrode the anguish and the longing.

'Stealth combines two technologies. The planes are built from materials and coated with materials which absorb or disperse most of a radar signal rather than reflecting it back to a receiver. And they are designed to have as low a profile as possible, so the actual surface area from the front or side is as small as possible and shaped with deflecting angles and planes.'

A different sort of excitement was growing in his voice. At last he could see what for him had always been the Promised Land of his intellectual and professional life, the chance to create something genuinely new, a real advance in the technology of radar. It was a bonus too to be doing it under these circumstances, untrammelled by bureaucrats, security and budgets. He went on.

'The signal an S-bend air defence transmitter emits is between two and three gigaherz, a wavelength of about twelve centimetres. It is transmitted from a dish which gives what we call "gain", the ability to focus the energy into a narrow beam a lot less than one degree in width and with a range of four hundred kilometres. But at that range the gain is not enough to detect a Stealth protected aircraft. If we increase the frequency of the signal to forty gigaherz, a wavelength of only seven millimetres we would then get a gain sixteen times better. Problem: above eleven gigaherz the signal bounces back off the moisture and dust particles in the atmosphere. But theoretically it is possible to find atmospheric windows in the EHF range, which would let a radar signal through . . .' He dragged tired hands down bristly cheeks.

'The rationale goes like this. The extra system gain due to frequency change would be in the order of two hundred and fifty times better. The loss due to atmospheric attenuation, even through a window . . .'

'These windows. What are they?'

'Attenuation of a radar signal due to atmospheric particles increases above eleven gigaherz as the frequency rises, but not in a regular curve. It dips twice, quite sharply, round forty gigaherz . . .'

'Why?'

'You'd need a very good background in physics to understand any explanation I can offer.'

Mansur waved a gracious palm which said: Okay, go on.

'The loss, even through a window, could be as little as twenty-five times worse, so the net gain would be ten times better. Now I don't know what the radar signatures of the Stealth airplanes are but I doubt if they go beyond a gain as big as that.'

'So you can do it?'

'Perhaps. But there would be other factors to be dealt with too. US Electronic Warfare systems, which, amongst a lot of other things, are listening posts, would pick up signals of this sort as soon as we tried to test them, and they'd want to know what was going on. And the front end, the transmitters and receivers would have to be rebuilt, though . . .' and here the excitement became almost palpable, 'they do exist, could be procured. SDI radar technology, you know, what they called Star Wars, has them because of course in space the atmospheric problem simply isn't there. Incidentally, it will be a bonus if our system is deployed in the Arabian desert, since moisture will not be a problem . . .'

He continued to think it through. 'Dish roughness would have to be improved to a sixteenth of what it is now. Tubes would have to be acquired capable of taking the increased wattage, though this need not be a problem if we trim the signal down to one micro-second. Our antenna would have to be carefully machined to improve tolerancing by a factor of sixteen . . .'

Opposite him, the beads stopped their tiny clicking, and the smile slowly broadened on the face of Jabreel Mansur. It was the word 'our', repeated once more, that gave him so much satisfaction. Clearly Cartwright was once more well and truly on board.

PART FOUR

CHAPTER 21

Uneasy lies the head that wears a crown. On the night of 30 October it's pretty certain that at least one head that did not wear a crown but yet held in its compass the mind of the most powerful man the world had ever known was lying a touch uneasy. Shame about the grammar, blame the Bard.

What medicaments do they give the President of the United States to ensure a good night's rest, sleep untrammelled by dream or nightmare? Do the potions exist in any pharmacopoeia capable of eliminating the obsessively repeated anxieties that can click round the stressed heads of lesser mortals as if on a malfunctioning carousel? How ensure that he wakes each sweet morning ready to improve the day, bright-eyed and bushy-tailed?

And which out of all the slings and arrows that beset him, many of his own launching rather than that of outrageous fortune, bothered him most? He was, after all, facing what the *Los Angeles Times* had described only days before as the 'Triple whammy of war in the Middle East, a recession at home, and spiralling oil prices', with the added problem that the mid-term Congressional Election was less than a week away.

But the election was already a disaster, a humiliation, a write-off. Republican candidates lost votes if he turned up in their support. One had attacked his policies and been applauded for it, with him actually sitting there on the platform; another had not bothered to turn up, and a third had insisted they met in private, not in front of the media.

One is tempted to opine that the President, if he were tossing and turning that night, might well have said 'Scrub the sons, and daughters, of bitches' and forced the creaking carousel on to the next nightmare he had to ride.

This could well have been a two in hand, the tandem of pusillanimous, lily-livered, yellow streaks who ran his goddamn army. No, I'm sure he didn't put it, even to himself, in the loneliness of the night, quite like that. Nevertheless, the fat one had recently gone on record, in *Life*, no less, as 'no fan of war, in a lot of ways . . . a pacifist . . . I know what war is. I am certainly anti-war.' And then again in the *Atlanta Journal and Constitution*, which the sleepless President no doubt conceded was probably *not* on the Butcher of Baghdad's reading list, with these words: 'War is a profanity because, let's face it, you've got two opposing sides trying to settle their differences by killing as many of each other as they can.'

And the other one, the blackie from Jamaica, who insists on rhyming his first name with 'rollin', affected SOB that he is, and always keeps 'touching base' to check out his woman and kids are okay, the milksop, all along he'd been for containment and strangulation, but never had the guts to come out and say it. But he did make a speech about Eisenhower the other day, saying Ike was no proponent of war but a Champion of Peace. He's a sight too fond of quoting Eisenhower: you can see who he reckons is going to be our first black president.

And meanwhile, Sweet Jesus, what is Saddam making of all this? He *shoots* generals who say things like this. A general who called a Holy War a profanity would have his butt kicked and then he'd be shot.

So how does this Laurel and Hardy act respond when told that we intend to kick ass, that we are shifting from defensive to offensive mode? They ask for . . ., and here our entirely imagined President ('imagined' for who would dare to assume he could enter such a mind and interpret it for later generations) tapped off the thumbs and fingers of his left hand with the index finger of his right hand, in the dark, above his face . . . double the Air Force presence, double the Navy carriers from three to six, double the Marine and Army ground forces and bring in the VII Corps from Germany with its fast tanks, and the Big Red One, the 1st Mechanized Infantry Division. And before any of these even fire a shot or do anything that might risk them ending up on the inside of zippered plastic, Laurel and Hardy want Stealth fighters to knock out all Saddam's command centres and all his air defence systems.

And what is Saddam going to do when he sees this lot coming for him? Even Mad Saddam is going to see some sort of sense. He'll back off.

The carousel lurched another notch. To the Nightmare Scenario. Saddam backs off. No Falklands. Margaret, just three months ago, on the very day it started, she said: George, this could be your Falklands. But if the SOB backs off, and thanks to Laurel and Hardy he's virtually certain to, no Falklands but a nightmare. We take the boys home, reinstall the greasy al-Sabahs, and boom-boom, back he comes again. But this time with a touch more subtlety, like saying to the al-Sabahs: 'We could come in but we might not if you give us the islands, redraw the frontier, raise the price of oil, write off our debts.' And Jaber will kiss him on both cheeks, the way those pervs do, and say: of course dear brother, help yourself, knowing full well that the Great American People will not wear an adventure like this a second time. And that will be yours truly (though had this particular president ever been anyone's truly?) that will be yours truly down the tube, definitively.

And at about this point we might guess that the medicaments that soothe even the most troubled brow began to take effect and the mind of the most powerful man the world has ever known began to slip into that spooky borderland where one's controlled thought and fantasy merge into dream and out again: that *terra incognita* where the waking mind can identify sleep by the way the fantasies come unbidden.

In the hypothetical dream, of the hypothetical president, which he knew was a dream because he could no longer control it, a big black butterfly hovered over an opening orchid, waxy and smelling of gangrene and burnt flesh — the sort of smell that comes from a tank that has been hit with a 'silver bullet' and has then fried its contents in the desert sun for a week. It was not its proboscis, though, which probed the evil flower but the ovipositor at the end of its long swollen abdomen. It laid its egg and a drop of viscous juice, and as it did the orchid became a poisoned chalice, a cup with a venomous pearl, which in its turn became an unbidden thought, almost verbalised. The dreaming President put it to his lips. It tasted of iron, blood and the sweet pus of a burst gumboil. He savoured it, and found the words which gave it meaning.

'I need the sucker to think he can win.'

CHAPTER 22

Later on the day that followed that uneasy dawn Sub-Committee Mid-East 3, Defense Intelligence Agency, reconvened on the second floor of the Pentagon. The ex-Colonel of Marines who chaired it looked around, beamed and nodded to each in turn.

'Bob, Mark, Louella. Louella? That promotion not through yet? Well, hell, I guess everyone's got just a bit too much to handle these days and no-one's clearing their in-trays as fast as they'd like. So, what's first?'

'The SISA operation out of Malaga, Spain.' Louella turned the cover of the orange folder in front of her, smoothed it flat with her chocolate fingers, day-glo cerise nails. Scratch my scrotum any time, thought the ex-Colonel.

'Two new factors. First a report from SIGINT City. Over the past month hundreds, possibly thousands of small packets of machine code have been transmitted as telephone signals from Spain to Iraq. They were picked up by the listening posts we share with the Brits on Cyprus and also from the Electronic War Stations Stormin' Norm has in place on the carriers in the Gulf and as of now also installed in the Saudi desert. Because they were in machine code and no-one knew what program was driving them it was some time before they cracked it, but it seems a reasonable certainty that they are the new builds Cartwright has created for SISA to update Ferlinghetti Advanced Radar Systems . . .'

'Louella, I don't think we have to waste any more time on this.'

'Pardon me, Sir, but think we do. Iraq now has the three Kuwaiti systems already deployed round their Command Centres together with updated HAWKs. This information that's being fed in updates the Kuwaiti systems —'

'Louella! That update relates to anti-radar-jamming devices and it won't be worth a wet fart to Saddam. The war starts with F–117A Stealth fighters taking out those ARSs and the command centres too.'

'Yes, Sir! But like I said. Two new factors. The other is this. A sub-branch of FADSI (UK), based on the Island of Wight, was commissioned by us, three years ago, to build a radar transmitter to operate at forty gigaherz in space. Part of the Star Wars programme. That's been virtually closed down and the FADSI (UK) subsidiary with it. But Gabriel Mansur saw the managing director in the SISA London Office on Canary Wharf three weeks ago, and the managing director went straight to the British Home Office who finally told Langley . . .'

'Three weeks? To get to us?'

'Well the Home Office cleared it through MI5 or 6 or both, and you know what they're like. We're lucky it came through so quick.'

'So, spare us the suspense, Louella, what did Gabby want from the Island of Wight? A forty gigaherz radar transmitter? No way even Gabby'd get a thing like that through the blockade.'

'No. He wanted all the paperwork, designs, back-up, specifications, blueprints, the lot. And the software. And he was offering a straight million US. Now all that can be sent down the wire like the other stuff.'

The ex-Colonel leant back in his cloth-upholstered chair, twiddled a gold pen beneath his chin. Problem was the usual one: how to ration one's time. He looked round, dropped the pen and lurched forward, smoothing his near-kipper tie as he did so. He measured the tone of his voice with care.

'Assess and comment, please?'

Shee-it, thought Louella, after six months we know his body language. The mean dick wants them to shoot it down. In flames.

Bob, dark, saturnine, Jewish, had his finger up first.

'The air war starts the middle of January. They'll never get a new transmitter, originally designed to be put in space, off the drawing board and working on land in two months and a half.'

Up yours, smart ass. GFY, Louella thought. She said:

'The basic transmitter is just . . . nothing. It was converted from the standard FADSI model. All they have to do is make a standard model work at forty gigaherz. It's a nuts and bolts job.'

'Mark?'

Sandy-haired, invisible eyelashes, the fourth member of the Sub-Committee slipped the bottom button of his vest, he'd had a good lunch, re-angled his butt on his seat and leant in towards Louella like he was on *Miami Vice*, cross-examining her or something.

'You know much radar, Louella?'

'Some. Enough to know that at forty gigaherz the gain would be good enough to pick up Stealth.'

'Radar don't work at forty gigaherz on earth.'

Fucking mother is guying my way of speaking.

'You know for why?' he went on. 'I'll tell you for why. Above eleven gigs the signal bounces back off dust and part-ee-culs of moisture in the atmosphere. I guess this is something maybe the mad butcher doesn't know about and Gabby is conning him. And not for the first time either.'

And not for the first time either Louella asked herself: just why do these fuckers take so much delight in putting me down?

'Screw you. I may not know all there is to know about radar systems. But Arnold Cartwright does. Cartwright is the best. He would have been Project Manager on the system to take out Stealth if he hadn't suddenly decided to take wing for Malaga. And the boys down at Ferlinghetti International reckon that without him FADSI (UK) is well up the faeces duct without a dirigible facility. So I guess he knows what he's doing when he asks Gabby to get him this stuff.'

My then, aren't we just that extra touch sassy this PM, thought the ex-Colonel of Marines. He made pencil notes in the margins of the folder, and looked up and round at them all — his children, he sometimes thought.

'I guess we have to leave this one open-ended and deal with the fall-out when it comes back to us. Send it up as it stands but with a digest of the analysis we have heard. Next?'

'Uh-uh . . . Sir?'

'Bob?'

'If this Cartwright really knows what he is doing, if he knows a way of making a forty gig signal find its way through earth's atmosphere, then I think we should recommend a terminator on the SISA project.' He paused. 'In my capacity as unofficial but approved liaison facility between this sub-committee and colleagues in Mossad, I also have to say two things. One. The Israel Defense Forces HQ is already deeply worried about the anti-radar jamming facility. Two. They're going to be less than happy about this new development. And another thing. This use of international telephone and satellite systems to send military information to Iraq is also in direct contravention of UN resolution 661.'

Does he mean it? Or is this just his cocked leg drop of piss making its mark?

'A-a-all right. The motion is does this sub-committee wish to recommend termination of the SISA project? Does any of you wish to speak again to this motion? No? Right. Vote.'

Since they knew the ex-Colonel had right of Chair's deciding vote, i.e. two votes, they knew they had to vote as one. They did.

'O-o-okay. We recommend termination of the SISA Malaga operation. Next?'

That way none of them knew how he would have voted.

Mark sighed and opened the next folder.

'The reports that the Israeli pilots flying Saudi F–11s have been black-marketing Scotch to their Arab colleagues appear not to be as unfounded as we originally thought . . .'

Bob lurched forward, banged a fist on the table.

'Oh, come o-o-on, Mac? This is straight bullshit from the PLO. From Ara-Fart. You know that!'

Louella leant back. This is going to be fun, she said to herself. This time I get the fun time.

CHAPTER 23

Ever since Watergate and the Nixon tapes the doctrine of Plausible Deniability has ruled the dark side of Washington's Defense Community. Plausible Deniability means that when something really nasty has to be done to protect the President's interests, or ensure his re-election, it must be done in such a way that he can deny having had anything to do with it at all, plausibly, so the people who want to can actually choose to believe him.

Under Reagan this was not much of a problem. No-one suspected for a moment that he knew of, let alone understood, half of what was being done in his name. Anyway, impeaching Ronald was always loony toons: he was far too lovable. But Bush was altogether a different matter. With his eyes on, hands on approach, his need to see the people he was dealing with, to be involved in what was going on, it was actually rather difficult to do things on his behalf without him getting involved. Another factor of course was the fact that he didn't really mind being naughty, probably liked it, and was loath to be kept out of things simply on the grounds that he might later be revealed to have been involved.

Which all added up to the fact that the people who had his best interests at heart, the ones who would lose their jobs if he lost his, had to meet in complete security in places where they could not be bugged and could not bug each other. Not a problem really. Room 208, the high-tech command center in the Old Executive Office next to the White House was as secure now as it had been when Ollie

North laid his career on the line for Plausible Deniability, and used it as a base from which to mastermind his operation.

Room 208 is a secure suite rather than just one room and on the day the decision to go offensive was publicly announced the Black Committee was convened there for just the one meeting. The Black Committee consisted of twenty-three men from all branches of intelligence and military, none under the rank of colonel, and they had one simple straightforward aim: to ensure that the nightmare scenario did not take place, that Saddam Hussein did not back down.

It was chaired by an Assistant Secretary — wild horses will not drag from us which, suffice it to say he had authority to requisition the room and enough knowledge of the Defense Community to know whose discretion he could rely on, who could safely be invited.

The ex-Colonel of Marines attended shortly after adjourning Sub-Committee 3 Middle-East DIA. He was just about the most junior person there and it amused him to see the bosses queue in front of two marines and an FBI agent at the entrance. Each was briskly frisked, IDs electronically scanned, voice-print checked before they were let in. A small pile of personal micro-recorders, electronic notebooks and so on grew on the desk by the door, like Colt 45s left outside a saloon bar in a Western. Once inside the windowless fan-shaped room they took their places in soft leather chairs scattered informally but all facing the apex. Here, on a low daïs the Assistant Secretary was already sitting beneath a large screen on which grey aerial pictures of Kuwait slowly shifted, real-time, satellite driven.

A general whispered in his ear, an admiral waited, one foot on the step, for his turn. The ex-Colonel modestly took a chair near the back. Presently, when all were in, and the general and admiral back in their seats in the front row, the Assistant Secretary took off his large gold wire-framed spectacles, gave them a brisk rub on a silk handkerchief, cleared his throat. The sound rattled impressively thanks to a discreet voice-enhancer, and everyone else shut up.

Now, they all knew why they were there and why the nightmare scenario had to be scotched. They knew they were passing sentence of death on at least some allied soldiers, for even if the Iraqis refused to shoot back when shot at, friendly fire would be sure to do its usual deadly work. They knew that many thousands of Iraqis would die. And they knew the underlying purpose of this slaughter. And the Assistant Secretary knew that their loyalty to the cause needed a better prop than that, that self-image needed a stroke or two; in short, they needed to be able to convince themselves they were taking uncomfortable decisions with the best interests of the United States at heart, nothing else. The Assistant Secretary's opening address did the trick.

'It comes down,' he began, 'to a simple matter of *realpolitik* . . .'

And immediately he had them. It was the buzz word, the word that made them feel like a nineteenth-century empire, the word that gave the New World Order and the *Pax Americana* a context, a history, a tradition. If it was *realpolitik* it was kosher.

'If Saddam just walks away, army intact, head held high, we've lost,' the dry voice went on. 'He'll do it again. That's why your president has repeated, again and again, no deals, no compromise, no linkage. Any of those and Saddam can report success back to his people and he's learnt the wrong lesson: he'll think he can do it again. Other options have been suggested. Assassination. Well, in the first instance, not easy. His own countrymen have had, at a conservative estimate, at least fifteen cracks at that one. But also contraindicated. Saddam leads a powerful clan of relations, the Al-Takriti, who have taken over the Ba'ath party. Kill him and another will pop up, much the same, could be worse. Obliterate the Ba'ath? No. Because then Iraq would fall apart. And that is the ultimate nightmare in this whole can of beans, er, worms.'

He paused, sipped water, dabbed his lips, went on.

'Why? I'll tell you for why. If Iraq falls apart the Kurds win the north-west and the oil round Mosul and Kirkuk. The indications are they would set up a socialist state, at all events a strongly nationalist one. I don't have to tell you the oil-rich states we like to deal with are monarchies, run by extended families, with brown-nose bureaucrats in tow and, if possible, a decent veil of something like a voting system. Saudi-Arabia, the United Arab Emirates . . .

'Kurdistan would not fit into that mould. And at the other end of a dislocated Iraq, in the south-east corner we have the Shias and oil capital Basra. They would take over, and within weeks Iran would have swallowed them up leaving Kuwait and the UAE exposed to Shia rebellion or annexation. Frankly it's better for the US to have Kuwait remain part of Iraq than have it become part of Iran.

'So we cannot let Saddam off the hook without a fight. But the fight must be a very carefully fixed one. We cripple him, especially economically, leave him one hell of a mess to clear up. We give him a bloody nose, such that he won't want to walk into shit like this ever again. Above all we take out his nuke capacity, his CBW capacity and his means of delivering either outside his own country . . .'

A rear-admiral leant across to the ex-Colonel and whispered: 'What's CBW?'

'Chemo-Bio Warfare.'

'Darn it. Of course.'

'But,' the Assistant Secretary went on, 'we leave him the means to continue to trample all over the Shias and the Kurds. That's the macro-view of the problem.'

He paused, sipped water again (at least, thought the ex-Colonel, it looks like water), cleared his throat.

'Focusing in on the detail, I guess we can see two clear aspects. We have to leave him confused as to our intentions right up to the last moment, even while he can see C-oh-lin and Norm building up a force he cannot possibly damage in any serious way and which will have the nuts off him as soon as it's used. That's tricky. And at the last moment we have to give him just the possibility in his mind that he can win, or if not win, at least inflict on us losses he knows will allow him to present himself as the Arab David who, even if he didn't actually cut off Goliath's head, left him with a nasty bruise on his forehead.'

Which, since David was a Jew and Goliath a Palestinian Arab, seemed to our ex-Colonel not to be altogether apt. But there you go.

Following the applause that came for this short presentation, the Assistant Secretary took questions and suggestions from the floor for a full hour before noticing the ex-Colonel's shy efforts to catch his eye.

'Sir, I chair various sub-committees in the Middle East section of the DIA, processing intelligence for upwards use. Well, there's one little number we've been looking at off and on for some time. Seems an outfit in Malaga, Spain, run by Jabreel Mansur, has a top Brit radar man on board. They're now looking at ways of enabling Saddam's radar to penetrate Stealth technology and feeding the information to him down the telephone. Well, we have just now decided to recommend termination, but it seems to me . . .'

The Assistant Secretary cut him off. There were things best left unsaid, even off the record. He tapped his spectacles against his teeth for a moment. 'General, come and see me after the meeting, would you?'

'Yes, Sir! But, Sir, it's Colonel of Marines on the retired list.'

The Assistant Secretary looked down at him over the rows of white and bald heads that separated them.

'Oh really?' he said.

Ten minutes later the meeting broke up. The Black Committee did not meet again. It did not have to. Twenty-three influential, intelligent men, some ambitious, others with small problems, domestic, financial, habits that were well known to Cabinet advisers, went away clear about what they had to do and who they could turn to.

'Louella? Come in, park your, um sit down.' He watched over the lip of his desk as she sat, switched her knees one way, then the other, made the dark nylon hiss. 'Well, girl, you got your promotion. I've been given an ACTCOMM, a full investigative committee with powers to initiate action, which if I were wearing a helmet would put a star on it. And I want you to be my Chief of Staff. It's the SISA Radar complex in Spain we're looking at, seems some of what you were saying is being treated very seriously by certain people . . .' He winked, pointed upwards, jabbing the air with his podgy finger. 'Are you on board?'

'Who else?'

'Well, neither Mark nor Bob.'

'I'm on board. Who else?'

'First thing is we need a guy on the ground out there who knows the scene. Langley had an asset was watching the Brit, Cartwright. Is he any good?'

'Phil Henley? One of the best.'

'Is he still there?'

'Cain't say I know the answer to that one, off the bat. I'll check and get to him if he is.'

'Clear it with Langley.'

'Oh sure. What next?'

'Well, Louella, I think the next thing I have to do is fill in the picture a little. Fact is the whole thing has now taken a very different tilt and since you're coming from behind the curve . . . Hold on to your seat now, this is going to come as a bit of a shock. We are no longer talking termination. Quite the reverse. Let me explain . . .'

When he had finished she had one very pertinent question.

'Chief, what about Mossad? They've already had one crack at SISA and lost a rated asset in the process.'

'They must be warned off the patch, kept right off the grass.'

'But we have to tell them why.'

'No, we don't. The tilt has changed Mossad-wise. No longer are they our anti-commie shield in the Middle-East. The commie scare is less than a paper tiger now. It's the Fundamentals we have to watch for, and the non-fundamental Arabs are our best allies in that area. Egypt, the oil states, even Saddam himself. We don't owe Mossad a thing. From now on we call the tune and they dance.'

An hour or so later Louella, walking down those long, clean, dull corridors, bumped into Bob. Since she was carrying files colour-coded in a way he was not familiar with, he stopped, acknowledged her.

'Hi there. Got your promotion then?'

'You bet.' And high on it all she couldn't help adding: 'And you know what? All possible technical assistance is now to be made readily acessible to SISA, Malaga. So screw you.'

She sailed on leaving behind her a wake of heavy fragrance, the odour of success.

Dark and saturnine he scowled, er, darkly. The servant of two masters whose interests no longer always coincided, he realised he had a problem. But habit, and maybe something deeper, won. By the end of the day the news had reached the Mossad headquarters, anonymously sited in a drab building above a bank and cafeteria in Shaul Hamalekh, East Jerusalem, that the US was helping an Arab arms dealer to develop a powerful radar system for onwards delivery to the Arab regime currently most hostile to them, and that they weren't to be told why . . .

CHAPTER 24

Cartwright kept up the Thursday evening meetings in the Caracas Bar through much of the summer and early autumn, though bit by bit they began to tail off. His life was now for the most part a pretty settled routine: off to the SISA facility, five sometimes six days a week, visits to Cartwright senior, then his kids came over. Then he was away for a week or so in September, took a flight from Malaga to Madrid with an onwards booking I wasn't able to check out, and frankly by then I was bored. You can do so much and I had done one hell of a lot. So I checked out the miniature video in his apartment every now and then, but he never had any guests, never did anything but fix himself simple meals, read a book, watch TV, so after a time I didn't much bother with that either.

No further visits from Killer Girl Roma.

Frankly this has happened to me before on a Langley job. They give you someone to watch, and it's all high key, fate of nations in the balance, they never let up nagging you for the first month or so. You send in the weekly reports and you get feedback, like an alteration in the contours of the assignment, but after a time these dry up, and three, four, months in you realise they've forgotten all about you. But you're still on the payroll, you send in the monthly invoice and back comes the cheque. And you look about for other ways to amuse yourself.

In my case a Brit widow called Jocelyne. Forty-five years old, which give or take put us in the same league. Her hubby, eighteen years older than her, retired TV presenter, had pushed his liver over the edge back in '88 and she was still in shock two years later when I asked her what was the matter in the Torre del Mar supermarket. She was weeping over a litre of Fundador brandy and said it had been hubby's favourite tipple.

One thing led to another. I discovered I knew a trick or two between the sheets beyond the capability or credulity of Brit TV presenters and next thing is she's suggesting I move in. And worse. And I have three wives already. One in Jo'burg, one in Santiago, Chile, one in Dublin, do I need another in Malaga, Spain?

So it was quite a relief when the summons to touch base came through, though it turned out to be the DIA block in the Pentagon rather than Langley, and a whole new brief. It got me out from under Jocelyne, literally. And I got to meet Louella. Lovely lady. I don't suppose I'll ever get my hand between her chocolate thighs . . . Dream on Phil Henley.

The upshot was round about Thanksgiving, not that I give a shit, I am driving up to Casa Sur with two big unanswered questions shaking hands across my mental landscape: how do I get Cartwright into Iraq? How do we keep Mossad at bay. Both carry supplementaries, the big ones always do. Like the Cartwright one splits into: How do we get him to accept the move? And how do we do it physically in such a way nobody rumbles that it's us, i.e. the US, want him to be there? And the Mossad one? Well, I reckoned a tethered goat was probably the answer, make them think they'd splattered him while we bring him off somewhere else safe and sound, and give them a good spanking into the bargain. And as often happens, the answers to all three melded nicely. 'Meld'? Does anyone out there still play Canasta? Get in touch if you do.

And one other thing to bear in mind I got from Louella. Roma. She showed me a mugshot and a coupla snaps someone had taken with a photo lens a yard long and then blown up up some, but it was her all right.

'Calls herself Palestinian, but it's not certain she's ever

been there. American University of Beirut and University of California, Berkeley. History, philosophy, economics. Then a course in armed and unarmed with Gaddafi's lot. Finally there's a very nasty place in Paraguay, second generation ex-Nazi consultancy where they teach you persuasion. And it's not all wrist slapping and spitting in your coffee either, there's a special course in sexual entrapment. In short she's a trained honey-pot.'

'So who's she working for in the current scenario?'

'Well, Phil, I guess that's the first thing you have to learn about her.' I can still hear the swish of Louella's legs as she rearranged them. 'Roma works for no-one, just the Cause. But in the loop we're now in what Saddam Hussein wants is good for the Cause, so we reckon she's working for Mansur. That disk-pack scam, getting Cartwright to take the RA 72 home, had two motives. One, it was a test to see what Cartwright would do and risk to get another sex session with her, and second to lay a bait for the Mossad section on the Costa. Mansur had already had trouble from them, breaking into Cartwright's father's apartment. I guess he was pre-empting any further hassle by taking out the one really heavy Mossad operative who also knew the region.'

She sat back, used her right pinky to rearrange the lipstick in the corner of her mouth, fixed me with dark, dark eyes, narrowed now and cool.

'Don't mess with her, Henley. She's a tough cookie. If you ever get to be in the same room with her keep your hand on your nuts. She'll break them otherwise.'

All that a fortnight back, in that far away fun factory, but still much in my mind as I drive the Renault 19 up the secondary road, little more than a dirt-track, into the hills above Marbella.

And here we are. Fortress Mansur. But the security is shit. These guys who come out with their machine pistols like they're 'droids, and look up and down the road, while the others frisk you . . . well, Sweet Jesus, they leave the pill-boxes EMPTY while they're doing that? So this might be the place to organise the Mossad . . . Uh-uh. I thought so. The small Merc convertible that was behind me most of the way after the slip-road to Malaga airport cruised by just as Mansur's toy-boy had finished feeling me up with his spare hand, the human one. Why do Mossad always use Kraut cars? Especially the brands Mein Führer liked? Maybe they think of it as cover, maybe they think everyone else is going to say: 'Can't be Mossad, not in a Merc.' Maybe they just like smart cars.

'He can't win. He can lose. He will lose.'

In the heart of Fortress Mansur now, neat office on the first floor, IBM PC with modem on his ebony topped desk, no doubt linked to a personal mainframe, fax, coupla telephones, Mansur himself snug in a black leather chair soft enough to cushion the gun he wears on his right buttock under the plaid jacket. I'm in an upright Bauhaus repro, though it could be original, with a view across lawns to a pool, a waterfall and some big dark trees. Quite a pad.

'But I guess you knew that already.'

He shrugs, no comment.

'Thing is,' I go on, keeping to the script Louella gave me, 'has he paid you? How much has he paid you up front? Because, señor, that's all you're going to get. From him.' Louella told me he likes to be called 'señor', now that officially he's Gabriel Sur. 'Not another dime will there be.'

'Why not? How do you know this?' Said lazily, not bothered. Okay, I lose seventy, eighty, but I'm Jabreel Mansur, and, since Adnan Khashoggi took a tumble, the biggest guy in the arms racket, why should I worry?

'Because by mid-February Iraq will have no industries, no road, no bridges, no airplanes, a debt as big as Brazil's, and just possibly no Saddam Hussein either. And certainly . . . no Kuwait. I guess it's time to think of hedging your investment on this one.'

The soft leather creaks, one corner of that angel-lip smile turns down, he takes a second sip at whatever it is he's drinking. Russian sixty per cent, sub zero temperature judging from the haze that keeps forming on the glass, but you never know. Could be cough linctus. Certainly he has a cold, clears his throat for the third time.

'Well. Clearly you have something to say to me — so say it.'

'The, er, guys who sent me here, want you to keep the enterprise turning over in such a way that the mother thinks he can win. Do that, and you'll be paid what he would have owed you if he had won.'

'Really! That much?'

He had seen the opportunity. Think of a number, double it.

'I'll take a hundred. Half up front.'

There we are — nice round number.

'I'll check back. But I have to say they're thinking more like thirty. They know what these things cost. An advanced radar system from Ferlinghetti, ex-factory, all legal is fifteen million dollars, US.'

'Phil,' he says, and leans back in his squeaky soft leather, smooths his silver lock and grins. Both sides of his mouth this time. He picks up a phone, the red one, hands me the set. 'Do that. Check back. And Phil?'

'Yes?'

'You're on two and a half per cent of anything over thirty they offer.'

Oh Sweet Jesus. Does he mean it? Will I ever be able to get him to pay up? And what did my grandad used to say. The only immorality on earth is to buy and sell in the same market. Shit to that. The Third World would not be a third world if folks clung to that sort of morality. And somebody has to be on the thin end. That's life. That's the market.

Lot of chat with Louella of the I'll get back to you on this one variety, but at the end of the day I reckon Gabriel might make fifty. Two and a half per cent of twenty million! That must be five hundred Gs. Not bad for twenty-five minutes' work, maybe I'll take a proper vacation when this is all over, out on the rim perhaps, the word is Bangkok still has a lot to offer . . . Those are the thoughts in my mind as Gabriel shows me down his sweeping stairs into that circular foyer he's got. And Cartwright's there, looking at a bust of Caligula and wondering what the guy had that he hasn't.

'Phil! No time long see. Shit.' So he's been at the sixty per cent too. Spacing the words more carefully, he goes on: 'Where have you been?'

'Here and there, Arnie.'

'And what are you doing here?'

'Arn-ie? I sell security and premises surveillance, correct?'

'Oh sure. But I should have thought Don Gabriel had all he needed.'

'You can't have enough, Arnie.'

'I suppose not.'

'See you around then.'

'You will be around?'

'Sure. I'll be around. Like you I'm on the pay-roll now.'

CHAPTER 25

A very nasty shock just half an hour ago. I'm not at all sure I should go on with this, even though in the end it turned out to be a false alarm. I'd just come back from a four-hour shift which yet again had drifted into six, seven hours: apparently my relief had a bad cold and the guards couldn't get his voice print to match, though actually I suspect more lay behind it than that. The fact is I have been de facto promoted to Presidential Adviser and he likes to have me around a lot of the time, but more of that in a moment . . .

Where was I? Can't be blamed for getting confused, these are confusing and tiring times, and I am, after all, over sixty and not as fit as I was.

I had just got back in, and had come through here to my study, my den, for a glass of the Johnnie Walker Black Label the Lion of Assyria was kind enough to thrust on me the other day after I had admitted that his company over the last months had given me a taste for the stuff, when the front door of our apartment was suddenly subjected to a most dreadful pounding. In Baghdad, indeed throughout Iraq, it is a noise which has only one meaning: the Mukhabarat have arrived at last. They always make it loud to frighten the neighbours, let this be a warning to you, you may be the next.

My wife let them in, told them straightaway where I was. Quite right. Standard practice among the intelligent in Baghdad. If one of you has to go the other should take whatever limiting action is available to protect her/

himself, and anything less than total co-operation is certain to be counter-productive.

He was the usual type: light grey suit, white shirt, no tie, Saddam moustache, and, in spite of the blockade which has most of us surviving on a diet of dates and cracked wheat, the glossy shine on his skin that goes with good living.

He had with him two sidekicks without jackets so you could see the bastinado canes, riot sticks, whatever they are, and the holstered Walther P38s. And behind them two older men in blue shirts and black trousers carrying small battered leather suitcases, the sort of thing you might expect your average torturer, third grade, might use for his electrodes, prongs and rheostats. And indeed, when a moment or so later they opened them, I thought that's it, that's what those wires and boxes with dials are for.

'Assistant Professor Dr Salih K . . .? I believe you have in your possession an apparatus called a modulator-demodulator, capable of receiving data on the telephone line from another computer so it can be read from your screen and stored in your computer?'

My heart spasmed. Pass the hemlock. They know about Beast 666 and how I and the CIA man at the Dutch Embassy had an arrangement . . . They'll flay me alive, hang my skin in Revolution Square, keep me alive until another has grown back, then flay me again.

'It's not precisely mine.' I measured my words carefully. 'It was provided by the Archaeological Faculty so I could continue to work at home on aspects of our glorious past, accessing data on the University mainframe. It is of course possible for a modem user elsewhere, if he has knowledge of the entry codes to . . .'

I was about to explain it was possible for a malicious outsider to store material on my computer without my knowledge. Fortunately, before I could get any further down the road of self-incrimination, he interrupted me.

'No longer. The State is requisitioning all modems not already deployed in the defence of our glorious country.

You will not have to do anything. It will remain where it is but disconnected from your computer. It will continue to receive data on the telephone line but these will be passed to another computer elsewhere. You don't have to do anything. These men will make the necessary connections and disconnections. Is that Johnnie Walker Black Label? Pour yourself a small measure and put the top back on.'

I did as I was told, and when he went the bastard took the bottle with him.

Meanwhile I felt a wave of relief. The stupid jape of allowing the CIA man to access Beast 666, via the University mainframe, in return for a promised post in Assyrian Studies at UCLA, had caused me many a lost night's sleep although he repeatedly assured me there was no danger to me in it. Although he disappeared from Baghdad some weeks ago, clinging to some western potentate or popstar's coat-tails, I realised of course he could still be accessing Beast 666 from outside, and much though I wanted to I could not quite bring myself to change the password. It was not because I felt my country deserved to be betrayed that I did this, but because I really do feel if Mr Bush and his advisers realise just what a muddle the Grand Educator of the Arab Mind has got himself into, they might find a way of getting us all out of this mess without bloodshed.

That I am now so completely in his confidence is because he trusts me to understand and interpret the niceties of the English language better than anyone the official School of Translators and Interpreters can provide. It is my knowledge of Anglo-Saxon culture that makes the difference. For instance it was I who suggested back in August that he should ask that little English boy: 'Did Stuart have his milk today?' knowing as I do what store the British and American middle classes set on milk as a source of calcium for young bones and teeth. Unfortunately the effect was a touch spoilt by the interpretation some western commentators put on the innocent question. Was the Butcher fattening him up for the table?

Culture and niceties of language? Interpretation of nuance? Believe me it's no easy job at all to comprehend the signals, so apparently contradictory, that have been coming through, and in some ways my heart goes out to the Heartless One as he struggles to make sense of it all. Let me record a more or less random selection of the things that have puzzled him. Though presumably since now the modem is no longer attached to this computer there is no chance that the material will be available to Mr Bush's advisers, I suppose there is a chance that it may be reconnected at a later date and in time to be some use.

First, on the subject of United Nations Resolutions, not really a matter of cultural niceties at all: it was the illogicality of it all, the cynical disregard of history that bothered him.

Tonight is the night of 29 November. In a few hours' time the United Nations will pass Resolution 678. What a mess! *A pause of goodwill to give Iraq time to get out of Kuwait before all necessary means are used . . . All necessary means can be employed on or after 15 January.*

'Salih, what does this mean?' This was just an hour or so ago, before I came off my extended shift. 'Tell me straight, because the lying mother-fuckers around me dare not. I can see it in their faces.'

As well indeed they might not: bad news is bad news for the bearers of bad news. Still, it seems he has placed me in the role of licensed truth teller, so I took a chance.

'It means, Excellency, that on or after 15 January they can use force to make you leave Kuwait.'

'You mean . . . they'll actually use all that *stuff* they've dumped out on the Saudi desert?'

'Yes, Excellency.'

He put his glass down on the table next to the gold mosque the Al-Sabah gave him to celebrate his (and the Egyptians', now his enemies) repatriation of the Fao peninsula and pulled in a large plastic-bound file. Tariq Aziz, our foreign minister, had had it put together for the World Leader of Pan-Arabism and it was a digest of UN reactions over the years to situations similar to the one we were in.

After first checking that we were alone, he pulled a pair of quite powerful half-lens spectacles from the top pocket of his battledress and slipped them on. I suppressed a memory of Groucho Marx, though I swear if the Father-Leader had raised his eyebrows at me I should have been done for. The water still splashed fifteen metres away in the Fountain of the Abencerrages. If I had laughed I should have been, I am sure, turned into *Duck Soup*.

'Why should this matter? Why should I take note of all this shit? The United Nations have passed similar resolutions against the Israeli occupation of Gaza and the West Bank, of Indonesia's rape of East Timor followed by genocide, which was a genuinely horrible business, and with nothing like the justification we had for taking Kuwait back into the Iraqi fold. And genocide is not something we contemplate against the Kuwaitis. Kurds maybe, but not Kuwaitis. Why don't they pass a resolution against me for genociding the Kurds?'

He looked up at me with that merry little twinkle in his haunted eyes, snorted, took a pull at the Black Label and moved on.

'Here we are again. Turkey's occupation of north Cyprus. That was decades ago. They're still there.' He ruffled the pages forward again. 'Here's our victorious onslaught on Persia. Not a single bleep did we get after they passed the resolution against us, against our invasion of Persia. Neither the United States nor anyone else lifted a finger to implement any of those resolutions. And the US flooded us with almost all the arms we wanted, even after passing laws that said it was illegal to do so, even after we'd accidentally exocet-ed one of their ships.'

He peeped over the top of his spectacles and raised his eyebrows. 'Indeed, Salih, one would think that the best way of getting the US to lay on an airlift of arms and *matériel*, is to have the UN condemn what one has done. Any historian looking at this lot would conclude that the US was about to pour billions in aid on us because we have invaded another country.'

I recognised he was being waggish and that I was allowed to laugh, which was just as well since his eyebrows were now fluttering above the spectacles and I expected him at any moment to say: 'Either this horse is dead or my watch has stopped.'

'Excellency. Look at five hundred and two.'

He did so.

'Las Malvinas. Shit. So sometimes they do mean it. Poor Galtieri. Nice guy. He didn't believe it either. Is that why the Brits are the only nation putting real guts into this US armada? US cashing a cheque?'

'Excellency, I think so.'

And ever since it happened he has rattled on about the Glaspie interview back in July, just before the invasion, indeed plays back the tape again and again, asking me where it went wrong, where his then interpreter (who took a dive into the fountain) let him down, what nuance in what the US ambassador said to him then was lost in the translation. And again I can't really help him. Here is a conversation I recorded back in October on the subject, which should have got to Washington. When we reached the point in the tape where she says: *I clearly understand your message. We studied history at school. They taught us to say freedom or death*... he pressed pause and looked at me with that hurt and puzzled look in his dark eyes that could be genuine.

He released the pause button, and she continued:

I think that you know well that we as a people have our experience with the colonialists.

He slapped his thigh. 'Exactly so. The same colonialists. It was the British who conquered Washington in 1785, and the Americans who drove them out in 1812, it was the

British who drew these fool lines in the sand which give all this wealth to the Al-Sabahs instead of my people, the people of Iraq.'

Not really my place to correct the historical detail in the first part, especially since the error does not vitiate his argument one whit. The only interpretation I can put on this statement of Glaspie's is that she, and the US government, sympathised with the border problem Iraq had with Kuwait; they'd had similar problems with the British in the past. But of course the clincher was when she said: *We have no opinion on . . . your border disagreement with Kuwait . . . the issue is not associated with America. James Baker has directed our official spokesmen to emphasise this instruction.*

'Salih, my friend, surely that meant that they would not interfere when I took the necessary steps to redraw the frontier a little?'

'I think, Excellency, that they did not expect you to take the whole country.'

And at this point he got very angry indeed, stormed about, chucked glasses, even bottles, kicked the furniture.

'The trouble with the Americans,' he shouted, 'is they are military simpletons. The Rumailah oil field is about the least militarily defensible place on earth. And what would be the point of fighting a battle on an oilfield one wanted to . . . to annexe, because it was yours anyway. At the end of the day whoever won it would have a graveyard not an oilfield. And the islands in the Al-Shatt waterway. If I put troops on them they'd be bombed and shelled to hell in hours. The Israeli pilots in the Kuwaiti air force would have annihilated them. The reason we went into Kuwait City was because no-one was going to bomb the shit out of us there. Surely that's obvious? The idea should have been clear to any idiot, it's the way we Arabs do things, have done them for centuries. They let us redraw the border, give us Rumailah and the islands, and then we give Al-Sabah a big kiss and give him back his stupid little country, now trimmed a little, pull out, and everything's back to normal.'

He calmed down, thought for a bit, took up another thread.

'Listen, Salih. The build-up started on 17 July, and went on right up to when we went in two weeks later. The US have satellites watching everything. Probably they are listening to us now. And not a word did they say to us that they didn't like what they saw. All we got was that Glaspie interview, which I deliberately ordered simply because I was so puzzled that they hadn't commented, or said a thing. I was massing troops, massing them, guns, tanks, the lot. If Bush had said then: wait a moment, Saddam, hang on . . .'

'Excellency, some commentators have said the US intelligence was misled because you had not brought up enough ammunition, enough logistical back-up for a full operation.'

'Al-lah!' He smote his forehead with that big fist I so much fear, so I thought he would do himself an injury. However, only his spectacles fell off, as far as his chest, suspended by a thin red cord. 'To invade Kuwait? This was not Persia, not the Zionist state, not the Saudis even. Did they think I needed more shells than each tank could carry to take out the Kuwait toy army? One in each gun would have been enough. Indeed was enough.'

'They have also said since that they thought you were just putting on pressure ahead of the oil talks . . .'

And then he got angry again. He knows some history. Some I have taught him. He shouted:

'Since 1945 the Americans have put together forces and then used them, to invade Greece, Korea, Guatemala, Iran, Lebanon, Cuba, Santo Domingo, Vietnam, Southern Africa, Grenada and Panama. So. When they see someone else massing almost their entire army, on one short frontier, they cannot possibly imagine that this is a mere gesture. They have been there themselves. They had every opportunity to say NO. And they did not. If there was a signal, and I am sure there was, it said YES.'

'Excellency. I think . . .'

'Yes, Salih?'

'I think . . .'

'Don't worry. You are only an academic, a writer, whatever. Not a serious person. I shan't put a bullet in your head.'

Yet.

'Excellency, I think one of the problems is just that. Their world view tells them that they are allowed to do that sort of thing. But no-one else is.'

'There, Salih. I told you you were a nothing, a mere thinker, an academic.'

'Sir?'

'We already know that they have done nothing to implement the UN resolutions to curb the Turks, the Indonesians, the Israeli occupation of Gaza and the West Bank. They let these people do these things. Why don't they let me?'

Back full circle to where we started. A pause while we filled our glasses. He raised his.

'Cheers, Salih. Who's coming tomorrow?'

'Edward Heath. He used to be . . .'

'I know. Well, we have a lot in common. Will you stand by, tell me if he is honest or a snake in the grass?'

'If your Excellency says so.'

And in fact we found him to be very straightforward, blunt, honest and compassionate. A good man. Well, I did. All the Leader Struggler could see was a man who had as much reason to hate Thatcher as he did. We gave him his hostage ration. Not as many as he would have liked, but then there were already several thousand British troops sitting on our borders.

Well, all that was several weeks ago, and now, today, they will be counting the days to 15 January.

But back to this business of how confused his fine-honed intellect is. It's getting worse. Bush's generals say they are pacifists. The Senate say they do not want a war. But then they bully the UN into this aggressive resolution. And all the time Bush refuses any compromise at all. Then an opinion poll, which the Sword of Islam is certain must be rigged, because ours always are, says the US people don't want a war . . . And so it goes on.

It's almost as if there is a deliberate campaign to keep him confused and uncertain as to whether or not they really are going to fight. And my own feeling is that it is all huff and puff.

CHAPTER 26

No-one told me how it can rain here on the Costa del Sol in December. Steady, heavy rain, still warm, though, with patches of mist or cloud drifting through it across the brown rocks as it splashes off them and forms silver runnels on the hillsides and down the back of my neck. Puts me in mind of monsoon time in Nam, and so does the smooth pistol grip of an AR–18, the neat sense of its perfect balance which makes its loaded bulk of nearly eight pounds as easy to handle as a pistol a quarter the weight, plus the truly delightful certainty that its high velocity rounds give me a hundred yards gain over anything the opposition has.

Who, I can now see through my enhanced vision nocs, have assembled at last across the hillside three hundred yards beneath me, and two hundred yards above the pill-boxes that guard Mansur's front door. They are later than expected, but clearly they too have, like us, received word that the Volvo got held up in Malaga by flooding following a night of rain, and is expected to be forty minutes late. ETA seventeen forty-five hours, it's now seventeen thirty-six.

There are four of them, all in combat gear, snaking very very carefully through the loose rock and bushes of the hillside, using routes they worked out from aerial photographs taken from the small Sikorsky that buzzed us a coupla days back. They're certainly thorough. Let's hope we've got the edge.

I think we have. Here's how it goes. Mossad flew out a

four man SAS-trained unit from Tel Aviv to organise the hit a week ago, and, as we expected, they've opted to take him out at the gate. It's the obvious place. Every day Cartwright is taken down to the SISA facility in a Volvo, armour-plated and stretched, wearing body armour beneath his jacket so he looks the way Maggie Thatcher used to whenever she did walkabout, we'll all miss her, great lady, they chopped her just the other day. Like her he has his human shield too which is why the limo is stretched, so he has one on each side, two behind facing backwards, and two in front, and in front of them the driver and an eighth man riding shot-gun. Literally. Short-barrelled pump action repeater. But when they come back after a hard day's work spent firing small packets of data to every spare modem in Baghdad, this is the point where Mansur's own sense of self preservation demands everyone gets out, is checked for unlisted weaponry, and the car too.

It's a deserted spot, away from main roads, and overlooked by hills covered with rock and low scrub, which look bare but which are a gift to soldiers combat trained on the Golan Heights, and not that different either.

We have nine men in the Volvo, if you include the driver, and last night we put three extra men in the pill-boxes as well as the four who normally man it and routinely check out arrivals. This gives us a four to one numerical advantage which, in a straight fire-fight, would be enough. But it's not a straight fire-fight. All these boys below me have to do is place one high velocity exploding round anywhere in Cartwright's body, and they've done what they came for.

Four to one? Better than that because finally there's me, behind a rock in their rear where I too have been since just after sunset last night with a thermo skinbag to keep me warm, a flask of brandy-laced coffee, a litre of Lanjarón mineral water, and some *empanadillas*, pasties stuffed with tuna. Almost all now gone. And as well as the AR–18,

I also have a flare gun. One thing about working with a guy like Mansur is the weaponry is not a problem.

The opposition's, however, might be, because shit and double shit, they've just unzipped what looks like the modified rocket-propelled grenade launcher they make in that Haifa factory of theirs. Now this is clearly a case of goal-post shifting. That mother can take the turret off most tanks, and it will certainly make a very nasty mess of the Volvo. It also means they can take out half our army, including Cartwright, with one round fired at the Volvo, and the other half with two more fired at the pill-boxes. Then they've got small arms to mop up any residue and cover their withdrawal.

Thirty seconds to go. I have RT comms with Mansur but not direct to the Volvo. Should I abort? But what happens if I try? I get Gabby, he gets the Volvo . . . there isn't time. Pre-empt, not abort.

I lay aside the nocs and immediately lose the mothers. At three hundred yards, in rain and mist, I am too far away. The AR–18 has a scope-sight, but it's not the same. Back to the nocs, there they are, this time I take a fix on a lichen-covered boulder whose markings resemble the man in the moon, back to the scope-sight, yes, this time I've got him. And now I can hear a vehicle. Not quite the right noise, but I daren't take my eyes off him to check, he's heard it too, up he comes . . .

And, just as I squeeze the trigger, down he goes again. My round skims the rock in front of him and whines on a further hundred and fifty yards before smashing into the windscreen of the school bus that's coming up the hill with the Volvo behind it.

We rehearsed this every day for a week, and no school bus. But no rain either, no hold ups, timing it for five o'clock, not five forty-five.

Hiatus, while everyone takes stock. The combat group below are redeploying to take into account a hostile above them, scurrying into a little ravine filled with bushes, but I count only three in, not four. Now that may mean I just missed where the fourth went before he got into one of the little caves or under a bush, but it also might mean he's working his way out and round to get behind and above me. I think it through. For all the loose cover this is still fairly open country. He could walk up to me in the open in three or four minutes, but to locate me first, and then get a good shot at me, without me seeing him at all, is not on. I decide to stay put until I can see what's happening. But first I raise Mansur on the RT and tell him the mothers have got an RPG. He already knows about the bus.

Down below about thirty children have spilled out of the bus, all shouting and pointing and milling around the way Spanish children do. They range in age from five to fifteen, boys and girls. I get the nocs on the windscreen. Modern toughened laminate so it hasn't starred or shattered, just a neat hole with the glass gone cloudy round it I guess, though at that distance I can't see detail. And the driver? Slumped over his wheel with another hole, but this time in his head? I reckon not. The way the kids are moving and the starling chatter I can just hear would have a different timbre if they had a dead body on their hands. No, here he comes, shooing and chivvying the children back into the bus. Then he does something odd. He turns the bus round, very slowly and carefully because the track is narrow, and goes back the way he came. Why? Maybe because one of the kids found the spent round and he recognised it for what it is.

And that leaves the Volvo very exposed, and the guy below with the RPG is very quick. I've lost sight of him and he gets in a round, a small ball of orange light with a dark vapour trail zipping at the speed of sound across the slopes, and CRUMP! the Volvo explodes in a ball of flame, black smoke, twisting sheetmetal. I miss the actual impact of course because I'm quick too and this time I don't miss, the rocket propellant exhaust behind him is a dead give-away and I take him out with a neat snap-shot that shatters his left shoulder blade. Give the guy a gold-fish. Then I shoot a flare into the ravine, and that's it for me, time to scarper, just in case the fourth man has been using that ten seconds or so of renewed noise and chaos to get nearer.

On the way down, well covered by assorted small-arms fire from all over the place, and not just the pill-boxes, I reflect: shit, Cartwright's gone. This has to mean end of mission, and I shan't get my five hundred K after all.

'Where are we going?' Is his first question, forty minutes later. We're sitting in the passenger seats of Mansur's MBB 'copter, cruising at eight hundred feet, well below the cloud which has begun to lift and over the big wide fertile valley of the Río Genil which presently widens into the Granada Vega, the great wide fertile plain which is where the Granadinos make their loot: tobacco and sugar beet for cash, but it raises three, four, crops a year, so there's wheat, maize and sunflowers too. Just now they're ploughing the end of the tobacco into the red soil and harrowing it for a winter sowing of wheat.

'You'll see when we get there. Basically it's a hideout, a place to hide you while we sort things out, make sure something like that doesn't happen again.' I reach forward, touch the pilot's shoulder. 'How long?'

'Half an hour.'

He's a Brit. A lot of Mansur's private army are. Ex-military mercenaries he hires through a London agency called Wolf Hound. I know because I've been used in the past as a contact between Wolf Hound and Langley. And they're real pros. Thing is, since the late fifties the Brits have had an entirely professional military which has been in almost constant action: Malaya, Cyprus, Yemen, Borneo, Africa, Ulster, Las Malvinas and maybe seven or eight more. And often, even while being paid by the Brit Government, they have been, in effect, mercenaries, not fighting for Queen and Country but for the big guys against the little guys. So, quite simply, they are the best. I guess that's why C-oh-lin and Norm were so keen to have the Desert Rats out in the Saudi desert. I only hope that

that La Billière character remembers our friendly fire record and keeps his eye on his back as well as his front.

All of which is also why the ex-SAS sergeant who was in charge in the Volvo had the sense to use the school bus and the kids as cover to get his men, and Cartwright, out and into the *maquis* before the bus moved. All in all it could not have worked out much better: two of the Israeli hit squad got away, which is fine by us as there is a fair chance they'll report back that they killed Cartwright.

Which means one, they might now leave him alone; two, Saddam Hussein will be very pleased to hear Mansur has taken out an elite Israeli unit and will be well convinced that there is no double deal going on. All of which adds up to the two main aims of the whole exercise. Still one problem though. I address it.

'Tell me, Arnie. Don't you have any qualms about providing this support to the Butcher of Baghdad?'

'None at all.' He's very cool these days, takes a shock like that fight we were in less than an hour away very calmly. I guess he's toughened up some.

'Why not? Not because you like the bastard, or think he's right?'

'It's six of one, half a dozen of the other. On balance, total shit though he is, I believe in this case he's more right than the other side, less wrong anyway. That's what my dad thinks, and he knows more about that sort of thing than I do.'

He looks down at the Vega. Shafts of sunlight pass over the red roofs of the big farms; a flock of sea-gulls, inland because they know a sea-storm is brewing up behind the rain, wheel silvery shards of white beneath us.

'And anyway, it's a scam isn't it? I mean it's not going to work.'

'It isn't?'

'No way. Squawking all those packets of machine code across a quarter of the earth's surface, up to space and down again, there are bound to be degradations, contaminations. Errors are bound to get through. And then there are the machinists and fitters at the other end. Nearly all this work in Iraq is done by imported skilled labour and he's let all his "guests" go. And among his own people, especially since he's gearing up to fight a modern war, he just won't have the skills to spare.'

'Is that right, Arnie?'

'Definite. But I suppose Mansur has convinced him it will work and he's being paid for it. And Mansur is paying me.'

'Question is, Arnie, is he paying you enough?'

'Enough? It's a hell of a lot.'

'Enough, if it becomes necessary to convince Saddam you're doing a good job, to persuade you to go out there and supervise the upgrading of the Kuwaiti Ferlinghetti systems and, if it comes to it, their operation?'

'No, Phil. No point in getting rich and dead. And that's what I would be. Anyway. Our lads are there too. I wouldn't want to be a party to anything that might make their lives more difficult. Or dangerous. Glory be. What's that in front?'

We've shifted onto a southerly bearing and, in a word, quite a view. Out to our left and quite close, the centre of Granada, most of it a modern sprawling mess, but the cathedral and the Alhambra glow red and warm gold in the sunset which has set the streaming high clouds above us ablaze. But that's not what he's on about. Twelve miles away and straight in front the north sides of the Sierra Nevada climb against heavy cloud, black where the sun doesn't hit it, so it must still be raining in the valleys on the south side, raining and snowing. And certainly on this side it has been snowing, heavy new snow way down into the forest and thick except on the sheerest rock faces above, and all bathed in this golden glow from the sun.

We're heading right into the middle of the line of peaks for one of the highest, the Veleta, a sloping rose-thorn well over ten thousand feet high, hanging above the ski station.

Which of course is where we're going.

'Do you ski, Arnie?'

'No.'

'Well, you're going to learn because the minder we've laid on for you is just about one of the best skiers I know.'

Presently we're dropping towards Pradollano, the actual resort where all the hotels and apartments are, and there has been a good fall of snow even as low as this. On the edge of the big carpark there's a handy little heliport put there for King Juan Carlos, but anyone can use it if *Su Majestad* is not around. As we touch down I give him the keys to a self-catering apartment we have him, them, booked into, and I tell him how to get there.

He jumps down, holding his hold-all, and his hair against the whirl of the prop, and gives me a wave. And what is it I'm feeling as we lurch back up into the darkening sky? Annoyed because clearly it's not going to be easy getting him into Iraq in a useful frame of mind, and, well, hell, envy. I mean . . . like it's not just pussy he's on his way to, it's *trained* pussy.

PART FIVE

CHAPTER 27

Not for the first time since he had left England nearly eight months before, Cartwright experienced the discomfort of moving into a place, a situation as strange to him as an alien planet.

'Climb the stairs,' Henley had said, 'then cross the big square in front of you. On the far side a road goes up and to the right, down to the left. Follow it up, maybe five minutes walk, and on the left you'll find a block called Apartamentos Europa, the name is big, over the door, you can't miss it. Here's the key to 4011.'

The stairs were a broad Meccano-like outfit that zig-zagged to an area above. Aliens in huge heavy plastic boots and very odd clothes clambered up them, carrying skis over their shoulders. When they got to the corners they swung their skis and he had to duck to avoid being decapitated. Already he felt cold, and very very tired.

At the top he found a square which was really a taxi rank, a bus station, another carpark, rather than a square, and filled with snow already smirched and slushy. On the far side brightly lit boutiques sold ski-wear and accessories, fast food and souvenirs to crowds milling round and through them. It was all new, all modern, though here and there a slope of varnished wood, a roof eave fret-worked like a cuckoo-clock, made a vague and unconvincing gesture towards the Swiss Alps. A haze of small snowflakes drifted through the orange street lights, and the grey slush, its surface already freezing as the sun dipped, crunched beneath his feet. Above and beyond the snow-filled mountains beckoned.

He followed the hairpinning road up the mountain and sniffed kebabs, pizzas, beefburgers all the way, realising that he was not only cold, wet and lonely, but hungry too. The Europa Apartments were on a lot below the road, a big brown stuccoed building with recessed balconies. He took the lift to the fourth floor, found 4011 just a short way down a narrow dark corridor, had some trouble getting the key to work until he realised it took two turns to open the lock, and then the time-switch light expired and he had to find the button for it in near darkness. But as soon as he got it open he sensed rather than smelled the hint of jasmine on the air and he knew it was all going to be all right.

She was in the bath, lying on her front with her elbows on the back of it, looking out through the open door for him, her pale brown body made russet by the hot water, her short cropped silvery hair beaded with steam.

'Hi,' she said.

He knelt in front of her and her long honey-coloured arm folded round his neck and drew him into a slow full kiss. Then she pulled back.

'We've got six days,' she said. 'Let's not waste any of it.'

In the morning they went shopping, bought him a yellow and red ski-suit, a woolly hat, shades with doeskin side pieces and mirrored lenses.

'You wear them whenever you go out,' she said, 'And coloured lip salve painted on your cheeks like war-paint. Everybody does, and the two together will make you virtually unrecognisable.'

Then they hired skis and boots. He could not believe the boots, heavy impact-resistant plastic, with ratcheted fastenings, gear for a robot to wear in a sci-fi fantasy, but designed by Torquemada. He said as much and she began to laugh, and indeed her laughter became the keynote to the week: she laughed a lot, and day by day, hour by hour he learnt to laugh too, a skill rediscovered, one which he had lost, and his father had too, when his mother became ill. She had been a great laugher, until they found the small hard lump in her left breast.

There was plenty to laugh at. First he left his ski sticks in the tiny white gondola that carried them up to Borreguiles, the actual ski station, and they had to wait until it came round again fifteen minutes later. Not a bad thing really, it gave him a chance to soak in the marvellous place he had arrived at.

It was a huge pear-shaped bowl of snow with the rose-thorn peak of the Veleta a couple of miles away and three thousand feet higher at its apex. It was bounded by two ridges to the west and east that came down from the crest. The slopes at the base of the bowl were very gentle indeed, with short nursery runs to the right. In the middle there was a four-person chair lift that went half way up the bowl, and then several smaller lifts to points even higher, one of them reaching almost up to the peak itself. Behind them was the gondola station and a large self-service restaurant. The sun shone now from an unblemished sky, the snow, a foot of fresh powder on a firm impacted base, sparkled like diamond dust, and what was best of all was that all round them everyone seemed happy, was having a good time.

In the first half hour, on a gradient of about three degrees, he fell over twenty times before learning to lean forward, knees bent, letting the front casing of the boots take the weight of his shins. Their laughter became hysterical. But he got the hang of it, and was soon moving under some sort of control, in a rigid snow-plough.

'Fine. I can start, I can stop. How do I turn?'

'Increase the weight on one foot. You will turn towards the other foot.'

He did just that, and fell over again.

'Lean outwards, away from the slope . . . that's it, you've got it. Now listen, keep doing that, one foot then the other. Zig-zag down the slope. And of course it's a better way of stopping than just doing a vicious snow-plough, instead you turn into the slope, make the slope slow and stop you instead of carrying you on down.'

'Like this?'

He turned too far, his skis began to slip backwards, and he was over again. Her laughter chimed like silver across the slopes.

Lunch was a splendid buffet: all the best things in Andalusian cuisine: mussels with garlic, paella, chunks of deep fried chicken also with garlic, tiny grilled cutlets, *tortilla*, mountain-cured ham and spicy *chorizos*, a huge array of salads, sauces and dips. They took their plates out onto the terrace where now it was hot enough in the sun to take off their ski tops. Beneath hers she was wearing a tight dark green jersey-knit polo neck, no bra, three quarter sleeves. Her gold bangles were hoops of fire round wrists as thin and delicate as a bird's, extraordinary how they could be so strong.

'You don't have to stare at me all the time.'

'I do, if I have only five more days.'

After lunch she declared he was ready to use the nursery slopes, which immediately posed a new problem — the bum-button lift. This was a disc about a foot in diameter, on the end of a three-foot stalk, which in turn was attached to the overhead cable loop. She explained: 'Put your sticks in your left hand, grab it as it goes past, put it between your legs so it pulls against your bottom, hold on to the stalk.'

He fell over as he grabbed for it, was hoisted up by a patient operator and righted. The next one he caught more or less correctly and allowed himself to be dragged up, his skis hissing through the now softly melting snow, enjoying the sensation of the pressure on his bum and the slightly vibrating stalk on his balls, until he fell over half way up on a bump. But he did manage to ski down, all the way, without falling over, and suddenly something of the magic of skiing got to him — he was hooked.

But also mortified. For now, even on that short nursery

slope, with only a touch of steepness near the top, he saw for the first time how good she was: it was like watching a swallow in slowish motion.

'It must be hell for you stuck down here with me, when you can ski like that.'

'No. I'd rather be with you than on my own. With you rather than anyone else for that matter. And tomorrow we'll take the chair lift, and the day after, if the snow holds lower down, we'll ski back down to Pradollano instead of taking the gondola.'

'I don't believe you.'

Again the laugh. 'You'll see. And on the last day . . .' she shaded her eyes, looked up at the peak, 'we'll go to the top and ski the mountain.'

Old friends now, they fell quickly into a routine that ran for the next four days. They did not get up early nor in a hurry. 'Four hours skiing a day, one before lunch, three after, are enough,' she proclaimed. After a long breakfast they made their way down to the gondola station where they had left skis and boots secure in lockable racks and lockers, did their four hours skiing and one hour lunch and then made their way back to the apartment, getting home at about five in the evening.

'Home'. Nothing, since he moved out of his parents' house, had ever felt so much like home to Cartwright as this big tatty room with its whip-cord worn carpet, its impossible sofa-beds that were as uncomfortable as beds as they were as sofas, so they put all the cushions and thin mattresses they could find on the floor and sat, made love and slept there.

Along one wall there was a kitchenette which they used only for coffee and croissants. Their evening meal they bought in from the wide variety of take-aways.

After the untrammelled lust of their first encounter, the romantic passion of their second, they now settled into domestic bliss. Or so it seemed to him. They nibbled pizzas and kebabs through the long evenings and into the night and drank a bit too, he more than she, and . . . read. Read books.

Cartwright did not often read fiction, and when he did it was usually Gerald Seymour or Tom Clancy. She was reading a British author he had never heard of: Angela Carter. Suddenly bored with Clancy (the world he had lived in since he had been employed by SISA exposed Clancy as a writer of fiction), he picked up the book she had finished, *The Infernal Desire Machines of Doctor Hoffman*, and found he was in a totally original, frightening and bewitching world that was as real (though totally different from) the one he now inhabited. Which was not the world he had previously thought to be real, the world of Nottingham, Ferlinghetti, children and a dull marriage.

They made love slowly, exploring with care and delight bodies that before had been taken by storm, but now they took their time, often eschewing the climax, saved it for later.

Cartwright was no longer demented by lust, overwhelmed with passion. He was, by the end of the third day, a day on which he had achieved, so she said, a parallel turn with pole plant and had got down from the top of the chair lift three times without falling over, he was . . . in love.

And then on the fourth day she spotted them, men as deeply disguised as she and Cartwright were in all the paraphernalia that goes with skiing. Spotted them not because they followed Cartwright and her up the chair lift, but because they waited at the bottom for them to come down. Three times. To Cartwright they were just two big men, like him in ski-wear, black and white stripes in their case, and shades, with painted faces, but to her they were vengeance, Nemesis.

She said nothing at the time, but on the way back to the apartment she told him to buy food in the supermarket, pasta, meat and tomato sauce in a jar, cheese, and fruit and two slabs of milk chocolate with nuts, two hundred and fifty grams each.

Back at the apartment she made him check that both

locks on their outer door were secure. Then she began to undress.

'You too.'

When they were both naked she took him into the bathroom and stood with him in the bath, turned on the shower. But this was not like Madrid. First she gelled his body all over, round his neck, across chest and back, made him lift his arms so she could soap his armpits. Then his genitals and his anus, but not to excite him, simply, it seemed, to wash him. Of course, he was excited, wanted her to go on, but as soon as his penis began to lift, she moved on down his legs, his calves, to his feet. She crouched in front of him, made him put first one foot then the other on her thighs above her knees, so she could meticulously work the gel between his toes.

Finally, she made him crouch in front of her, turned the shower on his head and creamed his hair with shampoo, occasionally pressing his cheek into her stomach. Feelings of loss, tinged with heart-breaking tenderness welled up in his chest and throat, and for a moment he could not remember why. Then it came to him. When he was small, six or seven, his mother used to wash his hair, she sitting on a stool by the bath, he standing between her knees so his head was over the bath while she held a rubber shower head attached to the taps. He remembered the warmth of her breasts against his back as she rummaged the soap through his hair. These were perhaps the last occasions on which he had been in prolonged physical contact with the only woman he really loved, and the memory of them now made him circle Roma's waist with his arms and tighten the embrace.

She looked down at him with slightly tightened lips, eyes a little sad. Of course she did not know what specific memory was in his mind, but there was a longing in the embrace for the things mothers give small children: security, freedom from fear, comfort, as well as the hidden passion, the desire for mutual possession in a never-never land where neither sons nor mothers grow old.

When she had finally rinsed away the last of the gel and shampoo, she climbed out of the bath and held a big warm towel for him. He was disappointed.

'Don't you want me to do the same for you?'

'No.' But she smiled. 'You can cook up the pasta and sauce. Big helpings, and then we'll read for a little, but we're going to go to bed early . . . and we're going to sleep well.'

They did those things and by nine o'clock were stretched out on mattresses and cushions, lightly covered with duvets. They read a little, she intently, he unable to concentrate. At last he said: 'I'm not going to find it easy to sleep.'

She folded down the corner of a page, put the book to one side, rolled into him.

'Oh yes you are.'

Throughout the night, whenever she sensed he was awake and restless, she stirred him into making love again. At about three in the morning he fell into a very deep dreamless sleep, a sleep of total relaxation, that lasted six hours. He woke feeling at first a little weak, but as soon as he had had coffee and croissants, strength flooded through him. He had never felt so fit, so strong, so alive.

CHAPTER 28

When he came out of the bathroom, he found her sitting amongst the cushions with the shoulder straps of her salopette still hanging round her hips. She was strapping a holstered gun into her left armpit over the top of a skimpy thermo-vest. She gave her shoulder and torso a wriggle to make sure it was properly seated, then she pulled on her polo-top and hoisted up the salopette. He could still see the gun's bulge, but this time, unusually, she put a ski jacket on over everything else.

'Why?'

'The men who followed and watched us yesterday.'

'Who are they?'

'The people who tried to kill you.'

'What are we going to do?'

'You'll see. Get dressed.'

When he was yet again fully geared up for skiing she looked around the room. 'Is there anything you brought with you you particularly value? I mean that you don't normally take skiing with you?'

He thought for a moment. Plastic, passport, keys, that sort of thing, some loose cash, were all either zipped into his ski-wear pockets or a small bum-bag. Otherwise there were his normal clothes, a sweater, trousers, a change of underwear, a pair of shoes he could easily replace.

'No.'

'Sure? Because we're not coming back.'

He went back into the bathroom and zipped his

toothbrush, toothpaste and a disposable razor into an upper pocket.

They went straight from the gondola to the chair lift and, for the benefit of the two men, still in black and white stripes like mountain tigers, established an apparent routine of skiing back down the blue run and then the red one. On the red one Cartwright had some trouble, did ten feet or so on his backside, got up but then came a real purler, losing a ski.

Roma looked down at him, chewed her russet-creamed lip.

'You're going to have to do better than that.'

He thought she meant that they were going to give the men the slip by skiing on down out of Borreguiles and back to the carpark in Pradollano.

They went up the chair lift for the fourth time that morning, but this time she skied off to the right, taking the green or easy piste. Without complaining he followed her. But then, in less than a hundred metres, she pulled up at the end of the queue to the drag lift that climbed the mountain to a point only three hundred feet below the peak of the Veleta. On the maps of the ski station the piste was marked as a red run, but at the top it looked impossibly steep, and lower down there were 'moguls', small mounds of hard snow. At every level there were more people falling about the place than actually skiing.

'I'm not coming down that.'

'No.'

'I'll wait here for you.'

'No. Listen. Have you got that chocolate with you?'

'Yes, I've not touched it.'

The queue moved forward, in a moment they would be in the single file lane and roped-off, no turning back.

'If we go up, we have to come down.'

She touched a finger to his lips.

'Shhhh.'

Then she unclipped her heavy ski-gloves from the

fastenings on her top, pulled them on. Normally she did not bother with them. The queue moved forward, two more and it would be her turn, then his.

'We have to come down, yes. But not this side.'

A bar shaped to be a handle, not a button this time, clanked round the wheel above his head, dropped towards her and she seized it as it passed her. He caught the next one, resisted the jolt, clung on, leant back. His skis hissed on the impacted snow, and a tight knot of anxiety, bordering on fear, began to swell in his diaphragm. He tried to remember maps of the area, recalled that behind the long massif of the Sierra Nevada was the valley system known as the Alpujarras: friends of his father spoke of it as one of the last unspoilt places in Spain. All too soon he was at the top. He let go of the bar and skidded to an awkward stop behind her; his skis overlapped hers and the people behind scolded him for half blocking their paths.

'Put off your skis.'

One of her very rare lapses in English.

She stooped to release her own bindings. He moved up out of the way of the other skiers, did as he was told, fastened his skis with the clip and rubber band he had learnt to keep in his zipped-up breast pocket. The effort left him breathless, with a raised heartbeat. He spared a look for the slope he was not going to be asked to ski down and felt relief.

'Are you sure this is possible?'

'Oh yes. People do it quite regularly. In parties. A bus comes up the other side to Capileira, takes them back to Pradollano the long way round. There is a road too, and in August you can actually drive a car over. But of course at this time of year the road is several feet beneath the snow.'

Capileira. The name meant something. Yes. That was where that English couple lived, with the two children, the ones he'd helped with their caravan. Cortijo San Mateo high above the village, that's what they'd said in Granada in June. Call in any time. Well, it looked as though he just might. If he survived.

'I'm sorry, but I don't feel too good.'

'We are nearly three thousand five hundred metres above sea-level. You have mild altitude sickness. Come on.'

She swung her skis on to her shoulder, he did likewise and followed.

There was indeed a ledge in the snow, a near flatness a few metres above them that marked where the road lay. It climbed to cut through the slanting edge of the Veleta just two hundred feet below the peak. High as they were and on the north side there was not much of the ice that forms where snow has melted. And, he said to himself as he trudged on in other people's footsteps, it's been done ahead of us, so maybe we shall live to tell the tale.

'Lean out!' she called, turning to see how he was coping. 'If you lean in, you'll go.'

The road had been cut into the upper sloping edge of the thorn and though the snow had almost filled the cut it was clearly there, about fifteen feet wide, fifteen deep on the higher side, ten on the lower, a hemisphere of sky framed in blueish white. A freezing gale blew through it. But when he got there his breath was caught not by the wind but by what he saw.

In the foreground fells dropped fold on fold, deep in snow, to a visual ridge maybe six miles away. Beyond them at a further fifteen, twenty, miles another massif spread across the horizon, lightly hazed with snow. Mist or cloud, from where they were as white in the sunlight as the snow they stood on, hung between the two mountain ranges. And beyond the distant mountains, and because they were so high it filled the space above them, the sea. It was pure liquid gold but merged into a deep violet, almost indigo haze that cut off the clear view of Africa which both of them knew lay within it.

They moved through the gap and the more immediate foreground became a horror. The track hairpinned out of the cut to run across the southern face of the Veleta, a huge, nearly vertical amphitheatre, sheeted with snow and ice. Ice, because now they were on the south-facing slope the snow did melt a little in the afternoons and froze at night. It was only twelve feet wide and sloped out and down. At the foot of the amphitheatre, two hundred feet below, there was a small tarn, a flat frozen disc covered with snow. And above the tarn there was nothing. Emptiness. Space. All the way to Africa. Cartwright had not known that he was prone to vertigo. Suddenly he discovered it. His head swam, he leant back into the rock-face behind him.

'I have to go back.'

'They'll kill you if you do.'

'I'm going to die here if I don't.'

'Have some chocolate.'

He ate and felt better.

There was one more really bad moment, very bad. People who, like Cartwright, do not know mountains, do not realise how thin they can get at the top, that those needle-like peaks and razor edges really are just that. Below the peak, the track passed along a swooping serrated edge, twisted gnarled teeth of rock with gaps between them so at times the wall between the two sides of the mountain was only two or three feet high and hardly any thicker. He realised he was on a ridge, a bridge. He looked between the teeth and into a deep black gully, black because it faced north and was too steep to support snow. Shreds of grey mist, close enough to be denied the sun, swirled beneath him. And on the other side he looked down to that tarn. And he had about three feet of more or less flat but slippery snow to walk along between the two. His head swam, blood pounded in his ears, drowned out the howl of the wind.

Presently the slope beneath became less precipitous and the track widened. She said: 'We could put our skis on here, you know. And ski down.'

'No.' Though already there were ski tracks among the footprints.

He knew she was irritated by the delay, but, damn it, he had been skiing for less than a week.

They trudged on, and eventually the track rounded out into gentler slopes and at last he felt, partly because his aching shoulders could no longer support their weight, that he could risk putting on the skis. He did so and fell over.

'Look,' she said. 'It's already half past one. If we don't get below the snowline in the next five hours, we'll die. Just try to remember a little of what you've learnt.'

He had not realised she could be so bossy. But he made better progress, following her turquoise blue and emerald green back, and making himself keep up, refusing himself the luxury of calling to her to go slower or wait.

After half an hour or so the track left the side of the mountain and began a long sweep across an undulating plateau where sometimes they had to take their skis off again and walk up gentle inclines. Always, and always it was a source of hope to him, there were ski tracks and footprints to show them the way.

He said: 'Who were those people? Why do they want to kill me?'

Already his breathing was easier, his heartbeat had slowed. They were back now to two thousand five hundred metres and going down.

'The Mossad,' she said. 'The Israeli equivalent of the CIA. They want to kill you because you are helping an Arab nation to put together an air defence system that will stop their planes from bombing Arab people.'

'I know who the Mossad are.'

A little later he asked: 'But aren't they on the American side of things?'

'Yes.'

'But all that . . . business I've been working for. Which I thought you were working for. Is . . . on the American side of things. I think.'

'That can't be the case. Jabreel is being paid by Saddam Hussein. How can you say the Americans have anything to do with it?'

The mountains in front seemed nearer and higher,

though still below them, the sea more distant and often hidden. But in front the blinding snow-fields stretched on for miles. He thought about her question, though thought was difficult. He realised that one of the reasons he had decided the Americans were in it all was because he thought of Henley as an American. But now he remembered, way back on the Plymouth-Santander ferry, Henley had described himself as Canadian. Did that make any difference? But there were other things too.

'Look, I can't think, talk and ski all at once. Can we stop for ten minutes, eat some more chocolate?'

She was already alarmed by what he had said, wanted to hear more.

'All right.'

She skied away from the tracks to where a low brown rock pushed through the snow, took off her skis. More clumsily he followed, sat beside her. As they talked they finished the first slab, ate snow to quench their thirst.

'So. Why do you think the Americans are behind Jabreel?'

'Every time I ask for equipment or specifications I get them. And from very different sources. Not just FADSI, but stuff that originated with Lockheed who make the Stealth F117A. They've even given me its radar signature. I was going to work on the same project in England, legally, and in my experience I'm getting this sort of information more readily now than I would have done if I'd stayed there. There's none of the endless bureaucratic hassle . . . It can only mean that someone very high up in the US government is supporting us.'

'I can't believe that. Why should they give the Iraqis the ability to take out Stealth?'

'They're not going to.'

'But you said . . .'

'Even with all this help, it's not going to work. Quite simply it's not possible. Not in the time available, not with the limited skills.'

'Why not? Why won't it work?'

'Because the maximum range I can get is twenty-five miles. A mile is one point six kilometres. Given the six to seven hundred miles an hour Stealth planes fly at we need fifty miles to process the signals and launch the missiles against them. And I just do not believe it can be done.'

She sat and thought for a full minute, then: 'So what do you think is behind all this?'

'I don't know. For some reason they want the Iraqis to think, to believe it will work. But it won't. That's why I don't object to doing the work — it's not going to hurt anyone.'

He sounded confused and almost wistful. A small boy playing a dangerous game, trying to convince a grown-up that there was no harm in it.

Roma was silent for even longer, silent and grim. It gave him time to realise how still and soundless the white wasteland was. He shivered, suddenly wanted to get on, on and down. She stood, leaned on one stick and with the other hooked a ski in under her foot, placed the toe of her boot in the 'shoe', and smacked her heel into the binding. Then she looked up at him.

'Is there any chance, any chance at all, that these systems could be ready in time, could be made to work?'

'No.'

'Not even if you were there, supervising the final . . . adjustments? On the spot to see how things might go wrong?'

He shrugged.

'Well. It's theoretically possible. Just possible.' He also stood, tried to get into his skis but his second boot had picked up too much snow. For a moment he put his arm on her shoulder while with his other hand holding his stick he banged his sole, trying to shake the snow free. His blood quickened at the nearness of her, the warmth of her cheek, but she stiffened, flinched away. He felt hurt, and added: 'But wild horses wouldn't get me to Baghdad. No way.'

CHAPTER 29

'Jesus sakes, what a mess! What happened?'

Poor Arnie still looks very badly shaken, even though the worst was two hours ago. I reckon he might feel better if he talks about it, help him to stop brooding on the nightmare. We're back in the MBB, night-flying this time, always a bit scary in a 'copter, especially over mountains, so maybe I too want something to keep my mind occupied. He turns away from the window, eyes dark and frightened in a tired white face, catches a glimpse of the bodies slumped in the small space behind us, filling it, flinches away, looks ahead.

'These English people I met, I don't really know them, but they gave me the address, said I should call any time. Well, they're renting that place, that house where . . .'

His voice tails away. Yeah, nice pad, but very, very deserted. The highest above Capileira, on a crag, close to the road, above the tree-line but beneath the snow. Just. Great views, great place to be in the summer, not much fun in the winter.

'So you recognised the name, Cortijo San Mateo, and as it was late afternoon you persuaded Roma that it would be a sensible thing to stop there for the night. And they didn't mind?'

'Not at all. Really they're very nice, Chris and Jenny and the two kids. I wouldn't have done this to them for the world.'

'Pleased to have the company, I guess.'

'Absolutely, they were all over us, straight away, drinks,

snacks and Jenny putting together a proper meal in the kitchen. It was all so warm and cosy after . . .' His voice catches on what could be a stifled sob.

'Then, I guess you heard the Sikorsky.'

'Yes, she . . . Roma, heard it first. She seemed to know straight away what it was, who it was. Phil, I still don't know how they knew where we were.'

Well, I know, having been over his apartment twice, with a very fine comb indeed, and they, of course, had done likewise.

'Arnie did you have that address written down anywhere in your apartment perhaps?'

'Yes, yes I did. Chris wrote it out and I left it pinned to a noticeboard in my kitchen.'

'There you are then. Once they rumbled you and Roma had gone over the mountain, they remembered that address, and guessed that might be where you'd hole out for the night. So what did she do then? She hid somewhere? Outside, I guess?'

'Yes. She told us to stay indoors, keep away from the windows. And she told me to say to them that she had gone on, and left me there because I was exhausted. Then she went out. She must have managed it without them seeing. And then, well, the helicopter came closer, was making a lot of noise, then the noise stopped and it had landed and everything was quiet for a moment . . .'

'Then the shots?'

'No, no. Not straight away. We heard some movement near the house, then a knock on the door. I opened it. He was still in the white and black striped ski-wear, shades and so on, but now he was carrying a gun, not a pistol, but not much bigger . . .'

'Uzi machine pistol. Nasty little brute.'

'After everything she'd said, and after that awful business when they tried to blow me up, I thought he was going to kill me there and then. Perhaps he was. But first he asked where she was, and I said what she'd told me to say. He turned round, called to the other man, I don't know what, I don't even know what language . . .'

'The other guy was covering for him. And he was saying, no need, she's not here.'

'I suppose so. Anyway, he came along the side of the house, the second one I mean, and just as he was getting near the door she shot them, both of them. From the woodstore.'

One in the head, the other in the shoulder. The wounded one managed to loose off a few rounds in her general direction but she kept her cool and took him out for good with her third shot. Living up to everything Louella had said about her.

'Then she came back in, told us not to go outside. And she used their phone, phoned you. And then we just sat there and waited.'

'How did your friends react?'

'Not really friends, I hardly know them. And certainly friends no longer. They were very upset, especially Jenny and the younger child. And Chris wanted to phone for the police, and an ambulance, in case they weren't dead. She said they were dead and he would be too if he touched the phone. Phil. It was horrible. I didn't know she could be like that . . . so, different, cold, brutal.'

Right, I say to myself, this needs some thought. Like the scales have dropped from his eyes and the honey-trap is blown, I'll have to dream up some other means of gentle persuasion if Arnie's going to stay in the ring.

But going back to the events he's describing, I was there in the hour, with Josh piloting the MBB this time — wasn't taking the Brit, knowing these were Brits we were going to. Speaking Spanish, we came on like we were Security Police, anti-terrorist, and the corpses were ETA, flashed some likely-looking ID, and I guess that Chris and Jenny swallowed it in the end. I doubt they'll stay there though. They looked pretty sick at the whole business.

We loaded up the corpses, but then there was the problem of the Sikorsky.

'I can fly it,' says Roma. 'I'll follow you.'

'Okay,' say I.

And that brings me to what happened just a moment ago, and the reason why I'm sweating on the report I'm going to have to give Gabby when we touch base again.

Just now Josh looked up into the big mirror which shows him the interior behind him.

'Phil,' he said, 'Look around, will you? She's not in my rear-view mirror any more.'

And he was right. She'd gone. Vanished.

'Is there any point in trying to pick her up, follow her?'

'None at all. She has a twenty knot edge.'

'Shit. Shee-it.'

She's blown. Something has happened, something's been said to give her the idea that all is not strictly kosher about the Mansur set-up. Now, maybe, considering everything, 'kosher' is not the *mot juste*. Anyway she's running, not running scared, girls like Roma don't run scared, but running. I should have flown with her. But I didn't like the look of Arnie, and I decided to stay with him. Now what the hell am I going to say to Gabby? And whatever else, I was right. No way is she the honey-trap that keeps Arnie in line, not if she's vamoosed. So that deserves serious thought too.

Problems, problems.

CHAPTER 30

'Dad, are you all right?'

'Of course I'm not. All right? Bloody look at me.'

Herbert was sitting in one of the low deep armchairs facing the portrait of his wife. He was wearing a dressing-gown pulled on over shirt and trousers. None of the buttons on either garment was done up, and the reason why was obvious. Both his hands were shaking, flickering almost, as if he were scattering seed or water over his knees and the floor. Occasionally too his head jerked up and to the left, and his left shoulder shot up to reach it. He looked very tired, very dishevelled and had clearly lost weight. There was a smell of stale urine in the apartment.

'How long have you been like this?'

'Arnie, I don't know. Five days? A week?'

'But . . . you've had a doctor in?'

'No.'

'Why not?'

'It's Parkinson's, isn't it?' Suddenly the old man was angry. 'Incurable. Just leave me be. When I can't bear it any longer I'll take an overdose.'

'Christ, Dad, this is ridiculous. Who should I ring? Doctor, hospital?'

Herbert said nothing, but the body language of head pulled down into his shoulders, the way he hunched up over his knees, said: no.

'Look. I am going to get you medical care no matter what you say or do to stop me. So you might just as well make it easy for me.'

'Centro de Salud. Health centre. Just down the road. Number's on the notice board in the kitchen. But it won't do no good.'

'At least we have to try.'

'Do we?'

Cartwright found the number, dialled it, gave the handset to his father.

'Make with the Spanish, Dad. And get it right.'

'No need. They speak English. Just start by saying *Habla Inglés,* and they'll find someone who can.'

A lady doctor, brisk, petite, young, black hair and unplucked eyebrows, was there in twenty minutes. Immediately she gave Herbert a sedative, then told Cartwright to pack him a bag of essentials. The ambulance would be there in under an hour, would take him to Malaga General, initially for observation and tests.

'And build his strength back up too.'

When she had gone Herbert began to worry.

'You'll come in and look at me plants, eh our Arnie? The water and feeding is on automatic, all you have to do is top up the reservoirs about once a week, but they must be checked for air and humidity too . . .'

He did his best to explain and Cartwright did his best to convince him he had understood.

'And me pills, me blood pressure capsules. I'll want them. They'll want to know what medication I've been having.'

And so on.

Twenty-four hours later Cartwright went to the hospital to see him. Herbert was in a private room, propped up on pillows. The shaking had subsided, though it was still there. His colour was better, indeed high, and he seemed sleepy, tired, but not dulled.

'Arnie? Flowers? Aye, mimosa, your mam loved mimosa. Mimosa in January? Mebbe it come from Africa. It is January, is it?'

'Just.' Arnie laughed. '1991 came in two days ago. That's

why I came round, wish you a Happy New Year. As well I did. You look better. They treating you right?'

'Aye. But listen Arnie. There's a problem.'

By now Cartwright had pulled a chair in close, and the old man reached out a still shaking claw of a hand and held on to his wrist.

'There is?'

'Now, don't be angry with me.' He paused, something like a twinkle drifted into his eye, something almost roguish. 'I'm going to say something I honestly don't believe I've ever said before in my life. I can't pay. That's the problem.'

'I thought you had insurance."

'No.'

'Why not?'

'Arnie, an old man with blood pressure? Can you guess what the premiums would have been?'

'Doesn't the E one eleven help?'

'No. I'm legally resident in Spain. It's only for tourists and short-stay visitors.'

'Well, you'll just have to dip into your capital.'

'Can't.'

'Why not?'

The silence lengthened. The muted but busy sounds of a large hospital became more insistent. Far away, a woman wailed, the uninhibited outpouring of Andalusian grief. Arnie squeezed his father's wrist.

'You don't have to tell me if you don't want to.'

'No. I don't. But I will.' He wriggled himself up into the pillows, took a deep breath, but shut his eyes.

'Two year ago, Tim Roberts, silly neighbour of mine, got a property company together, specially for the British market. I put half what I have into it. Property both here and in UK were going up five per cent a month at the time. You know what happened. By twelve months ago we was selling for two-thirds what we'd paid to meet the bank loan. Serve me right for behaving like a bloody capitalist.'

'But only half. Dad, that still leaves you a rich man.'

'No, our Arnie. It leaves you and your kids rich when I'm gone.' He opened his eyes, and again something like a sheepish grin lit his face. 'You see, I got such a fright, silly old fool, I said to mesel' you best not let that happen again. Meddlin' in what you don't know owt about. So I tied all that was left into a trust, keeping the income to live off, and the capital half to you and a quarter each to them when I'm gone. And I made sure it were bloody watertight. Ah well. There is a solution.'

'What?'

'You get me back to Nottingham. I'm still entitled there.'

'But you don't want that.'

'No, our Arnie. I bloody don't.' And he shut his eyes again, quickly, before the tear that was forming could spill.

An hour later Cartwright saw the doctor. Fortunately his English was good.

'We're almost sure it's not Parkinson's. It responds too readily to sedatives. What we would like to do is keep your father here for a fortnight or so, run some tests. It could be any of a number of complaints and the thing is to get it right, so we can prescribe the right treatment. Your father's insurance will cover it.'

'He hasn't got any.'

The doctor looked totally incredulous.

Cartwright assured him: 'Really. He hasn't.'

'Can he pay?'

'How much will it be?'

'Bed and board are ten thousand pesetas a day. I'm not sure offhand how much the tests cost. The blood ones aren't all that dear, but I'll want spinal fluid and that comes higher.'

Seven hundred pounds for the fortnight, and what? As much again for the tests? I can afford that, thought Cartwright. But will I be able to manage the treatment? That's a problem we'll face when we know the size of it.

'We'll pay.'

'All right.' The doctor shrugged. 'There is one other

thing. Your father's blood pressure is giving us cause for worry. At the moment we are leaving him on the medication he brought with him, which must have been prescribed with his particular condition in mind. But for some reason he no longer seems to be responding as we would expect. Are you agreeable if we run some tests in that area too?'

Back to Herbert. Cartwright sat with him for an hour, tried to make conversation that had some sense in it, wasn't banal. Early on a nurse came in, spoke in Spanish, took his blood pressure and then reached down the capsules from a locker over the sink, made him take one, flashed a smile at Cartwright and went.

Eventually he got round to the question that had been one of the reasons, perhaps even the main one, for his calling the day before.

'Dad, this Gulf War thing. Why would the Americans want to make Saddam Hussein think his air defence systems are far more advanced than they actually are?'

'Is this owt to do wi' the work you're doing?'

'Yes.'

'I told you it were mucky.' He sighed, then suddenly his face shrivelled as if he had had a pain and his fingers clutched the sheet. He was trying to stop them from shaking. 'This bogger's off again, Arnie.' '

'I'll ring for the nurse.'

'Aye, do that . . . Arnie, you may be clever wi' radar and computers and the like but you're an ol' daftie at everything else. The worst thing . . . the worst thing for Bush right now . . . would be, would be if Saddam pulled out. An' 'e won't if 'e thinks he's got any . . . any sort o' chance at all. 'An . . . an' thinkin' his radar . . . oh bogger this!'

All Cartwright could do was hold the old man's thin and shaking shoulders and wait.

CHAPTER 31

'Salih!'

He embraced me. Not always good news, and not just because of the garlic and whisky on his breath, but because he tends to embrace those who are about to die.

'Once again I shall need you for more than your four-hour shift. We have a long way to go, down to our nineteenth province.'

So, it was up onto the roof again, and into the big presidential helicopter, but only as far as the military airfield where we transferred rapidly across the blistering slipstream-whipped tarmac to the presidential jet. I have no idea what make it was, I have very little interest or knowledge of such things, but it was very well appointed with comfortable armchairs just behind the crew's quarters, bridge . . . cockpit, that's the word. Moreover, a couple of pretty girls in blue and red tartan suits with pencil skirts welcomed us on board.

We took off, and a flight of five Mirage F–1 fighter-bombers swooped alongside and above us as escort. I know that's what they were because he said so. Soon, however, they returned to Baghdad, to save fuel, and we flew on, strong in the faith that since Allah knew we had His best interests at heart, He would protect us. One of the tartan girls served us drinks, Black Label of course, on a tray with ice. The Supreme Eagle of the Arabian Skies reached up and lifted the hem of her skirt, looked across at me.

'They came with the plane,' he said. I am not sure if he

meant the actual girls or just their uniforms. 'Knock-down prices, the airline went bust.' He slapped her bottom as she moved back to the . . . galley? Yes, galley. 'Why can't they all be Caledonian?'

And he chuckled noisily. I did likewise, but I had not the slightest idea why or what the joke was. He drank, I sipped, he leant across the space between us.

'Salih. How long is a mile?'

'A mile, your Excellency, is the distance a man might walk if he took one thousand seven hundred and forty-six paces.' I banged my forehead with my open palm. 'No, sixty-four. One thousand, seven hundred and sixty-four.'

'So what does Mr Bush mean when he says "I will go the extra mile for peace"? I do not think he means he will walk a mile, all those paces.'

'No.'

'Does he mean that for the sake of peace he will go a short distance further than he has yet gone? Does he mean he will take steps, yes steps, that have not been taken before, explore a road that is new to him?'

'Possibly, Excellency. If Your Excellency could give me a little more of the context of this extraordinary remark . . .?'

'He has said that Mr Baker, his foreign affairs man, is ready to meet Tariq in Geneva. In a few days' time. But he has also said that Mr Baker will not be empowered to negotiate, compromise or accept linkage to the Palestinian problem. Now if he means all that, how can he talk of walking an extra mile? What is the point of the meeting, if he is simply going to reiterate the unacceptable? Could it not be that this mile he talks of is a signal, a hint that there may be some readiness to give way a little? After all they made such a big deal about that small step on the Moon, one thousand, seven hundred and . . . whatever you said, on Earth, must mean something.'

'Excellency, I think that must be the case.'

'Then I shall tell Tariq he should go. But we'll mess them about a bit over the actual date. The seventh, eighth or ninth? We'll make it the ninth, but only at the last moment.'

He looked out of the window and the huge hand pushed nervously at his moustache, pulled at it, mussed it up. Then, realising what he had done, he took a small pocket mirror from the top pocket of his combat jacket, almost always these days he wears his military clothes, and carefully, even daintily, twiddled the corners between finger and thumb, perked them up again. All this was done with complete lack of self-awareness, for it was the fate of empires that occupied his towering intellect.

'Salih . . . I don't think they mean to fight.'

'Excellency?'

'Ever since Vietnam they have paid other people to fight their wars, their real wars, I don't mean little things like Grenada or Panama. South Africa fights Angola and the Cubans for them, the Contras take on the Sandanistas, the Zionist mob are all over the place on their account, and while my Holy War against the Persian Serpent was entirely my own affair, they did at times give me aid, since I was punishing the viper who had humiliated them. Of course they helped the Persians too, but in the end they came out firmly on our side, clearing the Persian navy out of the Gulf for us.'

He looked out again and down, across the desert. It was a criss-cross of tracks as far as the eyes could see, monochrome tartan.

'Bush said, he's drawn a line in the sand,' the Master of Loquacious Wit remarked, and, with satisfaction added, 'but not as many as I have, eh, Salih?'

He chewed on his thumb, then sighed, the deep sad sigh of a child lost, confused, who does not know which way to turn. I imagine Hitler, in his bunker, was given to such sighs.

'Salih, I really do not understand the man. His senators support sanctions rather than military action and he hasn't purged them. His general, the fat one here, polluting the soil of Holy Arabia, also supports sanctions. His second in command announces to the world that he is not ready for a land fight. I shoot generals who say that sort of thing. It must mean he's not going to fight. That's what this Geneva thing is. He knows, all he has to do is set a date for a Conference on the Palestine Question, and I'll pull out and do my own private deal with the Al-Sabahs later. Ah, look.'

He pointed down again. Over to the left we could see on the horizon the skyline of Kuwait City, and beyond it a forest of six thin black columns of smoke which spread into a noisome canopy above, but below we were still over desert. It was now filled for ten miles in every direction with what looked like hemispherical *tels* left by some ancient civilisation — pre-Hittite, to my scholarly eye. Threading through came a convoy of cement trucks, all with their big drums turning, spewing diesel exhaust into the dust and air above them. A small fleet of armoured personnel carriers rode shot-gun for them though they were surely in no danger of attack with twelve days still to run before the deadline was reached.

'My Republican Guard,' the Lord of Hosts proclaimed. 'Dug in beneath concrete and the sands of the desert and ringed by the most advanced air defence system in the world. That's why he won't fight. That's the real reason this mother of all wars won't take place.'

He finished his drink, hauled himself up and lumbered towards the back of the plane, smiling at his aides and bodyguards as he went, slapping a shoulder here, pulling an ear there. I thought he was heading for the toilet, and so he was, but I must confess even I was surprised when he pulled one of the tartan-clad girls into the cubicle with him.

We travelled in a very long, I believe the 'buzz-word' is 'stretched', Mercedes from Kuwait airport for twenty miles out into the desert. The car was air-conditioned and very comfortable, with soft leather upholstery the colour of fine goat butter. The Wakeful Watcher took a brief nap, and woke apparently refreshed when we stopped in a small compound whose ancient brick walls suggested a caravanserai dating back to the Caliphs. Here we transferred to an open Land Rover. The Commander of the Legions of Arab Vengeance used the driving mirror to adjust the angle of his black beret and took his place standing behind the driver. I was motioned to get in beside him, the driver I mean. The bodyguards clustered around us. The driver then engaged reverse, and because the Adonis of Baghdad had altered the rear-view mirror, and the driver did not dare make the necessary readjustment, he shunted us into the back of a T55 tank. All fall down. I shut my eyes and hoped the driver's head would not splatter me too horribly, but, for the time being, the All-Merciful one was just that. Indeed, since very few people in the enclosed space had seen the incident, he gave way to laughter, and urged us all to do likewise. But, er, not too boisterously.

It was only a short drive, but the heat as we left the caravanserai was, just as the cliché has it, like a blow, a blow such as the Magnanimous One likes to bestow with his big raw hand on one's back — offered in a spirit of camaraderie but knocking the breath out of one. My shirt and the silly suit I was wearing were instantly soaked with perspiration.

Our mobile fortress trundled on across the desert, in the blinding sunshine, and around the backside of the Lion of Assyria, and the backside of his bodyguard, who was a lookalike near enough, I could see occasional passing soldiery, who sometimes cheered, more often prostrated themselves as we passed. Soon we were threading our way through the hemispherical *tels* we had seen from the plane, and I have to say I was mightily impressed: these were the only outward signs of a warren of fortifications protecting whole regiments of tanks and self-propelled artillery, brigades of foot-soldiers with armoured personnel carriers, all beneath concrete domes many metres thick, piled high with sand on top.

We were heading for the Command Control Centre, a labyrinthine palace of technology beneath the largest dome of all, just about, I would say, at the centre of the whole complex. Steel doors opened, a metre thick, then a second set, and we trundled into a low but brightly-lit indoor carpark, which was blissfully cool.

Blissfully? As we followed plain echoing corridors and stairs further and further into the heart of the bunker I felt the sweat that sheeted my body grow clammy, cold, and finally icy. This, I said to myself, means sciatica — something I dread almost as deeply as I fear the whims of the Great Healer.

We went to the very heart of the Centre, a big circular room which looked a little like those pictures of the NASA command centre at Houston one used to see during space events, though my memory of the NASA layout may be at fault. Here three circular banks of video displays in tiers surrounded an empty circle in the middle, much in the way tiers of seats surround a modern 'theatre-in-the-round'. This was carpeted a deep blood-red and was about ten metres in diameter. The walls behind the VDTs were filled with huge screens that followed the curve of the outer wall. One displayed a vast map of the southern half of Iraq in configuration that put the Centre at the centre. Others were real-time pictures taken from cameras placed in the empty streets of Kuwait City, in the forward positions of our army, on spotter planes flying above the burning oil wells near the port.

Two people stood in the arena. We did not go down to join them, rather Allah's Assessor on Earth prowled the highest gallery above them, behind the topmost tier of VDTs, with myself and sundry other aides trotting behind him, while, with the aid of some sort of hidden voice enhancement system, he conducted what at first seemed to be an enquiry, then perhaps a trial. Purer than theatre, this was real. As it unfolded I became quite caught up in it, and I have to say was slightly disappointed when it ended inconclusively. This in spite of the fact that neither of the protagonists was at all prepossessing in any way at all.

Both were below average height, five feet at the most, and that was where any similarity ended, apart from their general unattractiveness. The first to be questioned was a Korean called Tai-Won-Kun. She had a mass of thick, black but greasy hair, the flat face of her oriental forebears, was built like a tank: solid, hard, but bulky too. She wore denims, jacket and skirt, both cut along entirely utilitarian lines — for pockets and ease of movement. The way she gestured with her hands suggested advanced skills in martial arts.

The second wore combat fatigues, down to the lace-up boots, was thinner, yet, I felt, equally tough but more finely honed. She was, I soon realised, also female, though, in spite of her low stature, I had presumed her to be male. Her skin was sallow, but with that hint of reddish pigmentation one sometimes finds in those who come from the western end of the Arab world. Her bone structure was angular, symmetrical, and would have been beautiful but for the relentlessly thin, ungiving line of her unadorned mouth, the hardness of her eyes. And, most bizarre of all, her head was shaved, completely shaved — Brynner-bald.

The Last Trump boomed across the spaces above them, an adjustment was made, and he tried again.

'Madame Tai. Progress report.'

'Excellency.' Her voice, also amplified, was high, at moments of stress became very high-pitched indeed, a bat at dusk, a kitten in deep distress. 'Progress has continued to be good. We were, Your Excellency will remember, having problems in three areas. The first was the smoothness of the dishes, which had to be sixteen times smoother to receive accurately a return signal as weak as the one we can expect. The dishes are, as you know, made from a highly refined alloy of copper and zinc, closely related to brass, and the problem was that the machinists capable of doing this work, two homosexuals from Bradford,

England, left with the last of your guests in the middle of December. However, we were able to locate a Palestinian family of copper and brass-workers with a small workshop in the poorer part of Kuwait City and we are confident they will soon master the lathes and machine tools we have put at their disposal.

'Next, Your Excellency will recall that another problem was the strength of the signal our transmitters were producing. This is so powerful that it is bound to draw attention from the Electronic Warfare Systems the Imperialist-Zionist conspiracy have in place, particularly on the carriers in the north Gulf. Even emitting very short bursts at wide intervals when testing we felt there was a danger they would pin-point the exact site of the radar transmitter. Your Excellency will recall that Your Excellency opted for concrete rather than mobility as a means for making these secure, and they are now irreversibly dug in . . .'

At this point Our Master of High Technology's face became suffused with red, he turned on his heel and stormed back through the rest of us trailing round behind him in orbit above the Korean below. Much as if a comet had turned into its tail. Oblivious that she may have overstepped a mark, she continued.

'And so, after consulting with Cartwright by modem, we agreed to test only the radar system covering the north facing sector, knowing that a missile attack is not possible from that area and even a Stealth attack will require refuelling in the air . . .'

She continued thus for twenty minutes with technical data way beyond my comprehension, though the Intellectual Master of the Universe seemed to have sufficient grasp to be able to interject occasional questions that were not entirely impertinent. That's wrong. What I mean is that they had pertinence.

'Madame Tai,' his voice boomed, much in the way one may suppose the Angel's boomed when he dictated the Holy Koran to his Ancestor the Prophet, 'you must now say, once and for all, for the lives of many thousands of my glorious countrymen and particularly the heroes of my Republican Guard, depend on your answer. Will this system work? No matter what sort of holocaust is let lose across the rest of my beloved country, is my Republican Guard safe from air attack?'

She paused for a long time. Then: 'As of now, on a scale of one to five, three. Sixty per cent certain safe. Give us another fortnight, four. Eighty per cent safe.'

He who can read all minds roared like a lion in laughter and slapped his side: 'Madame Tai, if you had given me an unqualified yes, I should not have believed you. Now. Rumah. You have been with Cartwright in Spain and you believe all is not as well as Madame Tai would have us believe.'

The other woman now hitched herself off the low padded balustrade which surrounded the cock-pit, perhaps I should say hen-pit, where she had been studiously studying her nails, and strode half way round it, throwing a contemptuous glance at the Korean as she did so, then she flung up her head. The lights bounced off her pate.

'Saddam bey,' she called, in a clear high voice, like a baroque trumpet, 'Jabreel Mansur is betraying you. It is possible that Cartwright and this woman are also knowingly in this plot to bring destruction on you, certain it is they are unwitting agents.'

Madame Tai cringed against the balustrade, white-faced, her knuckles white too. She put me in mind of a cat, cornered and suddenly threatened.

'Rumah. This is a serious accusation. Prove it, or I will have you tortured until you confess your motives for bringing it.'

'Saddam bey. You know torture is something I have learned to survive. When I was eight years old, in September 1970, Jordanian thugs, the lackeys of King Hussein, whipped me with piano wire and my back still bears the scars. And I have been tortured often since.' She drew breath and went on. 'Now. I do not know how your political analysts have read Bush and the White House in the last few months, but has it occurred to you that you are being lured into a trap?'

Clearly it had. She could not see him, but I could. He leant against the highest rail and looked down at her, out of the blackness. His face went dark and his huge hands tightened. He shuddered, and suddenly a strange smell came off him, electric, feline, funky.

'Go on.'

'Bush must have Kuwait back, Bush must destroy your ability to threaten Kuwait or Israel ever again. But above all Bush must have his war, a war that only he can win. His greatest fear now is that you will withdraw, with your army intact, for then he will have no right to attack it.'

'He knows I cannot withdraw until at least he has conceded a date for a conference on Palestine.'

'He does not know that for certain. He does not know you at all. He understands you as little as you understand him. He has confused you with contradictory signals . . .'

Here Our Leader glanced at me, and I shrugged my acquiescence to what this extraordinary woman was saying.

'But even so, he still fears that you might realise that the forces arrayed in front of you are not to be beaten, that you might pull out unconditionally, at the very last moment, after the deadline has passed. So his people have concocted this plot, and everything around you now, in this room and throughout this Command Control Centre, is part of it, to make you think you can protect your Republican Guard, keep it intact and win a land war, even after Iraq has been destroyed in a fire storm as great as those that swept Germany in 1945. But you can't. The final phase of the fire storm will be the destruction of these bunkers, the destruction of your Guard . . .'

'No. No-o-o-o. This will not be.' The hemisphere around him echoed to his manic bellow. He smashed his fists into the balustrade, signalled to the little man who is the only doctor he trusts and who was already at his elbow. With a heroic act of will, sustained by the little yellow pills the doctor gave him and which he ate out of his palm as if they were sweets, he regained control of himself. 'Rumah. Prove it.'

She unbuttoned a top pocket in her combat blouse, and produced a small mini-recorder.

'Saddam bey,' she called, 'Do you have with you someone who can understand English, someone you can trust?'

'Lives there a soul in this Vale of Tears, my Rumah bayan, one can really trust?'

I uttered a polite cough behind my hand. Mind you, I was shivering with cold and fear, but ... I was curious too.

'I have Doctor Salih K ... here. He speaks English. And so far I have had no cause to distrust him.'

'Then I would ask you, Saddam bey, to come with me, and Doctor Salih, to a room where we can listen to this in private. It is a conversation I had with Arnold Cartwright.'

The Korean woman circled her, looked as if she might make a lunge for the recorder, but instead came to a stop beside her, looked up in our direction.

'Let me be there too. I insist.'

CHAPTER 32

An aide took me to a small room furnished with armchairs, a table, a portrait of Guess Who, a viciously cold air-conditioning outlet and nothing else. Presently he returned with a jug of lemonade, glasses, a brass bowl of dates and another of *locum*, Turkish Delight. A moment or two later the other three joined me. I poured lemonade for all of us. The Shield of Islam added whisky to his from a hip flask, took three dates, chewed, spat out the stones.

'Right, Rumah. Let's hear it.'

She pressed buttons, and a male voice, educated English with a slight accent began: '*Every time I ask for equipment or specifications I get them. And from very different sources. Not just* FADSI, *but stuff that originated with Lockheed, the people who make the Stealth* F117A . . .'

I held up my hand. She stopped the tape, and I translated.

'*They've even given me its radar signature . . . It can only mean that someone very high up in the US government is supporting us.*'

Then Rumah's voice, but, of course speaking English.

'*I can't believe that. Why should they give the Iraqis the ability to take out Stealth?*'

'*They're not going to.*'

'*But you said . . .*'

'*Even with all this help, it's not going to work. Quite simply it's not possible. Not in the time available, not with the limited skills.*'

I translated again. Our Leader's face grew darker, his

giant fists clenched. A date stone he had secreted in his palm was exuded by the pressure like a small hard turd and zipped an inch or so across the table. I think I was the only one who noticed. Madame Tai had now assumed a pose of oriental inscrutability, perhaps concealing panic as to how what was to come might incriminate her.

'Why not? Why won't it work?'

'Because the maximum range I can get is twenty-five miles. A mile is one point six kilometres . . .'

When I translated this The Master of Tongues gave me a look as if to say: Now why couldn't you have said that?

'Given the six to seven hundred miles an hour Stealth planes fly at we need fifty miles to process the signals and launch the missiles against them. And I just do not believe it can be done.'

When I finished interpreting this, despair settled on the room like a mantle. But Rumah indicated that there was more.

'So what do you think is behind all this?'

'. . . For some reason they want the Iraqis to think, to believe it will work. But it won't. That's why I don't object to doing the work – it's not going to hurt anyone.'

'Is there any chance, any chance at all that that these systems could be ready in time, could be made to work?'

'No.'

'Not even if you were there, supervising the final . . . adjustments? On the spot to see how things might go wrong?'

'Well. It's theoretically possible. Just possible.'

Sounds of tapping, a little like pipe ash being knocked out. Then the male voice came nearer, much nearer, as if it were speaking directly into the microphone. *'But wild horses wouldn't get me to Baghdad. No way.'*

The Wrath of Allah turned on Tai, who cowered.

'In your report, you did not mention there was a problem with range. Why not?'

She improvised, I'm sure of it, but convinced him.

'Because I do not believe there is. There are three ways

we can improve the range. It is simply a matter of implementing tuning-up improvements in three separate areas. I am already working on them . . .'

'Would it help to have Cartwright here?'

She thought for a moment, and then bowed her head in a recollection of oriental female submission.

'Excellency, yes.'

'Then we must hire some wild horses.'

Rumah intervened.

'That won't be necessary.'

'Why not?'

'The Americans will get him here.'

His brow furrowed.

'Why should they do that?'

She kept the irritation out of her voice, for the answer was obvious. Even I had seen it.

'They want you to believe this system will work. If the man who designed it stands here in front of you and says that it will, then you will believe him.'

There were two more thoroughly unpleasant incidents to be lived through, in that long unpleasant day.

The first occurred almost as soon as we, the Last Great Caliph, the Palestinian woman and I were back in the middle of his fortress outside Baghdad. I sat at my desk in the secrecy of the colonnade and watched while he and this Rumah continued to talk, but quietly, so I could not hear them. No doubt they were discussing what had gone before, weighing the pros and cons of the situation. Basically, I suppose, whether or not to continue with Operation Haroun al-Rashid, the codename for the Most Advanced Air Defence System in the world, or forget it, and forget Kuwait too. I was not sanguine. Whether out of design or artlessness she had left him with a tiny nugget of hope — if it really was true that the Americans would get Cartwright out of Spain and on the spot.

Presently there was a buzz, a messenger was on the

doorstep, had been cleared. Who from? Jabreel Mansur. His name? Joshua Mendoza.

Rumah stood.

'It would be better, Saddam bey, if he did not see me.'

He ushered her through the door behind the settees, a privilege granted to very, very few. Then he pressed a buzzer and the doors at the far end of the room were thrown open, and a large dark man in a black turtle-neck sweater, pale grey suit and black loafers padded down the long colonnade towards me, passing the Fountain of the Abencerrages as he came. He was carrying a hard document case fastened to his wrist with a long bright chain.

Clearly he knew the formalities of the Divan. Having reached my desk he began to move crab-wise out into the main hall. When he was in the middle he bowed low, offered the *salaam aleikum*.

'Greetings, Excellency, from your friend and servant, Jabreel Mansur.' From the side I could see gold flash from a capped canine.

The Fount of Wisdom and Justice waved his big hand to the settee in front of him.

'Jabreel wants his money?'

'That was the arrangement, Excellency.'

'He should have come for it himself.'

Joshua Mendoza merely shrugged, said nothing.

'Jabreel is a lying treacherous viper. And when I have the chance I shall crush his head beneath my heel.'

Mendoza offered a small, uneasy smile.

'Excellency, if that is the message you would like me to take back . . .'

'Instead of the dollars you intended to pack away in that case? Yes. That is the message you will take for me. Tell me. Can you run, can you run fast?'

'I . . . I am quite fit.'

'Let's see. Let's see how far you can get before I shoot you.'

Mendoza, encumbered by the case chained to his wrist,

rose and turned as the Avenging Angel pulled his big pistol from its holster. I watched only for a short time. Then I was sick. He got about ten yards down the hall before the first shot hit him low on the outer thigh. He ducked in behind the pillars and began to weave between them, staggering, bleeding like a pig and of course screaming like one too. The case swung and banged against the pillars. The Butcher followed, shooting casually, often missing, and never aiming for a fatal wound. The repeated reverberations bruised my eardrums even though I covered my ears with my hands. The bullets screeched round the room, bounced off the toughened glass of the outer wall, so I feared they were as likely to hit me as Mendoza. I got under the table. The smell of cordite, blood, faeces and vomit tainted the air.

At last silence fell and I looked up. They were far closer than I would have liked. Mendoza must have doubled back, blindly, no doubt. He was certainly blind now, blind and dead, the side of his face shot away. Dark blood spread in a pool around him. His Executioner crouched above him, knees splayed, smoking pistol still in his right hand dangling between them. A bodyguard had appeared behind him. Without looking up the Father of the Al-Takriti Clan said:

'Cut off his hands. Put them in that case and send them back to Jabreel.'

Then he shifted his gun to his left hand, and quite delicately removed the gold-capped canine from the mess in front of him and put it in his pocket.

It is not really to be believed but there was one last moment to this dreadful day still to come, worse than all the rest put together.

I got home to Amiriya just as dusk was falling. It's a pleasant suburb to the north of the city, which I have not perhaps sufficiently appreciated in the past, my mind prejudiced as it has been for so much of my life by memories of those years in Cambridge, the Backs, the cherry-trees in blossom above the red tulips behind King's College, which I dutifully admired but which to me looked like blood in snow when the blossom dropped, the greenness, oh all that English shit. Anyway it's a nice place, Amiriya. Academics, doctors, lawyers, engineers live here in pleasant enough detached villas. We make our gardens flower and fruit. There are trees. Birds. As I came down the street I even saw a little owl, *Athene noctua*, flying down ahead of me in her swooping flight before rising up to perch on a telegraph pole above the weeping willows, just coming into leaf. Above her a sickle moon lay on its back in a sky of purple velvet.

I let myself in with my latch key and found myself confronted with a distasteful tableau. My wife appeared to be entertaining the Mukhabarat officer who called some weeks ago to redeploy my modem. They had coffee, already a black-market commodity, in front of them, served, Arab-style, from our best coffee service of good quality brass and porcelain. He was, I have to admit, a handsome, well set up sort of man, which I am not.

It took me some moments to realise that I had not stumbled on an illicit romance, but when the officer said the magic words 'Beast 666', I realised that something far, far worse was afoot.

'Dr Salih, I just called round to say that we of the Mukhabarat would like to congratulate you on the present favours you enjoy in the Shadow of the Enlightened One.'

Still believing that they were taking refreshment after an afternoon of erotic delight, I tapped my foot.

'And also,' he went on to say, 'to communicate to you our curiosity regarding Beast 666.'

I made great efforts to compose myself.

'I do not know what you are talking about.'

'Ever since your modem has been in the hands of the security forces we have had urgent requests coming up on it for access to a secret file code-named Beast 666. We have no way of being sure but they seem to originate from . . . abroad. What do you know of all this, Dr Salih?'

'Nothing, nothing at all.'

'Then you won't object if I watch while you go through the procedures of accessing on your computer a hidden file with that entry code.'

With heavy heart filled with dread and a premonition of sciatica in my hip joint as well, I took him to my study and did as he asked. To my amazement the message came: 'Invalid command. No such file exists.' I tried three times always with the same result.

And at that moment a siren went off and my wife came in, carrying our gas-masks.

'I'm sorry,' she said, 'but the regulations are very clear. Although this is clearly a practice, we are bound by law to comply.'

As we hurried down the street towards the air-raid shelter by the mosque, along with a thousand or so of our neighbours. I managed to quiz her.

'How did that happen? What has happened to Beast 666?'

'Days ago I changed the password.'

'To what?'

'Georgy Porgy.'

I stopped her in the street and embraced her. Truly, a good woman is worth her weight in rubies.

'But how did . . . how did you . . . why?'

She broke back from the embrace.

'Let's just say I know what an idiot you are and I do my best to look after you.'

CHAPTER 33

Cartwright found Henley waiting for him in the hospital carpark. As he unlocked the door of his Ford Sierra, Henley got out of the Renault 19, already parked two slots away, put his elbows on the roof.

'Arnie? Long time no see.'

'Phil. Yes, I suppose it is.'

'They're missing you down at SISA, and, frankly, Gabby is a touch pissed off with you. Three days now is it since I brought you back from your paid holiday with added nookie? And they say you haven't clocked in at all.'

Cartwright, his heart suddenly pounding, bit his lip, opened his door, got into the driving seat. But Henley moved fast, wrenched the door open again before Cartwright could move or even lock it.

'Buster, just what the fuck do you think you're playing at?' Cartwright looked up into the red angry face, the broad shoulders spread across the grey sky. Henley went on, spitting so saliva sprayed Cartwright's face. 'You know the deal: money in the London branch of the BCCI the day after the land war starts. Otherwise not a dime. Now listen, Arnie. We know just how bad your old man is, how he's tied up his dough and how much the treatment will cost. Can you risk losing your salary? Your job? Fuck with us now, and I guarantee you'll never work in the defence field again.'

Cartwright turned away, clenched the steering-wheel, gazed out through the windscreen at wind-tossed palms, their branches knotted up for the winter in unsightly bunches. He took a deep breath.

'Henley, I'm through. I'm tired of being manipulated and bullied. I feel deeply . . . sick, and hurt, that that woman was there all along just as bait. I have seen people killed. I am not going to go through with this. I am certainly not going to Iraq. I am not leaving Malaga until my father has made a complete recovery. And as for working in what you call defence, I'm not taking blood money any more, either legitimately or from gangsters like Sur. Now close my door and let me go.'

'Arnie.' This time the softly, softly approach. 'Let me in. We have to talk, talk this thing through. First, there's no question that Haroun al-Rashid is going to kill anyone. We told you. It's not going to work . . .'

Suddenly Cartwright was angry, really angry. If he had been in a position to do it he would have cracked Henley's skull open.

'Listen, Henley. I've got a brain, a mind. It's not just a calculating machine working out programs. It thinks. Right? If Saddam Hussein thinks Haroun al-Rashid will work, he'll stay put and there'll be a war. And I want no part of it, I won't have any part of it. Now piss off before I get out and hang one on you.'

He started the engine, gunned it.

Henley, with a swinging gesture of anger, smashed the door shut, watched with clenched fists as the Sierra swung noisily out of the carpark.

'Fucking limey bastard. But we'll get you. We'll get you there. Just you wait and see.'

Then he allowed himself a small laugh and a grin, turned, shook out a Chesterfield, felt for his Zippo.

'Performance over,' he murmured to himself, 'give the guy a big hand.' Then: 'I guess I have to touch base with Louella on this one. Give her a bell, anyway.'

'Right, gentlemen, and er, lady, we have a complex situation right here to deal with, and perhaps if, Colonel, er

General, er, would like to fill out this, er situation, then we'll evaluate his recommendations.'

Vice-Chairman (Joint Chiefs of Staff)'s Sub-Comittee, Middle-East Intelligence, had reconvened, but this time with Louella and her ex-Colonel, now a General and chairman of ACTCOMM ME 18/A, present.

'Point of order, Chair, before we start?' Louella, at the end of the long table, leant round her neighbour.

'Er, Miss, er, yes?'

'Sir, it has now been established throughout this building that no-one has to suffer passive smoking? Isn't that the case? I mean, I have no desire to make waves, but I guess what I am doing right now is passive smoking? Yes?'

Air Force looked across at her with stunned disbelief. No-one said anything. The silence extended, was at last broken by the sound of Air Force banging his pipe on the side of a large ceramic Coca-Cola ash-tray sited in the middle of the table. Black sticky ash, some of it burning, spilled across the table towards Louella. The pipe stem broke. Air Force left the bowl in the ash-tray where it continued to smoulder throughout the meeting.

The ex-Colonel General, sitting at the end of the table, facing Chair at the other end, shuffled papers, smoothed them, cleared his throat, began his presentation.

At the end of it Air Force scarcely waited for permission to speak before jumping in.

'Sir, this is loony toons, all through. It's worse. It's a load of horse faeces. If you are asking me to validate this request to kidnap one of the best radar scientists there is, smuggle him into Kuwait, and let him fine tune Saddam's Ferlinghettis to pick up Stealth, then, then . . . Well, Jesus I won't. That's final.'

Louella leant forward again.

'Sir? If I could just interject an observation or two here? You see one thing my Chairman did make quite plain, I think, in his presentation, is that no way is it possible for Cartwright actually to . . . Look. There's an aspect of this we haven't fully developed. May I?'

Half an hour later Air Force withdrew his objection, mainly because the argument had become too technical for him and he found he could not oppose it without exposing his ignorance.

The Man from State now intervened.

'Okay, I grant you it's neat, very neat. Even elegant. I like that. But this Cartwright doesn't want to know. Which is why he has to be kidnapped. But what makes you think he's going to co-operate once he's there? I mean as of now he's lost motivation, how does he get remotivated?'

The ex-Colonel General smiled benignly, all round.

'We make him hate us. Already he hates us. But now he is going to really hate us. May I explain?'

Another half hour went by. It left the Texan general shaking his head in disbelief.

'That is nasty,' he murmured. 'My, that is really just about the nastiest thing I ever heard. Who cooked this one up? Neither of youse two, I guess. You ain't evil enough.'

'It came from our field man out there, a guy called Phil Henley. Er, Tex, does this mean you don't want to go along with it?'

'Hell, no. I just said it was evil. That don't mean I don't go along with it.'

Navy coughed, looked round, raised a finger.

'We have to hope he lives long enough to do it?'

'How's that, then?'

'Is this the Henley the Israelites are in such a tizzy about? The one they've lost, how many is it now, four operatives to? What the fuck was the point of that? We're meant to be friends, aren't we?'

The ex-Colonel General was blunt, straightforward.

'No. As we all know, the tilt Mossad-wise is on an entirely new kilter. They got a clear directive to keep their hands off of this one, they didn't, they got their fingers burnt. It was a lesson for them, show we meant it.'

'Nevertheless,' Air Force pulled a new pipe from his pocket, began to stuff it. 'I wouldn't give a wet fart for Henley's chances of making it through to the Victory

Parades. Eh? I'm sorry, Miss, but I guess the meeting just now terminated.'

He flicked the cap off his Zippo, sucked flame into the bowl.

Night-time. Cartwright naked, for he always slept naked and was ready for bed, moved through his father's apartment, carefully checking that everything was as it should be. The timer for the heating and hot water was set for seven in the morning, the freezer indicator was precisely in the middle of the green band, the doors and windows were locked. And the humidity and temperature on the closed-in balcony where the fifteen orchid plants grew, were spot on. In the bathroom he cleaned his teeth and then moved to the master bedroom where there was a full-length mirror. A touch drunk as he was he leered at himself for a moment, fiddled with his prick and his scrotum, thought about Roma, whore though she was.

He moved back into the living room, poured himself a last large Soberano brandy, took it to the sofa, swung his legs up and pulled the duvet over them. He hated the spare rooms with their views into the sights, sounds and smells of the *patio de luz*, preferred, in his father's absence to be where he was. Using the remote control he flicked through the satellite channels looking for soft porn, found none, finished his brandy, switched off both TV and the light.

A long buzz, loud, repeated, thrashed across the darkness, just as he felt he might, after all, sleep. He groped for switches, got the lights back on, staggered across the deep-pile carpet, caught his mother's reproving eye, reached the telephone.

'¿Señor Carrrt-richt? Hola. Señor . . . I am very sorry to have to tell you that your father is now very seriously ill indeed, and has been moved to the intensive care unit. Under the circumstances . . .'

'I'm coming. I'll be there. I'll be there just as soon as . . . Listen. Please. Tell him to hang on until I get there.'

Knowing he was drunk he took a taxi. Because he could not speak Spanish he could not get the driver to understand that it was an emergency. Either that or the driver was a bastard. Herbert was dead when he got there, already in the morgue in the basement, slotted into a wall of stainless steel niches, already refrigerating. They hauled him out, and Cartwright looked at the tired dead face, realised that what he was looking at was nothing. Nevertheless he touched the old, arthritically knotted, mottled hands, folded on the sheet that covered its chest. The impression left by his finger lingered.

'That's not my father,' he said.

'¿Qué?' The doctor was alarmed.

'I'm sorry. Yes, of course. That was my father.'

It was now two o'clock in the morning. He was deadly tired, still drunk but in a cold sick way, that blurred his speech, caused him to sway a little when he walked, but his head remained cold and clear. He wanted to weep, but could not. He wanted home, but he had none. He wanted comfort and there wasn't any.

He began to walk, almost aimlessly but keeping in mind the general direction of the Paseo del Parque, the quays and the sea. He could not face the idea of bed, of darkness, of loneliness. He moved away from the main avenues with their bright street lights into an area of shadows, of low stuccoed buildings with gaps where they had been reduced to rubble, cleared for redevelopment. He walked into one such space, sat on crumbled brick for a time with his face in his hands, resting legs that suddenly ached. But there were rats and he hated rats.

He moved away too quickly, his toe caught a cracked paving stone, and he felt as if the pavement had swung up like a rake handle when you tread on the head and smashed him in the face. It took him a moment or two to realise he was on the floor, with a mouth full of grit. His whole body felt badly jarred, as if the connections within it had been loosened or twisted, but it was his face, and one knee, that really hurt. He hauled himself to his feet, touched his face, felt the blood. He got himself beneath a dim street-lamp, an unshaded bulb mounted on the wall by a corner, and saw that his hand was covered in blood. He leant against the wall, and began, at last, to cry.

A waiter, on his way home from a café-bar, passed him, asked him if he was all right. Not understanding, he said nothing. The waiter was near his own home, had a telephone and rang the police. A quarter of an hour later a patrol-car picked Cartwright up. Again the language problem got in the way. First he gave his own address in Torre del Mar, then he remembered the keys were in Torrox, in his father's apartment. The police were puzzled and suspicious when he gave them the second address, especially since they could not understand his attempts at explanations. Nevertheless they took him there, watched him use the keys and finally left him. He collapsed on the settee without taking his clothes off, and slept, at last.

They were back in the morning, at least that was what he thought when he was woken by the door buzzer and saw, through the Judas hole, two policemen in Policia Nacional uniform with a man in plain clothes between them. He did not know that the car that had picked him up belonged to the Municipal Police: he just assumed that they had come back to check he was all right, perhaps to get an explanation of what he had been up to, perhaps the one in plain clothes could speak English. These at any rate were the thoughts that stumbled through his confused, numbed mind as he led them into the sitting room. On the way he caught sight of his face in the hall mirror.

'*Momento.*'

He dodged into the bathroom, made some sort of effort to clean himself up, but it was a painful and not very successful business. He had a rash of grazes above his left eye and across his left cheek. Presently he became aware that one of the policemen was in the doorway, watching him.

Back in the sitting room he found they were already

sitting in the armchairs. He sat on the edge of the settee. The plain-clothes policeman straightened, put his arm along the arm of the chair, drummed with his fingers for a moment. He was about thirty years old, tall, lean, tough, short-cropped dark hair, well-cut dark grey suit.

'Mr Cartwright, first let me say I am sorry to intrude on your personal grief at this time.'

His English was perfect, too perfect. Educated but with a slight cockney accent. Cartwright accepted it gratefully: he remembered Herbert had said that there were one or two policemen who spoke excellent English, and dealt with the ex-pats' problems. The thought lurked at the back of his mind that he had seen this man before somewhere . . . lurked, but stayed there.

'I am afraid I must ask you some questions regarding your father's death.'

What followed was a long, detailed and occasionally acerbic interrogation regarding the capsules Herbert took for his blood pressure. Did Cartwright know what they were? Did he know how long his father had been taking them? Where in the apartment had he kept them? When was this particular lot made up? Which pharmacist had they come from? How often did he take them? Did he ever forget to take them? And so on.

Then the questioning changed tack. Was Cartwright in work? What was his financial position like? How much money did he have in the bank? What outgoings did he have?

Cartwright broke up. He managed not to weep, converted his misery to wrath.

'Get out, go away,' he shouted, 'can't you see the state I'm in? Either tell me what this is all about, or get out. I can't stand any more.'

'One more question, Mr Cartwright. By how much do you expect to benefit as a result of Herbert Cartwright's death?'

'Oh, for Christ's sake! You can't think I had anything to do with why he died? You really can't mean that!' He stormed, then he began to laugh, a wild high laugh. The 'policemen' watched, impassively. As the laughter turned to choking he managed to stumble the words out. 'I really don't know for sure. Two hundred thousand pounds? Is that enough for you?'

The plain clothes policeman stood.

'Arnold Cartwright. The contents of the capsules your father had by his bedside had been tampered with. They did not contain the medicaments that were in them when they left the pharmacist. The actual substance is a complex organic alkaloid compound. Preliminary tests show that in small doses it could cause the nervous and muscular malfunctions which your father was suffering from, and in larger doses could cause death. All these facts have been put before an Examining Magistrate and he has issued a warrant for your detention while inquiries are continued. I must ask you now to accompany us back to Policia Nacional Cuartel in Malaga . . .'

CHAPTER 34

But Cartwright never made it to jail. As they hustled him across the small gap between the entrance to the apartment block and the waiting car, men in black hoods and armed with machine pistols spilled out of an unmarked van parked behind it. One of the uniformed Policia Nacional went for his gun, but an order barked in Spanish across the space made him freeze and saved his life.

That, at any rate, is how the charade was played.

Cartwright was seized from behind, he struggled for a moment, but they dropped a black bag over his head and bundled him into the van, smashing his shin on the tailgate on the way. The pain, on top of shock and everything else, left him shaking and longing only for oblivion and an end to what had become a relentless succession of nightmares.

The oblivion was granted — for a time. As the van began to move strong hands rolled him onto the side, pushed up his right sleeve, fingers probed for a vein.

'Just a small prick, old son.'

His last thought before he collapsed into narcotic stupor was that the voice was that of Philip Henley. But later he felt less sure about this.

He woke six hours later, but only briefly, enough to take in the fact that he was in a narrow but comfortable bunk, and that his ears were filled with a steady but not intrusive droning sound, overlaid with at least one higher pitched buzz. He opened his eyes. The ceiling above him was a low narrow vault, the light was cool, diffused, but bright. It took him a moment to realise he was in a plane. Another sound: very close, a page being turned.

He turned his head on his cheek and became aware that his skull was filled or almost filled with what felt like a rock or sphere of pain. When he moved it lurched and thumped into the side of his head.

There was a woman sitting beside him. He made out two things about her. She was in pale khaki fatigues and had a shoulder flash: a red crescent on white; and she was reading a magazine — it looked like *True Confessions* but the script was Arabic.

He tried to say something but no sound came: his tongue felt swollen and his mouth was dry. He closed his eyes and the blackness swept over him again like a wave.

Hours later he was still in the plane, but now it was lit by dim electric light. Strong, capable hands were hoisting him into an upright position. There were two of them this time. They murmured to him, softly, gently.

'Up you come now. There's a good feller. How do you feel now? Not so good, eh? Well, we'd like you just to take a drink of this, restore your body fluid and sugar levels, okay?'

The English was the sort he associated with British Pakistanis, but though these women were dark, they were not what he called coloured.

The drink was in a plastic beaker with a spout. It was chilled but not really cold, slightly sweet but with a distant acid tang, lime or lemon or a mixture of both. Again he slept, and this time it really did feel like sleep.

The next time it was pressure from his bladder that woke him. Tentatively he pushed back the light sheet and blanket that covered him, got his feet to the floor. He discovered that he had been undressed and put into a long plain white cotton night-shirt.

The nurse looked up from her magazine.

'I need to . . . to urinate.'

'Can you make it to the toilet?'

'Where is it?'

'The door at the end of the bunk.'

'I'll try.'

The pain in his head was now bearable, but came back with a thud as he got to his feet. He looked round, managed for the first time to take in his surroundings. He was in a cabin about twenty-four feet long, with three bunks along each side, all made up and ready for use. At each end there were bulkheads with closed doors. There was a general air of antiseptic cleanness and he assumed he was on some sort of hospital plane, possibly as big as a Boeing 737, but no bigger. He wondered what lay beyond the doors: more cabins like the one he was in? An operating theatre? The toilet was tiny, he could only just close the door behind him, shutting himself into a stainless steel cupboard, but he managed.

He got back on the bunk and the nurse pulled the covers back over him. For a moment she hung over him, a warm smile in a plain face, strong hands holding the hem of the sheet and blanket.

'The bastards killed my father.' He felt his eyes fill with tears.

'Did they, dear? I'm sure they didn't mean to.'

She's treating me like a loony, he said to himself. Then: Perhaps I am.

It was still dark when they landed. He woke with the change in pressure on his eardrums, then he was conscious of busy purposeful movement around him. He opened his eyes. The nurse was securing doors and cupboards, finally she leant over him and fastened a strap with a safety belt clip across his chest.

'Five minutes, and then we land.'

'Where?'

She smiled, returned to her seat and strapped herself in. He felt the altered tilt of the plane, the swing of it as it circled through ninety degrees, then the change in pitch of the engines as they whined in reverse. His ears popped again, and he swallowed, discovered his throat was dry and sore. Then at last a quite hard bump and the long decelerating rumble. Again the swing, but this time on a sixpence, and then the whine died and near perfect silence for a moment before the creak and bang of hatches opened.

She stood up, yawned, unstrapped him, hoisted him into a sitting position, looked at his bare feet, muttered to herself in a language he did not know, opened a locker beneath the bunk and found a pair of black canvas slippers with orange plastic soles. They were too small, so she scissored the canvas heels.

'Best we can do for now, dear. All right?'

He stood, and she wrapped a red blanket round his shoulders.

He paused at the top of the steps. Although it was still dark the sky was lightening to his right, opal on a distant horizon of low hills, nearer a handful of palms silhouetted against it. It looked just like one of the small watercolour miniatures you can buy in French sea-side boutiques for forty or fifty francs according to size. Biarritz, Hossegor. His children. How many centuries ago? How many light years away?

'Come on please.'

He looked the other way. Low concrete and glass buildings, lights, a control tower. Then he began the descent, slowly, carefully, because his head was still not quite right, his limbs ached and the slippers felt insecure. With the fresh air, he was aware of hunger, like a fox hidden beneath his night-shirt, gnawing into his stomach.

Three men, all in combat fatigues with black berets and black moustaches, waited at the bottom of the stairs in front of a small jeep. It looked like a real WWII general purpose vehicle, such as he had seen only on movies shown on TV between two and four in the afternoon.

At the bottom he turned back. The nurse was still at the top, making sure he got down safely.

He called up to her: 'Thanks.'

*

There was still a long way to go. They travelled by jeep, in a sand-coloured ambulance with a red crescent on a circle of white, in a helicopter. They gave him food: a sticky paste made from ground sesame seeds and honey, grey bread with big holes in the crumb and a tooth-wrenching crust, dates and black milkless tea. Later it was more of the bread but this time with thin slabs of a white cheese, slimy with the weak brine it had been kept in, and the same bitter tea again.

At last, with dusk, the helicopter, large, military, harsh, noisy and uncomfortable, clattered down into a vast patch of desert littered with saucer-shaped hummocks, barbed wire, tents, mounds of detritus. The surface was criss-crossed and scarred with thousands of tracks, and many different sorts of vehicle, jeeps, armoured personnel carriers, trucks, tanks and transporters were parked haphazardly here, there and everywhere.

Still clutching the blanket round his shoulders, still hobbling and curling his toes in desperation to keep the slippers from slipping off, and buffeted now by a chill wind that blew out of the red eye of a distant sun and whirled grit and debris about his shins, he followed his escort down the sides of the mound they had landed on, and so to the big double steel doors. Long curving corridors walled, floored and roofed with rough concrete bearing the marks of the form work that had shaped it, lit by bare bulbs, swung round some still unseen nucleus. A door on the outer side of the curve was thrown open.

'Mr Cartwright. This is not comfortable. We recognise that.' The oldest of the men who had accompanied him ever since the hospital plane had landed, walked in ahead of him, gestured around at a basin, a seatless toilet, an iron-framed bed with a thin mattress. And a mirror. 'But no-one who sleeps here gets anything better.'

Cartwright looked round.

'Is this a prison?' he asked.

This seemed to make his guide, guard?, quite angry for a moment.

'This,' he said, 'Is the crucible in which our final victory is being forged.'

He saluted and left.

On the bed there was a dark grey suit made from some coarse but man-made fibre, a cotton shirt, briefs, socks, black cracked shoes. They had been made for someone fatter than him, so he could get them on, but shorter too, so once he had them on he felt a fool.

CHAPTER 35

9 January 1991, well, actually two o'clock in the morning of the tenth and here I am back inside Georgy Porgy, tapping away. I don't know why, but I feel light-headed, almost 'high'. No reason for this at all, indeed very much the reverse: there is going to be a war and I have had dreadful sciatica for nearly a week. Maybe the pain-killers, which are hardly efficacious at all as such, also contain elements capable of inducing euphoria. The Healthiest Man in Town's doctor gave them to me, and since he seems able to maintain the Arabian Jupiter's joviality at all times, that is probably the case.

With luck we shall all die giggling.

One thing: there have been no more trips out of Baghdad. I don't think I could have borne travel on top of the pain. It seems that from now until the crisis is over the Shield of Islam is going to remain holed up at the centre of things. 'It is important, Salih,' he said to me the day before yesterday, 'that the Americans know where I am, so when they want me to know that they are withdrawing from the Mother of All Wars they can reach me without a delay to ask for the necessary cease-fire.'

He has also been told that the Americans have rejected the assassination option, on the grounds that they do not wish to de-stabilise Iraq, fearing that by doing so they will let in the Kurds and the pro-Iranian Shias. So, he is staying put, and has told them where he is staying put, to be sure they don't assassinate him by accident. But that's all by the way.

The Ghengis Khan of the Twentieth Century spent most of this morning in conference with the Englishman Mr Cartwright, Tai-Won-Kun and the Palestinian Rumah, all of whom had been flown up from Kuwait for the occasion. The night before, Allah's Avenging Angel took me on one side and explained to me my part in today's proceedings.

'Salih, the Englishman has no Arabic, so your first duty will be to translate, in summary, what it is necessary for him to understand. However, all three of them speak English and it is possible they may speak amongst themselves in that language. If they do, you must listen, and make sure they are not using the tongue of infidels to conceal from me clandestine thoughts or plans. Finally, this Englishman. Is he a spy, is he a deceiver? Is he sincere? Observe him closely, Salih, use your knowledge of the serpentine ways of the cunning Anglo-Saxon, interpret for me his every gesture, every nuance of what he says so I may really understand not only what he says, but what he signals, and what he conceals.'

At ten o'clock then all four of us were sitting on the settees waiting for the Lion of Assyria to appear. The Fountain of the Abencerrages tinkled behind us; beyond the inner wall of toughened glass and above the ornamental orange trees, now laden with golden orbs, the white doves tumbled in the winter sunshine. I took the opportunity to acquaint myself with this Arnold Cartwright, reputedly the greatest radar technician in the world.

He was a little over forty I should guess, allowing for the fact that he was in very bad shape. His face was severely grazed, the skin round the scabs inflamed with sepsis. He looked very tired, hollow-eyed, wretched. He was wearing clothes of poor quality that did not fit him and his hands shook. Most strange of all he kept casting looks of such ambiguity at Rumah, that I began to wonder if he were not slightly touched. Sometimes these were full of hate, sometimes full of adoration, but always they were filled with longing. Which is odd, since whatever beauty she has is mannish, and she is, as I have already said, as bald as a billiard ball. Once he reached out to touch her, but when he made contact, his hand flew back as if it had come in contact with a strong electric current. I had been given a brief curriculum vitae and now made use of what I remembered of it to strike up a conversation.

'You are from Nottingham, I believe?'

'Er, yes. I suppose I am.'

'I have not been to Nottingham, but I had a friend at university, Cambridge actually . . .' For some reason he shrank from me when I said this, as though I had confessed to leprosy rather than laying claim to a connection with a great seat of learning, 'where I took the Bachelor of Arts honours degree in Archaeology and Anthropology, passing in the first division of the second class. I am sorry. I have lost myself. I was saying, I had a friend who came from Nottingham.'

'Oh, really.'

'Yes. He had a very droll story to tell about the stone lions that flank the city hall. Apparently they roar only when a virgin passes. Perhaps you have heard that story?'

He looked weary, passed a shaking hand across his pale brow.

'Yes. I have. Often.'

I cast about for a new topic.

'Lord Byron, a fascinating character, came from nearby, did he not? Something Abbey?'

'Newstead Abbey.'

'An abbey. But Lord Byron was not, I think, a monk.'

He did not seem aware that this was intended as a pleasantry, a humble joke. Fortunately at this moment the Scholar General of our Glorious Armies made his entrance from the inner quarters, dressed as usual in fatigues and with his black beret tucked under his shoulder strap and, of course, his pistol on his thigh. He had a morning freshness about him, redolent with after-shave and bonhomie, shook hands with each of us, with a warm embrace added for both Rumah and me.

Then he settled in the big settee opposite us.

Rumah began the debate. In short asides I passed on the gist to Cartwright.

'Saddam bey, over the last two days I have had long talks with Mr Cartwright and Madam Tai-Won-Kun and I have no doubts at all now about the nature of the American-Zionist trap that has been laid for you in the shape of the Advanced Air Defence System code-named Haroun al-Rashid. Their intention was to make you think that you could protect your Republican Guard from air attack, even an air attack spearheaded by Stealth-protected fighter-bombers. They were always afraid that you would withdraw from Kuwait on or shortly after the deadline of 15 January, leaving them with no option but to do likewise from Saudi Arabia, lift the sanctions and call an end to the whole affair. But they knew that if you felt you could win, or at least inflict serious casualties on their land forces, you would never withdraw. To that end they gave Cartwright every possible assistance, and when they judged that you still needed to be convinced that Haroun al-Rashid would work, they kidnapped Cartwright themselves and passed him on to agents of our movement for onward transit, facilitating the move for us at every stage. And they believe they have given Cartwright a good motive for doing all he can to help you.'

'How did they do that?'

'First they arranged for his father to fall seriously ill with an illness requiring very expensive treatment, which only he, Cartwright, could pay for. That was to make him continue working for them. But when he refused to leave Malaga until his father had made a full recovery, they arranged for his father to die in such a way that it would appear that he, Cartwright, had murdered him. Thus in one stroke they achieved two ends. They made it a matter of importance for Cartwright to get as far from Malaga as he could as soon as he could, and they gave him a motive for doing his utmost to damage them.'

When I translated this last bit Cartwright tried to intervene, but Rumah looked at him, gave her head a slight shake, and mouthed the word 'later'. I made a mental note of this apparent act of com- if not actual dup-licity.

'Did these two know what was going on?'

'I think not, or not entirely. Madam Tai has been here for some months now, and did not know how easily Cartwright was getting information, nor where it was coming from. Cartwright himself believed all along that the plot was headed by Jabreel Mansur and its aim was to extract large sums of money from you, paid up before the system was actually put to use. He believed Mansur was paying backhanders to American experts and technicians, who had no qualms in passing on the information since they knew, as indeed did Cartwright, that Haroun al-Rashid could never shoot down a Stealth-protected plane.'

The silence extended long after I had finished my English summary for Mr Cartwright. The fountain tinkled on, wings mutely clapped outside. Then the Giant of Iraq shifted a little on the sofa and he, or someone else, and it wasn't me, emitted a brief fart.

'And the reason why it won't work,' he said at last, 'is because it has a range of only twenty-five miles, and we need it to have fifty.'

Rumah, who had been sitting very upright on the edge of the settee, now leaned forward, and the thin point of her tongue briefly flickered over her top lip.

'That, Saddam bey, is why the Americans think it cannot work.' She emphasised the word 'think'. 'Let Madam Tai explain.'

The Korean woman's Arabic was good: I complimented her on it after our first meeting back at the Revolutionary Guards Command Centre and she told me then that she had worked on our French Thompson CSF Tigre systems for eight years during the war with Persia. Again, I found her plaintive kitten voice much at variance with the hard chopping gestures of her hands.

'I have been discussing the possibilities with Mr Cartwright over the last thirty-six hours and we believe there are three strategies open to us. If we maximise the effects of all three we should get an increase in overall performance range efficiency of 3dB, that means the range is effectively doubled.'

I whispered to Cartwright: 'She is going through what you and she together have come up with. Do I need to translate?'

'Yes,' he whispered back. 'I need to be sure she is getting it right, not cheating.'

'I will do my best. It is very technical.'

And probably what I am now recording in Georgy Porgy is a travesty of what she said, but I will again do my best. She had politely paused during this brief exchange, and now continued.

'First, Mr Cartwright believes he can make improvements in the circuit boards carrying the phase-locked loop decoders thus enhancing the threshold or weak signal performance of the radar receiver. This will give an extra 1.3dB. Secondly, we specify a "red-alert status", that is a set of parameters describing the likely contours of a Stealth attack. When those parameters are met the system closes down all functions irrelevant to a Stealth-led attack, the computers refuse to handle all comms not Stealth-relevant. If I fine tune the relevant software, which I think I can, the net effect is that the computers will handle the information received, and issue directives to the missile sites, very much more quickly. We believe this will give us further 1.2dB.'

She reached forward, drank water, tossed back her greasy locks.

'Finally, we are both very impressed with the skills and diligence brought by the Hakim brothers to their work. They may not understand radar but certainly they understand metal, and the lathes, polishing and milling tools we have put at their disposal. Much of the metal is in fact brass which of course is what they know best. Particularly we were having trouble with the "feed". This is the part of the apparatus mounted on a simple frame in front of the dish. The outward-going signal is fired from it and bounced off the dish in a focused beam, and when the signal, now very very much weaker, comes back it is the feed that collects it and sends it down the line to the computers for interpretation and assessment. Now, at forty-two gigaherz we are firing a signal of twenty thousand megawatts . . .'

The All Powerful One made precisely the sort of intervention I have come to expect.

'A megawatt is a million watts?'

'Yes, Excellency.'

He nodded wisely at his own mastery of the subject and allowed her to continue.

'Even fired in short bursts, pulses lasting only millionths of a second can cause the metal in the feed to overheat, and even melt, especially if there are any irregularities in it. And it is through their skill in honing and polishing the metal in the feed and the surface of the dish itself that the Hakim brothers can, we believe, give us a further full dB. This brings the total possible enhancement up to 3.5dB, a range improved by a possible thirty to thirty-five miles, and the gain of more than the three minutes we need to get the HAWKs in the air before the Stealths can loose off their laser-directed bombs.'

Another long silence. Then he shifted again, without the fart this time, and directed his gaze at Mr Cartwright.

'Ask the Englishman if he can make it work before 15 January.'

I did so, and passed back the answer.

'On one of the three systems, yes. But then the work would have to be repeated on the other two. Since this would simply be a matter of copying work already done he thinks it should be possible to have all three functioning by, say, the twenty-first.'

'How safe are my Guards while only one system is working?'

'Theoretically one, covering a three hundred and sixty degree sector, a full circle, should be enough. However, if we do that, the signals from each sector are coming back to us less frequently by a factor of three, and more information is being fed into one system, more than it might be able to handle even on red-alert status. However, if we know from which direction the attack is likely to come, we can focus the one system broadly in that area and leave the rest unprotected. It's a gamble.'

This time it was I who reached for the water.

'We have asked him if he can do it. Now ask him if, to avenge the memory of his murdered father, he will do it.'

Mr Cartwright looked at me with eyes as haunted as any that appear in the works of Lord Byron. His answer was simple enough.

'No.'

The Pinnacle of Arab Culture reached for his pistol and I held my breath.

Mr Cartwright continued, and I translated.

'My father was a good man. He was a socialist. He was a pacifist. If you believe you might win then there will be a war. If you realise you cannot and back down, then maybe there will not be a war. Above everything else my father would want me to say: stop the war.'

The Assyrian Lion pounced to his feet, moved round the low table that separated us, and still supported the toy gold mosque, the gift of the Al-Sabahs . . . and oh dear me, I thought, here we go again. Bye-bye, Mr Cartwright. But somehow he caught a signal from Rumah, and it was my arm he gathered up, me whom he hurried down towards the Fountain of the Abencerrages.

However, we surged past the fountain, galloped arm in arm (a recollection of something called a Barn Dance that I attended in England forty years ago came, bewilderingly, into my head: Should we doseedo at the far end? Make a chain?). When we got there his trembling fingers rolled up his left sleeve, then he tore off my tie, made a tourniquet of it which he made me tighten until a vein protruded. Into it he injected the contents of a small pre-prepared syringe.

Then he took my elbow and we walked slowly back to the other end, exchanging comments as we did on the beauty of the orange trees and budding espalier roses beyond the glass.

When we got back to the Divan, Mr Cartwright had his head clasped in his hands and almost between his knees. Rumah was standing.

'He'll do it.'

'Why?'

'I convinced him that you will not withdraw without a date for a conference on the future of Palestine and pointed out to him that war was inevitable if you believed you could win, and the Americans knew you could not. But if Bush knows he can only win at the expense of many, many body bags and the loss of Stealth aircraft, he will back off, because the humiliation will cause him to lose the next election. I told him the only way to stop this war from happening was to make Bush believe that he could win it only at that sort of expense.'

He looked at me. I knew he was asking me for my assessment of Mr Cartwright's sincerity. I nodded. I have met English people of this sort, men who revere their fathers and the very old-fashioned sort of socialism their fathers clung to, even if they do not actually espouse it themselves. Even in Cambridge there were one or two of them around, back in the early fifties.

Tonight the BBC World Service tells me that the Geneva meeting between Tariq Aziz and James Baker came to nothing. Tariq refused to accept a letter from Bush whose language, he said, 'was not compatible with the language that should be used in correspondence between heads of state.' There is speculation apparently that Saddam asked only for an extension of the 15 January deadline to 22 January, which was refused. I am not sanguine. I am not at all sanguine that things will turn out for the best in this best of all possible worlds.

Perhaps the euphoric effect of the pain-killers is wearing off. Certainly my sciatica is playing up 'like nobody's business'.

CHAPTER 36

Returning that evening with Tai-Won-Kun and Rumah to the Air Defence Operations Centre which was sited close to the Command Control Centre near the Kuwaiti border, Cartwright looked round and fought back a tide of exhaustion and despair. It was a foul place, a set for one of the nastier circles in Dante's *Inferno.*

His earlier reaction, when he had first set foot in this rectangular cavern dug into the sand and rock of the desert with its floor twenty feet below the surface, had been tired relief: nothing sophisticated could be made to work under these conditions. The roof which lay like a tortoise shell just above the surface of the desert was reinforced concrete and very thick: supported on thin concrete walls buttressed by the Earth's crust. However, the sands, rock and rubble outside had not been properly impacted, and the walls were already bowing outwards and cracking. Occasionally small falls of damp grey aggregate would skitter down the sides, right from the top. It was clearly only a matter of time before the walls crumbled and dumped the carapace on the floor.

Meanwhile dampness was the major problem. The rainy season had started and the walls and floor sweated continuously; shallow brown brackish puddles covered with a crusty scum formed in patches on the uneven floor; when the temperature dropped towards nightfall a fine haze formed and drizzled down on everything below. The air was foetid with smells of mould and must. Within twenty-four hours all the people who worked there had sore throats, eyes that felt hot, and they ran slight fevers.

He looked around it, at the litter of tables, boxes and benches stacked with video displays and terminals, Vax clusters of DEC computers, cabinets filled with disk packs and manuals whose paper was floppy with wetness. Instead of a snake-pit below the floor, cables in all sorts of sizes and colours flowed over and under each other: they were like the matted roots of a mangrove swamp. The whole was lit by four unshaded bulbs suspended from the roof.

'One week. Less than a week. It can't be done. Not in all this . . . mess.'

'It has to be done.' Tai-Won-Kun pushed past him, headed for a row of master switches fastened to the wall below fuse boxes.

'Why? There's no way all this shit will make the Americans back off. However clever we are, they'll get round it.' His voice rose in mockery. 'What are you doing it for, Tai? The money?'

She shrugged. 'Of course. But, Meester Cartlight, survival too. When the attack comes, we have to shoot them down. If we do not the bombs will kill us.'

She threw the switches and the consoles began to glow, the click and hum of the computers filled the air.

Assisted by eight inadequately trained technicians they worked eighteen hours in every twenty-four through seven days and nights. For most of the time Cartwright worked on the actual hardware, particularly the circuit boards carrying the phase-locked loop decoders. The purpose of these was to isolate the very weak incoming signal from the enormous amount of 'noise' that the parabolic antenna would be picking up, especially in the middle of a war, enhance it and lock on to it. The circuit boards themselves were six by eight inches, and he calculated he could raise their performance, and hence the distance from which they could interpret the signal, by changing the values of the resistors and capacitors. This involved the application of a lot of electronic theory in intense calculations and then extremely fine practical work with a micro-soldering iron.

He was permanently tired now, emotionally drained, numb. The actual work became obsessive, filled every cranny of his mind, blocked out all memories of the horrors that had gone before. He clung on to it as if he were a small child and the work his comforter. He dreaded the brief hours when he had to rest because it was then that the dreams flooded in. But never in his entire life had he worked so well: it was as if demons possessed him.

Tai worked nearby with a Vax cluster modifying the software executive programs so they would respond to the 'red-alert' status and ignore all other program interrupts. She was doing this by preparing software 'patches' on floppy disks and then slotting them into the main system. Throughout the week she kept the same quiet, deferential distance between them that she had maintained in Malaga, but always, now as then, undercut by a barely visible sly knowingness, a reservation that seemed to say: 'All right, you are the boss, now, but . . .'

Outside, and five minutes walk away, the nearest of the Ferlinghetti AR 3Ds captured from the Kuwaitis had been parked in a compound which had over the months taken on the appearance of a roofless bunker, surrounded by a concrete glacis, rising to a low pentagonal wall with triangular redoubts. The trailers and containers inside were almost exact replicas of the ones Cartwright had tested in the Mauretanian desert, though the trucks that had hauled them there had disappeared. This freezing them in one place seemed absurd to Cartwright: the whole point of a mobile air defence system is that it should be mobile, as difficult to find as a Scud missile launcher.

On the third day, walking from one installation to the other across a space filled with a litter of used oil drums, burnt-out engines, and heaps of empty food cans black with flies, he brought it up with the woman he still thought of as 'Roma'. She too was always around, a presence for the most part silent, padding into the hangar in her soft-soled laced-up boots, watching them work, with her legs astride, her thumbs snagged under her webbing belt. With her shaven head and ochre and brown fatigues she looked like a skin but the comparison was not apt: as well compare a black-phase jaguar with an overfed and neutered ginger tom.

'Saddam is afraid of movement, afraid that things and people who can move can run away or betray,' she murmured, and Cartwright realised she was talking of someone she knew well, a familiar. 'Always he digs in, fastens down, issues over-elaborate instructions, kills off initiative. Someone free to act independently is for him someone who can acquire a knife and stick it in his back.'

She stood aside at the gate to the compound, made him go in first. Somehow she made it a gesture of dominance, control, impersonal authority. The compound was dominated by the antenna reflector, a parabolic section sixteen feet high. Mounted on its vertical axis it shone now with the intensity of gold polished to perfect smoothness, blinding, if your eye caught the right angle, almost as surely as the sun it reflected.

The Hakim brothers were working on the microwave feed assembly, a conjuror's nest of brass cylinders, the outer one about nine inches across, narrowing to the disc at the back which fed the collected return signals into a cable that led back to the processing and enhancing computers and so to the visual displays. The outer cylinder already glowed like Parsifal's Grail, the inner one like the Ring of the Nibelung.

Lean, dark, but with grizzled hair, indistinguishable apart from the fact that one had a broken nose, wearing oil-stained denims, they saluted Rumah as a superior, but without overt deference. She turned to Cartwright.

'They want you to check the tolerances. Apparently there was a groove in one of the cylinders and they had to grind it thinner to get rid of it. If they've gone too far they will have to cannibalise from one of the others.'

He made the necessary checks, asked her to congratulate them on their skill and dedication, then turned to get back to his bunker. He had been away too long, the sunlight, the open air, laden though it was by diesel fumes from hundreds of generators, and the ventilated stench of several thousand men kept underground all day (they came out only at night, to train and exercise) became more difficult to handle each time he emerged. He was, he supposed, developing agoraphobia.

On the way back he asked: 'You are determined, as determined as are the Americans, that he should fight. Why?'

'The best result for my country is that he should fight and win. If he wins they will concede us a homeland, however, small, but still a homeland, a foothold. And he cannot win if he does not fight.'

'He cannot win.' He gestured with the exaggerated wave one associates with the slightly demented. 'Even if we succeed here, the rest of the country will be destroyed.'

'Anything short of annihilation will be a victory. Annihilation will be almost as good for us as victory.'

'Why?'

'If he is annihilated the Arab people, and I mean the people, will rise at last. The uprising will spread from the Atlantic to the Indian Ocean. Victory or annihilation — either way he must fight.'

He felt sick, turned away, clattered down the fifteen concrete steps that took him to the doors of the cavernous womb where the work, like amniotic fluid, waited to embrace him.

CHAPTER 37

15 January, but counting the minutes to midnight. The deadline came and went at eight o'clock in the morning local time, midnight Washington, but no-one had expected an attack an hour or so after dawn. But now as the first midnight after the deadline approached, a black, squat, reptilian aircraft waited with warming engines on the tarmac of its very own personal airstrip. Painted black, in a black night, on black tarmac it was already invisible. Suppose though that it was seeable: then from above it was a black paper dart sixty-five feet long with wings swept back so their trailing edges or rather angles were only a few feet ahead of its tail, and at the widest point only forty-three feet in span. It was almost a flying wing though the superstructure did extend in a lozenge-shape a few feet behind and supported two tail-planes mounted in a V shape. Seen from the front, triangular pyramidal planes sloped back to an apex above and behind the cockpit giving it the look of a snake's head designed by a committee obsessed with an arcane geometry.

Behind the three angled panels of his windscreen (coated with gold beaten to an airy thinness to dissipate radar), the single pilot checked his instruments. He was nervous. Not because he thought there was any chance the Iraqis would catch him, but because the 'Wobbly Goblin' was notorious, even in its improved versions, for its instability. He had heard on the grapevine of two of the four fatal crashes that had taken place on test flights.

The second hand on the illuminated clock amongst the

many dials and discs of greenish light in front of him flicked to the twelve, the minute hand flicked to the three. Twenty-three hundred fifteen. He murmured into the stalk microphone fixed like a fine rigid proboscis two inches in front of his lips, received confirmation through his cans. The fatherly tones sounded so deep in his skull they might have been the voice of a benevolent god. At all events they wished him 'God Speed.' He opened throttles, felt the strain of the jets against the brakes, watched the needles climb, then let go. For the briefest moment those on the ground saw a cigarette glow of exhaust behind him, then he was gone, as if the plane had been dissolved into molecular particles, beamed up to an equally invisible spaceship in the sky.

Less then than a shadow he swept on through skies kept empty so he alone inhabited them, a black nothingness in the night. Even inside the cockpit the displays were so dim that they scarcely shed any light at all: he was enabled to read them only by virtue of his helmet's night-vision visor.

After four minutes in the air the myriad lights of Riyadh swung by on his right, ten thousand feet beneath him, and he checked the visual display that showed his exact position, sliding slowly, a tiny worm of light, across a map, more a simplified picture than a map, of the Saudi desert. He was flying on two automated navigational systems. High Precision Inertial Navigation computed his speed and height from take-off and instructed him to make minute adjustments in course and speed to keep to the pre-ordained and programmed flight-plan. It was backed up by GPS, the Global Positioning System, a satellite based precision navaid, integrated in a Digital nav/attack system. Neither used tell-tale radar beams.

In the foetid shed north of Kuwait, Cartwright, Rumah and Tai watched the digital clock on the wall flip through seconds and minutes. The message had come, they did not know from whom or how, that the F117A had taken off at twenty-three fifteen which meant that its ETA within their extended radar range was, give or take a half minute or so, dead on midnight. A major with the Republican Guard eagle shoulder flashes stood behind them, hands on a field telephone linking him to the nearby Command Control Centre. Twenty-three forty-eight. Twenty-three fifty. The square black clock glowed on the shiny wall, dimly reflecting the glow of the dull unshaded bulbs. Sweat filled Cartwright's palms. Rumah chewed her lip. Only Tai seemed completely unphased by their situation. Yet if their radar failed, if all their work proved to be faulty, then the very hangar where they sat on high stools watching blank screens and the clock, would almost certainly be the first casualty of the air war, of Desert Storm. Twenty-three fifty-five. Cartwright nodded. The only technician who was any good threw a heavy master switch. Outside generators accelerated, new ones cut in. Cartwright and Tai moved through the consoles throwing switches, the displays began to glow.

Out on the dark waters of the northern Gulf, calm, black, streaked with the slicks Saddam had released months earlier, a giant carrier, its exact position also honed by satellite, shifted minutely. Linked dishes and aerials, a cat's cradle of meshed wires and cages, strung across its superstructures, swept the skies, fed every electronic whisper they could catch to the computers deep in its heart. Processed, enhanced, they formed themselves into blips on simulated three-dimensional maps, numbers streaking down screens, or were spewed from whispering printers in carpets of concertina-ed printout. The white-shirted personnel monitoring this unceasing stream of information moved with studied ease, professional casualness, passing comments in the convoluted jargon of their trade, feeding what the programs told them was important to the admiral and general who sat above them in the ultimate control room of this floating Electronic Warfare Centre.

Twenty-three fifty eight, and the display which held the

commanders' concentrated gaze, a circular map, its centre the Air Defence Operations Centre north of Kuwait City, three miles inside Iraq, came alive with semi-circles of thin light that streaked in ripples across the graded concentric circles, each registering a five-mile interval. Diminishing swiftly in intensity, they nevertheless reached the fifty-five mile mark on the south side of Kuwait City.

'Well, I'm darned,' murmured the general, as the ripples came again and again, at intervals of one point seven seconds, sweeping a hemisphere to the south of the centre in steadily repeated pulses. 'They've done it.' He relaxed, grinned at the Admiral. 'Hell, Buster, we're going to have our li'l ol' war after all. Well, I am doggone!'

Suddenly, he stood up, took off his baseball cap and hallooed a raucous hunting cry that rang across the brightly-lit spaces.

'Saddam, you thievin' bastard, hold on to your nuts, we're coming for them.'

More contained, somehow more *responsible*, the admiral turned to an aide.

'Let Commops know Sand Blind is on course, will you?'

'Commops?'

'Commander of Operations, Norman Schwarzkopf, dumkopf!'

Twenty-three fifty nine, sixty, fifty-five, the second hand fell through the figures, four, five, six, began to climb, seven, eight, nine. The pilot was scared now, too much aware during the last ten seconds that he was the soft machine in an incredibly complex web of interlocking systems, a web that was also a web of deceit that could easily go wrong. And then, dead on midnight, the end of 15 January, the beginning of 16 January as he passed across the fifty-mile line, it came. Simultaneously, a spectrum analyser like a small TV set, to the right of the console in front of him, with a noisy green horizontal line, began to blip, sharply, intensely, right in the middle of the line; a bright red light flashed close to the centre of the displays;

and a high pitched bleep screamed deep in his skull. All said the same: the unthinkable had happened, a radar beam had found and locked on, and the whole weapon system of which he was the only truly sentient part, was reacting like a scalded cat, insisting he should take action, prescribing what it should be.

This was the worst moment, the most dangerous. First he had to watch that second hand move once more round the dial, putting him ten miles nearer the HAWK (Homing All the Way Killer) missile that would, even before the end of that minute, be streaking towards him. Then, and only then could he put the Wobbly Goblin into the sort of turn and shallow dive that had dumped at least one prototype on the floor of the Arizona desert, open the throttles of the twin General Electric F404 engines, and, exhausts flaming, spewing scatter behind him that might deflect the missile, crash the sound barrier and what little remained of his Stealth cover, heading south, yes, like a bat trying to get back into hell.

Back in the hangar, with the sticky dew falling round them, they watched second by pulsing second the blip turn as the second one sped towards it in a faultless curve. There was a moment when the gap seemed to be closing quickly enough, it did indeed continue to close right to the end, when only a mile separated them, then the second blip abruptly disappeared, just as the first blip was getting fainter, fading, and then too went out as it crossed the fifty mile threshold.

'What happened?'

He felt her strong hand grip his arm, the warmth of her body, her breath.

'His instrumentation told him we'd locked a radar beam on him and he got out. The missile self-destructed when it knew it could not catch him. But still. It's good news. Very good news. He didn't jam us, didn't even try. His jammer won't be on the right frequencies. And it'll be a matter of weeks at least before they can override that. That'll be our next job. Do what we did before, what worked in Mauretania, but on these higher frequencies. We're looking for a further 6dB, but as I said we've got weeks, maybe a couple of months.'

He turned, looked round them, through them.

'Well done. It worked. Christ, I'm tired.'

The major cranked electricity into his field telephone, spoke quietly, insistently, but there was intense excitement there too. For him, then, one way or the other, his war was won.

Two and a half hours later the first bombs and missiles began to fall on Baghdad, but none, none at all anywhere near the Republican Guard.

CHAPTER 38

23 January. Three o'clock in the morning, and the first night in a week I have not spent in that hideous shelter by the mosque. I've had enough of it: the bombs and missiles seem to be uncannily accurate, very few civilians have been killed, I believe I am as safe here as in the shelter. And what if the enemy took it into their heads to think it was some sort of military bunker, what then? Anyway, my wife and daughter and all the women and children of the neighbourhood are in it and I am free to bring Georgy Porgy up to date. Mind you I have half a mind to go back to the old label. My modem is operative again and about three times a day I get the repeated message, in one form or another. It's very worrying, as they actually now use my name. If the Mukhabarat are still eavesdropping on this number then I am doomed. I can only hope that at this time of crisis they have more important considerations. The trouble is, since the Dutch Embassy closed, I have no number to ring to tell him to stop this dangerous nonsense. At this very moment it is bleeping for an incoming call . . .

There you see, I flipped over to receive and what did I get. 'Come on Salih, give us a break, why don't you? Tell us where you've hidden Beast 666 and when it's all over we'll make you a professor with life tenure . . .'

Tempting, but frankly I have had enough of the West. I was too easily seduced by Cambridge, and it left my mind, my soul even, tainted with an ingrained snobbery, an ineradicable sense that I was somehow better than anyone else around. It is only in the last few months that I have been aware how deep this went and have begun finally to root it out. There you go, you see: I am still incapable of splitting an infinitive. Indeed, I think the overly mocking, lampoonish style of the earlier entries in Beast 666, indeed even the choice of that name, may be attributed to residual Oxbridge habits.

It's never an easy moment when the scales fall from your eyes and you realise you've been had. I have a recollection which dates back to when I was a very small boy, perhaps eight years old. At the time we lived in the old Ottoman apartments on the west bank of the Tigris, just across the river from the market. These had once been grand, the homes of the Turkish administrators before the First World War. When they left the area was taken over by the rising middle class, of which my father, a doctor, was a member, but they were already falling into decay and the inhabitants were a very mixed bunch.

Anyway, I set off one morning for market, not running errands, we had servants for that, but just for fun, when a door to one of the older apartments opened and an old widow we knew slightly called to me. She gave me a very small sum of money and asked me to get her some dried fish. When I got to the market the fish cost twice what she had given me, and I made up the difference from pocket money I had hoped to spend on liquorice and other cheap sweetmeats, maybe a wooden toy. When I got back with her fish I asked for the money she owed. She laughed at me. Black, cracked teeth, and she laughed. Then slammed the door.

The way I felt then is a little like the way I feel now about Cambridge, and UCLA for the matter of that.

What an absurd reminiscence to indulge myself with while the bombs thud around us, and the spent rounds from useless anti-aircraft fire rattle on our roofs!

I was in the Supreme Headquarters from eight o'clock in the morning of the fifteenth until an hour or so after midnight on the sixteenth. There was a great deal of busyness going on for most of the time, much to-ing and fro-ing of ministers and military. Should we evacuate Baghdad? A lot of argument about that, but in the end the answer was no. Too difficult, the people did not want to go (that was true), if there were civilian casualties on any scale then that would be a propaganda victory.

Which led to the next big dispute between rival ministers: should the foreign correspondents be allowed to stay? Yes, they can report the damage, the wonderful morale of the Iraqi nation, the ruthlessness of the enemy attack. A few days later, I can't remember exactly when, this decision was reversed: the attacks had been so deadly accurate it was assumed that someone amongst the foreign correspondents was directing them from the ground. And I must say they were amazing. One morning I saw a missile, a long white tube with fins, cruising towards the hotel where most of them were staying, when suddenly it turned through ninety degrees to go a further few hundred metres before crashing into the Defence Ministry. It was indeed hard not to believe that it had not been redirected by someone in the hotel with one of those radio things the children of rich Arabs, I mean the oil ones, use to direct their model planes.

Where was I? Back to 15 January. I have to say all this was conducted in an atmosphere of efficient calm. There were no histrionics, no outbursts, no trips to the Fountain of the Abencerrages. This indeed mirrors the behaviour of the population. I am proud of the dignity, forbearance, the willingness to put up with it all, our people have displayed.

At about seven in the evening a sort of niggling, restless anticipation settled over the place: no-one had expected attack during the day, but now dusk was falling and at any moment we expected the bombs to come. Then suddenly a message arrived which electrified everyone. I should have said that we were all now in the War Room many hundreds of feet (judging from the time it took to get down there in what felt like a high-speed lift) beneath the central gardens. It was much like the one in the Revolutionary Guards Command Control Centre on the Kuwait border, though smaller I think, since it was not actually linked directly to weapon systems, and certainly very much more comfortable. Lots of quality basketwork chairs, potted plants and little fountains, discreet lighting and marble floors with good quality rugs, as well as all the computers and screens and displays and all that stuff. There were also caged birds, goldfinches, that sang constantly — not to please the ear so much as to reassure us that the air stayed healthy.

Anyway, here it was that the Shield of Baghdad, surrounded by his Chiefs of Staff, with their aides, received an encrypted message from somewhere south of Riyadh, that a flight of three Stealth F117As had been wheeled out of their bunkers and on to the aprons in front of them, were being fuelled up and armed. Similar reports came from other areas in Saudi Arabia: our network of observers, I will not say spies since it is the Saudis and especially the Ibn Saud family who are traitors to their people rather than the other way round, were performing even better than we had expected.

Then at about eight o'clock came confirmation that the first strike, aimed at making the Sword of Islam sheath his weapon and give in, would be against the Republican Guard. This made sense. If the aim of the enemy was a quick, clean, clinical war, and they had the means to do it, then the immediate destruction of our best troops was the way. No real need to drop a single bomb anywhere else. And this was the contingency for which we were prepared: significant damage to the Guard on the first night would have led to acceptance of all UN resolutions and our immediate withdrawal. That at least is what I had been told.

The next four hours were of course painful, but ended at last with wild expressions of joy from everyone present, except for the Saviour of his People himself. He did allow himself that shy smile of satisfaction that so puts me in mind of a small boy who has pleased his mother while all these generals, and whatever, clustered round him, shaking his hand, cheering, embracing him and each other and knocking over the potted plants.

The reason for this extreme euphoria: the leading F117A had been detected by the Englishman's radar and had turned back, pursued by a HAWK missile. Some reports said it had even been shot down. The message, the signal, was clear: the Republican Guard was safe from air attack.

When all at last were calm, the Eighth Pillar of Wisdom announced the war was won.

'We can all go to bed,' he declared. 'Tomorrow the negotiations will begin. For the first time in earnest. There will be the temptation to heap humiliation on the paper tigers of Zionism and America, which we shall resist. We shall simply ask for what is our due, what we have always said were our War Aims. The re-drawing of the frontier with Kuwait, and a Middle East Conference on Palestine . . .'

Since all military vehicles were bespoken and public transport ran only for limited hours each day to conserve fuel, someone was kind enough to phone for a taxi for me, which of course had to come out of Baghdad to pick me up. I was thus half-way home, on the ring-road round Saddam City, the huge suburb built for our workers, when suddenly, in seven, eight or nine places all around, explosions rent the darkness of the night with orange and scarlet, the cab itself shook with the vibrations and the sky erupted with tracer and the explosion of shells.

You know, for just one very brief moment, I really did think it was a firework display specially prepared and now let off to celebrate our victory.

And it has gone on ever since, with very little respite, day and night. As I have said the bombing here in Baghdad has been remarkable, with very few casualties. This is not the case elsewhere. We still have the TV company that relays news all the time, and one or two sympathetic newspapermen have been allowed to remain here in Baghdad, so — no civilian casualties. But elsewhere mosques, schools and even hospitals have been hit. And the targets here are by no means all military, indeed no. We have no water, only very intermittent electricity (my computer has a built in back-up battery which recharges when the electricity does come on), the Dora oil refinery has been blazing for days.

Of course Our Leader is overwhelmed with conflicting advice and I am afraid is suffering badly from the strain. The Black Label is much in evidence again, and the little yellow pills (incidentally my sciatica is almost better, just a nasty little nag deep in my hip joint, but bearable), bleary eyes, shaky hands and outbursts of foul temper, none of which has yet taken him to the Fountain, I am glad to say. More and more he uses his sound-alike for his radio broadcasts, which I have to say are becoming more and more misjudged and having ill-effects on the will of the people. It's no use saying that things are worse in Tel Aviv, following his Scud attacks. People just don't believe it.

Conflicting advice? The Military say we cannot give in while the Guard survives: it would be political suicide, it would mean the loss of any pretension we have to lead the Arab Nation. On the other hand the civil ministries want an end to it. We are being bombed back into the Middle Ages, or anyway the way things were under the Ottomans which is really the same thing.

And I agree with them. In spite of the war with Persia a tremendous amount has been achieved in the last twenty years. Life expectancy and literacy have soared. Commerce and industry have expanded. Even learning and the arts were healthier in spite of rigid censorship. Women have gained more and more rights — nothing like enough my wife says in private, but then she forgets what it's like for them in Riyadh and the Yemen. Islamic fundamentalism is virtually dead except in the south-east. We were on the point of becoming a developing nation, on the scale of Korea or Taiwan, investing our oil revenues not in foreign subsidiaries, as do the Ibn Sauds and the Al-Sabahs, or foreign banks as does the Sheikh of Abu Dhabi, but in our own infrastructure and industries. And now that is all being torn apart before our very eyes: and perhaps that is the reason for what is happening, the real reason, perhaps the forces against us want to achieve just that. Under the New World Order we are to remain mere oil producers, to fuel the industries of others. No-one wants another Korea or Taiwan in an already overcrowded market-place.

Ah well, the ramblings of a tired old man must cease. Dawn is still marked by bird-song, and I hear a key in our latch. My wife and daughter are safely home after another night of consciousness-raising with their gossips in the shelter and it's time for us all to get a couple of hours sleep.

She looked in on me with bad news. Apparently I was missed in the shelter and she admitted I was at home. The police will take me there by force, if I don't go willingly, that's the new law they say. So there we are. For the foreseeable future I am doomed to days at Supreme Headquarters, nights in the Amiriya shelter.

Time to switch off. *Exit to DOS.*

CHAPTER 39

12 February. Twenty-three ten, twenty-three twelve, the same pilot, in the same F117A, on the same airfield twenty miles south-east of Riyadh, switched off his cabin light, turned down the intensity of his console displays, pulled his night-vision visor off his forehead and onto his eyes. No nervousness this time. He had flown the Wobbly Goblin fifteen times in the intervening three weeks and never a wobble. Also this time he knew there was no chance of having to evade a HAWK missile snapping at his heels.

Why? Because at twenty-three fifty-nine and thirty seconds, when the green line on his spectrum analyser showed the blip that meant he was in the beam of a powerful radar signal, and the red light came on and the bleep screamed in his ears, this time he was allowed to flip the switch that had been denied to him the first time, the switch that activated the Rockwright AN/ARJ2000 jammer that used a high power amplifier, developed for Star Wars, to counter the tube that emitted the signal that was hitting him. The warning signals disappeared, he dropped fifteen hundred feet, took a wide arc to the east. Four minutes later the exhaust of a HAWK tracked across his vision high and to the left, targeted on the course he had been on, heading for a collision the computers below could only now predict, could not determine. He grinned behind goggles and the silk scarf he affected. This was the moment he liked, the Luke Skywalker moment, the moment when he felt like Shane riding into town on his white pony. Only difference was instead of two six-shooters he had two 2,000lb BLU–109 low-level laser guided bombs to deliver, and no way was he going to ride away at the end of it with a bullet in his shoulder. No way.

Geronimo.

After three weeks of nothing in the concrete shed that housed the Air Defence System Control room, it was not to be believed. It all happened so quickly. For two seconds, for two seconds only, the blip was there, and then it disappeared. Cartwright could not believe his eyes, but all the back-up instrumentation told the same tale. They had picked up a Stealth, and immediately, and impossibly, it had jammed their signal — either that, and it was equally possible he had to admit, considering the conditions they were working under, there had been a serious malfunction.

Moving rapidly, and cursing Tai who had left twenty minutes before to take a leak, she had said, he activated all the emergency procedures. His feet splashed in water often an inch or more deep — it had been raining intermittently but heavily for a week and the walls ran with seepage from the earth outside. Alarms rang, a HAWK was fired at the point where computer prediction said the Stealth should be heading, he ran three more checks and got the same result. His signal was jammed. He looked at his watch, the Rolex Oyster his Dad gave him on his twenty-first (the digital wallclock was now five minutes slow). Twenty-four, zero two, eighteen seconds.

Dizziness swept over him and he sank to his knees, heaved a black vomit of stale dates and olives onto the filthy floor. Unbelievably, a steady cool hand cradled his forehead, an arm supported his shaking shoulders. Not since his mother had nursed the bilious attacks of his late boyhood . . .

'What's wrong? What's happening?'

He lifted his head, his cheek closed on hers, he felt the warmth of her breasts on his damp back.

'We have two, perhaps three minutes, then we die.'

'That's a long time.' Rumah stood. Speaking Arabic she got the ten-person crew into the middle of the shed, beneath the highest part of the roof, made them all lie down, all but one. She told him to turn off the main power supply. Two dim emergency lights, battery operated, continued to glow.

When all this was done there was still a minute to wait, the longest minute of their lives.

The explosions were close, very close, but it was not the shed that had been hit. The first had been aimed at the Republican Guards Command and Control Centre, the second at the Ferlinghetti AR 3D itself. The Command Centre was badly damaged but eight more bombs, delivered later that night, were needed to take it out completely. The radar containers and their crews were destroyed by the one bomb.

In the Air Defence Command Centre it felt like a quake and the results were similar. The roof shed huge pieces of concrete, which splashed into the pools below. Loose aggregate tumbled down the walls and one of the lights went out. Then the wall to Cartwright's left began to bow out, then in, and finally concertina-ed into a pile of rubble only six feet high. The roof followed it, and on the other side gouged its way down the inside of the other wall, which held. Rivers of wet slurry poured through the cracks and spread deltas of muck across the floor.

Rumah stood.

'I think we should see if we can get out. How long is it since Tai left?'

'About half an hour.'

She stepped across the snaking cables, squeezed between two computers. She went on:

'Well. That was quite brave of her. She could easily have been held up somewhere. Knowing what was going to happen I would have wanted a better margin than that. Good. The door has fallen in. We can get out.'

They clambered over the toppled steel plate (it echoed

like a stage thunder-sheet beneath their feet) and he followed her up the concrete steps into the chill drizzly night. Two huge fires spewed flame, debris and black smoke from what looked like volcanic craters, each a hundred yards away, one to their left, the other to the right and a little behind them. Something exploded in one of them, and a blast of hot air swept across them.

'Where are we going?'

'Kuwait City.'

On the way (she found a Land Rover and no-one challenged her until they got to the perimeter, and then only to ask her what had happened behind them) they crossed a ridge, an escarpment. On the top there was a police station occupied by Iraqi troops. Rumah pulled into the side of what was now a six-lane highway, and for a brief moment joined the soldiers, frightened, underfed youths, to watch the fires and explosions that were now erupting all over the area occupied by the Guard ten miles behind them and to the north. The glow from the fires was bright enough to pick out on her cheek the runnel left by a tear. Cartwright said nothing but followed her back into the jeep.

Many months later, when he was learning to cope with everything that had happened to him, he realised that this was the infamous Mutla Ridge. The implication was clear. The point-blank massacre of the convoy that left Kuwait City two and a half weeks later, the infamous 'Turkey-Shoot', had not been aimed at fighting troops which were all in the rear. After two more nights like this one the survivors of the Guard had been withdrawn to positions well inside Iraq, from which they were later deployed to crush the Shia rebellion in Basra. The victims of the Turkey-Shoot were the third or fourth rate troops who had held down Kuwait, Iraqi police, collaborators and, yes, Palestinians with their wives and children, who wanted out ahead of the returning Kuwaitis. They had been no threat to anyone. Every account of the slaughter that he read bore this out.

Meanwhile, they drove on, down through Al Jahrah and Subahiya and into Kuwait City.

Baghdad was also bombed that night. For Salih it was perhaps no bad thing. Earlier that evening, shortly after he had left the Supreme Headquarters, a senior officer of the Mukhabarat described to the President how the CIA accessed through a modem a hidden file on Assistant Professor Salih K . . .'s personal computer. At five o'clock the next morning the Amiriya shelter was hit by a laser-directed clone of the bomb that had hit the Revolutionary Guard Headquarters five hours earlier. Salih, and his wife and daughter, were among the four hundred incinerated inside. It was probably better to die thus than kneeling over the Fountain of the Abencerrages with neat whisky boiling in his stomach, but it was a dreadful death for the four hundred, mostly women and children, who had no reason to die at all.

Cartwright saw the newsreels later that same day. Rumah knew where Tai had gone: two days earlier she had found a small bunch of keys, with an addressed label attached, in the Korean's purse. The address had checked out as the apartment of an American diplomat, long since evacuated. She drove straight there, arriving at about one in the morning.

'Wait here,' she said, slamming the door of the Land Rover.

Cartwright stayed in the passenger seat. He looked up and down the well-lit but deserted street of expensive apartment blocks. There were small acacia trees just coming into leaf beneath a haze of gently falling rain. At first sight there was little evidence that he was in an occupied city, indeed there had been little to see on the way to suggest it apart from very old Russian tanks parked on occasional street corners and a parade of looted luxury shops with smashed windows. But now, in the stillness and silence, no longer moving, he took in more detail. There was a lot of litter. The few cars parked beneath the little trees, BMWs, Mercedes, a Toyota Celica, were all damaged, vandalised. There were graffiti everywhere, but always in Arabic: much like the graffiti airbrushed in the concrete walkways round Waterloo Station and similar areas in London. But presumably those were the work of exiles from Saddam, and carried, he reflected, the opposite message to these.

A body fell from the fifth floor above him, crashed through the branches of an acacia, thudded onto the paving ten feet in front of the Land Rover. A very lean dog, ribs protruding, which had just a moment before lifted its leg against the tree, leapt away in fright and with a squawk rather than a bark. The body did not move. It was obviously dead. He recognised Tai's denims, her black hair. He stared at it through the sparkling raindrops which had begun to merge and trickle down the windscreen. Presently the dog came back, sniffed at it.

His door opened.

'You can come up now.'

On the pavement, out in the open air, he became aware of a distant, deep, unchanging roar. There was a rosy glow in the black sky to the north.

'What's going on?'

'B52s. Now your radar has gone they're carpet bombing the Guard. Come on.'

She took his elbow, but he resisted, nodded back at the body.

'Did you have to do that?'

'Yes.'

The apartment was spacious, well-appointed, but anonymous, impersonal. The pictures were large art photographs framed in satin-finish steel, the seats and sofas white, buttoned, imitation leather, the carpets deep-piled but patternless. The only object that suggested in any way at all where they were was a large beaten copper alloy bowl. The work of the Hakim brothers? Why not. Three South African peaches, whiskered with mildew, rotted in it.

The electricity was working, the water still ran in the taps, though both, they discovered in the remaining three weeks of the war, were intermittently cut. As she checked out the rest of the apartment, the kitchen, bathrooms, bedrooms, Rumah laughed, but with bitterness.

'Kuwait City,' she remarked. 'Probably the safest place in the whole area.'

She went out as soon as the dawn paled the street lights below.

'I have friends in the Palestinian quarter I must see,' she explained. 'You must stay here. Don't show yourself, don't go out, don't let anyone know we're here.'

He couldn't sleep, he could not even rest. He found a collection of compact discs: Lloyd Webber, Sondheim, Broadway Hits, Your Kind of Beethoven, and he left them untouched. There was a radio and he found the BBC World Service, but it seemed remote, unreal, and even the bulletins of the Gulf War were like news from another planet, totally unconnected with where he was, what he had seen and what he had lived through.

By ten in the morning he was hungry. He found frozen seafood pizza in the freezer and a microwave oven. He did not appreciate the significance of the pool of water beneath the freezer. By eight in the evening he was wracked with stomach cramps, at nine the vomiting and diarrhoea began.

But first, Rumah came back in the early afternoon, turned on the big screen television. There were pictures of people pulling charred bodies out of the Amiriya shelter.

'It must have been a mistake,' he said.

'I don't think so.' She did not look at him, her cold eyes remaining fixed on the screen, but she went on: 'Do you remember the Iranian airbus, how missiles from the US cruiser *Vincennes* shot it and its two hundred and nine civilian passengers out of the sky on 3 July 1988?'

Of course he did not, said as much. She shrugged.

'They said that was a mistake. But it convinced the Iranian leadership that the US was not only now taking a more active role as Saddam's ally in that war, but was prepared to attack civilian targets. Because of it the first Gulf War came to an end. So perhaps this was designed to have the same effect.'

She nursed him through the food poisoning, which did not get better for ten days and nearly killed him, and then through the desperate weakness that followed.

One day, towards the end of February, she said: 'I have to go now. The Americans will be here soon. They'll look after you.' She kissed him lightly on the forehead. 'Take care.'

He often wondered: was she a casualty of the 'Turkey-Shoot'?

It took Cartwright more than a year to recover, much of it spent in a private psychiatric ward. He could afford it. He cashed his cheque on the BCCI account before the bank collapsed and he claimed his father's inheritance. There had been no police enquiry into his father's death: the police who had come to arrest him were not police at all but Jabreel's men.

He is now what I would call a rich man, but you would not think so to see him. He has bought a small hardware shop in a New Forest village where he is very popular with the poorer gentry: he fixes their lawn-mowers free of charge, and has been known to get old TV sets back to life, even when the local repairman has written them off. This does not mean he favours the gentry, just that the poor who are not gentry are usually capable of fixing things for themselves. His children spend half their holidays with him.

He is also having an off and on affair with a local policewoman, whom he would like to marry. But she is not sure she can cope with the occasional depressions that swamp him, nor with his deep cynicism about human nature in general and politicians in particular. She is a good woman and a good police person. She believes in the Great and the Good and she believes they have ordered things for the best in the best of all possible worlds. In a small village where even most of the rich have roots going back a generation or two, and the poor remain sturdily independent and meet the rich on equal terms in the pub and social club, this is not quite as naïve as it sounds.

The problem lies in the fact that a good police person needs to believe in the probity of the Great and the Good, has to believe that the interests of all are well served by protecting the interests of the few. Doubt that and all can fall apart. A police person who has lost faith in the system s/he serves must be either bent or wretched, and she does not wish to be either. On the other hand she has recently expressed an interest in a smallholding that has come up for sale where goats are reared for their milk, hens and ducks for their eggs, and even the potatoes are raised both organically and successfully. So I see them thus in the future: he selling nails by weight and fixing failed appliances, while she cultivates . . . her plot. And for as long as they are able to forget where his money came from I suppose they will be tolerably happy.